NEW ROMAN TIMES

NEW ROMAN TIMES

Evan Brown

gatekeeper press

Columbus, Ohio

New Roman Times

Published by Gatekeeper Press

2167 Stringtown Rd, Suite 109

Columbus, OH 43123-2989

www.GatekeeperPress.com

ISBN: 9781732010130

ISBN: 9781732010123

Printed in the United States of America

Contents

Chapter 1

Braxton Alexander, newly reduced in rank from sergeant to specialist, downed his sixth shot of whiskey and lit up a hand-rolled cigarette made from a special blend of Turkish tobacco and dried *Sarpa salpa*, otherwise known as dreamfish, a sea bream with psychoactive qualities that smelled like burning eraser when it was lit, tasted like bleach, and felt like fiberglass when it was inhaled.

He'd bought the dreamfish in a fit of desperation. Alexander's coping mechanism had gone on holiday, taking ever more reckless turns with the potential for a bigger reward. Like moving up the ranks, he graduated from alcohol abuse to pot to huffing keyboard cleaner, and while he had the good sense to stay away from heroin, he only hung by a thread.

There were only so many soldiers he could watch die, only so many brothers in arms he could hold one last time in his own arms, and only so many enemies he could lay waste to before it started to feel like the war was a ghoulish, repetitive waste of time.

Alexander had spent the first eighteen years of his life in Abilene getting into trouble, treating foster homes like a revolving door. School expulsions were the norm. He was on a first-name basis with several juvenile parole officers. On his eighteenth birthday, he robbed a Flying J truck stop with a butterfly knife. Five truckers held him pinned against a wall until the police arrived.

And while the Christian Republic of Texas was a country of strict laws and treated criminals with what some other countries regarded as barbarism, they were known on occasion to give someone a second chance. It must have been luck that Judge Roy Springs Jr. was assigned to Alexander's case. After scanning his lengthy list of infractions and weighing the gravity of a federal Texan offense that carried with it a mandatory twenty-five years in prison with no parole, Judge Springs decided not to throw the book. Instead, he offered a choice.

"Now, you've done nothing good up to this point. It might have been the way you fell out of your mama, and it might have just been bad luck. But I'm guessing no one ever did you a good deed. So I'm going to do you one, like the Lord tells us to, in the hopes it changes your life for the better. You've got yourself two choices: either ship up north and work on the chain gang to build the new Edmonton pipeline, or serve your country in the world's finest army and build some discipline."

Alexander chose to join the Texan army. He spent one week in jail while they got his papers in order and gave him a thorough physical and mental exam. After that he was escorted with forty other prisoners 345 miles north for basic training at Fort McAlester.

He spent two weeks getting in shape and getting his head right. Thirty of the prisoners failed out of basic because of attitude, ability, or both. The ones who failed out went straight to the federal jail just outside McAlester city limits. On the drive in, Alexander noted that the jail was twice as large as the base. He made his decision early to pass with flying colors and made good on it, graduating as a private first class.

Somewhere during the endless mud crawls, 0500-hour runs, and orders and insults barked from the drill instructor, Alexander discovered he not only liked discipline but also craved the respect and reward from his superiors. He was an expert marksman, took all orders and endured all reprimands with the same amount of fervor, and impressed those around him. At night he dreamed that one day he might even become a leader. He'd fall asleep thinking, *If they give me a chance, I'll show the world what I'm made of.*

One afternoon while he was running with the platoon, singing back the cadences the leader would holler, the weight and power of his fateful decision hit home.

I broke the law in Texas
And got my ass in trouble
They'll made me join the army
And turned my hair to stubble.
I'll fight for God and country
Fight the evil man
Fight to keep our ladies safe
In this great Texan land.
Now I'm proud to be a soldier.
Proud to be a Texan.
But most of all I'm proud
I'm in the 51-7.

Though the division was actually the Thirty-Sixth, it was long ago nicknamed the 51-7. Various theories abounded as to why this was. The most popular was that back in the war that annexed the oil fields in what was then Canada, fifty-one soldiers from the Thirty-Sixth Division arrived at the Alberta pipeline to find just seven Canadian civil servants standing guard. With fifty-one against seven, there was no way they could fail—which was just as well. Since its inception, the Thirty-Sixth was always a place where criminals went as a last-ditch stop on the reformation trail before eternal damnation in prison.

"The SEALs are the best of the best," his drill instructor would yell. "You're the best of the worst."

His first tour of duty lasted six months. He was stationed in southwestern Iraq with seven from his graduating class. The learning curve became much steeper. Here, grizzled vets mocked them without reprieve. The firefights were sporadic. They mostly spent their days disabling IEDs to make sure the supplies kept coming.

In the sixth month, Alexander and his squad found themselves in a combat situation in which they were pinned down. A private's MK16 jammed. Unable to return suppressing fire, the soldier got one in the face.

Alexander pulled him to safety, killed six insurgents, and wounded one. They took that one as prisoner, covered his head with a black hood, and did unspeakable things to his genitals until he sang. For his efforts,

Alexander was given two medals and a promotion that came with a raise in pay. He was a brave soldier and a good leader. He went on leave thanking God for his country and kissed the ground when he landed.

On his second tour of duty, Alexander experienced the opposite side of the coin. For starters, the duration was three times as long. As any soldier will tell you, the breaking point often comes around the thirteenth month. Up until that point, his second tour was uneventful. The enemy had retreated or focused efforts in other parts of the country near the Syrian border. With nothing to do most days and nights, they spent their time getting drunk, playing video games, and trying not to die from boredom.

The men and women fraternized in ways they shouldn't have, but no one was there to stop them or care. One soldier got pregnant. Another tried to slit his wrists. The heat got to them. The flies got to them. They gained weight, got bloated, and lost their discipline. Gone were the shining days of the armed saviors in green fatigues. Nobody remembered why they were there in the first place.

This was the first time in the service Alexander saw anyone shoot heroin. He stayed away, determined to keep himself on the straight and narrow. No one in boot camp had prepared soldiers for the horrors of war. Perhaps the biggest horror was what soldiers did to cope with their boredom. Verbal and physical harassment of the locals was not uncommon. Nor was theft. If the devil found work for idle hands, those accustomed to combat were only too happy to do dirty work.

He was on patrol one morning when an IED exploded underneath the joint light tactical vehicle in front of his own, killing four men. The body parts that weren't melted into the seats and ceiling were turned to dust by an instant, violent cremation. The smell of smoke and burning flesh and bone made Alexander retch. When he finished, he got down on his knees and prayed that God would save their souls.

He found the strength to make the calls and fill out the debriefing reports, even overstepping his duties by taking pains to make sure someone notified the next of kin in the most expedient and sympathetic way. Alexander knew the only good thing about deaths over here was that they were handled with care when it came to civilians back home. From the soldier who showed incredible valor to the dirt bag who overdosed on heroin with his gun between his legs, everyone was given a hero's burial, and the parents were none the wiser.

One gray morning, he sought out the chaplain.

"I never much gave a thought to God growing up. Wasn't raised in any church; didn't care much for religion. But when I saw the way those guys ended up…" He let the rest of the sentence go unfinished. Tears came without warning. The chaplain stayed with him for an hour. He listened. He nodded. And he shared appropriate words of comfort.

For a month or so, Alexander was able to carry those words like a security blanket, until the words stopped working, because he couldn't get the sight of four charred soldiers in a truck on fire out of his head. He saw them every time he closed his eyes. And they were there when he woke up. His mind was a pressure cooker, threatening to explode at any moment.

It wasn't that he felt he should have done more to save them; nothing could have been done. It was just the sheer senselessness of it all that immobilized his psyche. If Alexander's truck had been the first in the convoy, it would have been his number instead of theirs. War was hell because it was arbitrary.

Alexander spent the remaining few months of his second tour in a codeine-induced fog. He was depressed and angry and bored. It was all he could do to get out of bed in the morning. But when it was time for lights-out, he couldn't sleep. They sent him home at Christmas. But without a family to go home to, there was nothing to do.

He went to a titty bar on Christmas Eve. The dancers wore Santa hats and red G-strings. He spent some money, took a girl home, and woke up alone.

She left him a note on the motel nightstand that read "Thanks for your service, soldier. Merry Christmas. God bless you, and God bless Texas. Xoxo."

Alexander sat on the bed, not moving for a half hour. For a fleeting moment, he thought about blowing his brains out, but the darkest of those clouds passed. He looked for a phone book, thinking it might be good to talk to someone about his feelings. But he couldn't interrupt someone on Christmas Day. Not his fellow soldiers enjoying respite with their families. For a few blessed weeks, they could put aside the horrors and atrocities. The idea of chatting to some no-name angel on a suicide prevention line wasn't appealing, either. Instead, he drove to a roadhouse bar and drank until he was numb. Alexander spent the rest of his furlough watching cartoons and waiting for orders.

Like some sick joke, they shipped him back to Iraq, this time just outside Mosul. The area had been cleared for months, with locals trying to put back the pieces of their shattered lives and achieve some sense of normalcy. Far from liberating the oppressed and making the world safe for Texan democracy, the mighty 51-7 was reduced to living in an outpost where the locals were hostile and mistrusting. They'd seen their fair share of carnage and suffered collateral damage as a result.

Alexander's outpost was situated on a stretch of road pockmarked by bombs and mortar projectiles. In this decrepit concrete oasis, their orders were to help rebuild the roads. In oppressive heat, Alexander and his company would first sweep for IEDs, neutralizing them if necessary, and then spend painstaking amounts of time shoveling and repaving.

He'd go through two hydration packs' worth of water a shift, even on the days when his only job was standing guard, waiting for insurgents that never appeared and waving off locals who hurled insults at them in the regional Arabic language. Alexander would return their curses with even more vitriol, waving his M16 as he did so.

His bitterness only became worse when he remembered turning down the judge's offer to work on a chain gang, thinking the armed forces would be more virtuous. Now his job was more or less doing the exact same thing in hotter weather. He wasn't a soldier. He was a construction worker with a gun.

Alexander spent the next year descending into a thick and heavy haze. He became adept at swallowing a handful of pills without water. Though the president declared progress in the war against terror on the nightly news back home, Iraq seemed no better than when they'd first arrived. If anything, it had even deteriorated more. The accomplishments were cosmetic at best. They might have been rebuilding roads, but the hearts and minds were unchanged.

He withdrew from the company, spending as much time alone as possible. When Alexander wasn't killing, he killed time. When he wasn't rebuilding, he was building a wall around himself: feeling nothing, thinking nothing—a perfect zombie soldier shuffling in his desert boots.

In some of his more coherent moments, he'd eavesdrop on his fellow soldiers' gossip. If one were to believe it, the 51-7's latest tour might be twenty-four more months. When the gossip became verified fact, he upped the drink and drug intake, until his tolerance went from alarming to legendary.

It was at this point that Alexander tried dreamfish for the first time. While the Mosul locals wanted nothing to do with the Texans, the Bedouin soldiers were more pragmatic. Texan GIs were paid every month. Some had Texan currency, which was worth seventy times that of the Iraqi dinar. The Bedouin were all too eager to sell what they had. And if they didn't have what the soldiers wanted, they'd find it all right. Alexander was amazed with the speed with which they'd procure everything from hashish to a bootlegged blockbuster movie release.

It was one such Bedouin named Hatim who supplied Alexander with dreamfish. A member of an unidentified tribe, he often traveled through the region. Neither spoke each other's language very well, but Alexander pointed to his head and his heart and made the Bedouin understand how much he was suffering. Hatim's eyes showed concern. He nodded like a sage and said, "PTSD, yes. Survivor's guilt."

He then handed Alexander a bag with the bone-dry fish inside. "You smoke. Just a little. Little only." He repeated the warning.

Alexander rejoined his squad, explaining away the fetid smell by telling the other soldiers it was a Bedouin custom to present valuable gifts as a sign of their hospitality.

Getting the correct dosage took a bit of experimenting. When he first tired it, Alexander used a mixture of half tobacco, half dreamfish, figuring that would be the equivalent of "just a little." But as it turned out, 0.4 grams of dreamfish was closer to the "much too much" end of the spectrum. The experiment plunged Alexander into three days of a waking nightmare, where all he could was endure.

At first he thought the desert sands had turned red from the blood of soldiers and terrorists alike who'd died in his tours of duty. The bobbing headless bodies then turned into dolphins.

Then a sound came he hadn't heard in weeks: the very real sound of gunfire from insurgents. While standing guard during infrastructure rebuild, six men appeared dressed in Bedouin clothing. This wasn't in itself unusual. But there was something about them that seemed off. When they got about thirty yards away, Alexander realized what it was. They were wearing boots, not sandals. Before he could warn the others, their Kalashnikovs appeared.

He shouted to take cover, diving behind the vehicle as he did so. When he was sober, the sound of bullets hitting metal came like deafening white noise. But in his current state, Alexander's paranoia made him associate the sound with specific visions. He scanned the tops of palm trees, believing the sound was coming from crabs as big as a man, hiding in the treetops, crabs with giant castanets clutched in their pincers. They played for him alone. With a junkie's warped sense, he thought the minute they stopped playing the castanets, their giant pincers would reach out to decapitate him. Somehow he and his squad fought through the ambush, killing all six insurgents, with only one solder suffering injury—two if you counted Alexander's mental state.

He was taken to sick bay, where he vomited for twelve hours, hallucinating the entire time. He was curious to see the ocean and nautical hallucinations replaced with more nonsensical visions.

Alexander was convinced he'd turned into a can of snakes, the kind sold at joke stores. With each spew of vomit, another snake popped out. When his stomach was empty and only bile came up, he lay shivering in a cold sweat. He was ready to die.

As war in the Middle East progressed, the medics saw with startling regularity two types of patients in sick bay. Soldiers who were wounded in battle were to be expected. But the soldiers who were damaged by what they saw and what they did to themselves—casualties of the war and the failing war on drugs—were a different kind of demon to fight. These brave men and women would shoot up, snort, drink, or swallow anything they could to get away from reality. The medics had thought they'd seen and treated it all, until they saw the effects of too much dreamfish.

First they gave Alexander something to stop the vomiting. It worked. But that still left the hallucinations. For the next two days, Alexander alternated between screaming in horror and fits of uncontrollable laughter at the movies playing for him.

It was only after a medic had the idea to question the squad that a soldier who'd witnessed the ambush remembered the Bedouin's gift. Hatim was located and brought to base. They explained through an interpreter what had occurred. The Bedouin shook his head, reached into his bag, and brought out some dried herbs. They watched as he prepared a special tea, which they forced down Alexander's throat. Twenty minutes later, he was as close to normal as he'd ever been.

With only a slight accent in his otherwise perfect English, Hatim screamed at him. "Dammit, man. I said only a little bit! Are you thick? What the hell." He spat on the floor for good measure and turned to leave.

Then Alexander's commanding officer had a go. The imposing figure stood over his pale, stinking body and yelled for a half hour. When he lost his voice, the commanding officer took Alexander's jacket from a chair and stripped him of two ranks.

"Sergeant Alexander," he rasped, "if it weren't for your exemplary record and the bravery shown during your first tours of duty, you'd be a complete worm all over again. And it's only because we need bodies out here that I can't afford to court-martial your sorry ass. Consider yourself blessed and get back to work." As an afterthought, he added, "*Specialist* Alexander."

Alexander responded with a weak, "Sir, yes, sir."

It would have been a nice time to take stock of the situation and get his life in gear—a come-to-Jesus moment, as they say. But Alexander had seen little of Jesus since he'd been fighting the terrorists who'd shoot to kill, die for their fanatical cause, behead without compunction, and lay IEDs on every square inch of pavement.

It was another week before he could stand up without seeing light trails. When the drugs finally left his system, Alexander went back to work. Each week, he experimented with the dreamfish dosage, starting at 0.05 grams. Then he moved it up to 0.1 grams, and this seemed to be just enough to create some level of dislocated reality without leading to torment.

At this dosage, the high started off by making him queasy. This was something he found avoidable if he first ate a starchy vegetable like mashed potatoes. It took an hour or so for the effects to come on, lasting anywhere from four to six hours. While the hallucinations were odd, they weren't disturbing or severe. It felt like someone had left the TV on mute in the background. The images were interesting enough to distract and amuse his brain, but harmless enough to allow normal mental function. He settled into a daily groove. He was at least maintaining composure.

And then one afternoon, the country rap star showed up wearing rhinestone and leather pants, a white wife beater with a flak jacket over it, and a red felt pimp's hat. He also had with him an entourage of fifteen musicians and hangers-on in tow, as if a surreal field trip were taking place.

Alexander was lounging in his bed, counting cobwebs real and imaginary when a burst of feedback blared from the PA system. He could tell the difference between cobwebs because the real ones weren't bioluminescent like the imaginary ones. The fake ones reacted to the feedback swell by rearranging the patterns. He shook his head to clear them.

The announcer's voice came over the PA, beginning with a mumbled apology for the feedback. His delivery was stilted as if someone had just handed him a printout to read, which was most likely the case.

"Soldiers of the Fifty-One Seven, listen up. The USO has seen fit to bring some astounding entertainment to this fine base to help us keep up morale. This evening at twenty-one hundred hours will be a special performance from Fort Worth's very own MC Jeb." Alexander cringed when he heard the female soldiers giggle and shout like pop fans.

He hadn't planned on attending the show. But after a few shots of whisky and his special cigarette, he changed his mind. MC Jeb might not do anything for his morale, but the entertainment value of watching a shit show sure would.

Someone had erected a makeshift stage for MC Jeb and his backing band, which consisted of a dwarf who scratched records on two turntables and a country guitarist who looked like he'd been born in a honky-tonk. Standing in some unpronounceable location in Iraq, in an outpost base nowhere near the front lines of the war, the band could not have been more far removed from their normal concerts with light shows, laser projections, giant amplifiers, and people who actually paid good money to see them perform.

Alexander had to hand it to the guy. MC Jeb might have been smarmy, but at least he was a consummate professional. With a grand salute, he took the stage promptly with his dwarf and country guitarist filing up the steps behind.

"Before we start the show, I just want to say thank you for your service. I know I speak for Willard and L'il Miggy here when I say it's people like you who serve our great Texan nation and keep us safe at night, and we appreciate it so much."

Polite applause.

"You know," MC Jeb continued, "we just flew in on a Black Hawk helicopter, and I have to say—holy shit, that's fucking loud." He put his fingers in his hears.

The soldiers laughed.

"But I'll tell you what: we're gonna see if we can out loud the helicopter tonight. This first song is about making out under the stars in the heart of Texas, with a good old-fashioned country girl who ain't afraid to drop them short shorts and bend over."

With that, L'il Miggy dropped the bass, Willard plucked an acoustic-electric guitar, and MC Jeb rapped about making out with the girl who wasn't afraid to drop her pants and bend over. It seemed like half the song was nothing more than MC Jeb shouting, "Drop your pants and bend over." And when he got tired of that, he'd shout, "Drop your pants," and then point the microphone at the crowd, so they could finish singing the lyrics for him.

Alexander managed to get through two songs before giving up and heading back to his footlocker. He was running out of dreamfish; he'd have to be careful from now on. His whisky stash was still in good supply.

He took a swig, passing it to two soldiers who sat playing cards on the bed.

"Here's what pisses me off most about civilians," he said. "Every time I see one of them, I don't want to protect them. I want to shoot 'em myself."

"Tell me about it," one of them answered. "Whenever I'm home, they want to thank me for keeping them safe and buy me a drink. I want to say, 'If you knew what I really did, you'd never look at me again.' But I tell you what: I don't mind taking a beer off their hands."

Alexander nodded. "They all think we lead these amazing, heroic lives of bravery, like we're all SEALs who brave the elements and cheat our deaths by chewing off our leg, just so we can crawl away and live to fight another day." He took back the bottle and took another swig. "Shit, you'd sooner get your leg blown off than ever have to chew it off anyway."

He'd just tucked the bottle into the footlocker when his commanding officer approached.

"Specialist Alexander."

"Sir, yes, sir."

"What's the matter? Not enjoying the morale booster? Well, never mind. You'd best turn in early because you'll have a big day tomorrow. Something's happening in Hammam al-Alil. Know it?"

Alexander shook his head, waiting for him to continue.

"They've got sulfur springs there. Used to be big business for the locals. Matter of fact, it was the first business in the area to resume the moment we pushed back Al Qaeda. Locals claim the sulfur spa is good for healing and detox. Maybe you should try it while you're there, Alexander. Might do you some good."

The commanding officer allowed the soldiers to laugh before continuing.

"Now, you know how some of these villagers are superstitious. They're claiming a demon is hiding in the sulfur springs, making a great noise and scaring the locals away. Go down there and take a look."

"Yes, sir."

"And, Alexander, try and lay off the shit fish, or whatever it is you smoke. Otherwise you might get smoked."

More laughter came from the other soldiers.

"It's either a buncha bullshit, or it's Al Qaeda come back to put the fear of Allah in 'em. My money's on the latter. At ease."

When he left, Alexander flopped down on his bed. "Hey, what'd you do while you were in the army? Well, I'll tell you: I investigated sulfur mud. That's right, fellow civilian. I investigated literal shit. Don't it make you feel proud to be a patriotic Texan?"

They set out at 0400 that morning, driving three hours to Hammam al-Alil. Alexander was hung over. Coming down from dreamfish didn't help. Above all, he was more than a little angry, because his commanding officer had also assigned Ramos to the patrol, and that was a very bad thing because Ramos was a magnet.

Every company has a soldier who's been chosen by life's dark jester to be the one who attracts the most danger when they're out on patrol. Most soldiers can go out on patrol for months without incident. Then all of a sudden they go out with a magnet like Ramos, and their Jeep runs over an IED, or they get ambushed or caught in friendly fire from a wayward drone. Ramos was the 51-7's magnet. With incredible luck, Alexander had managed to avoid him like the plague until now.

Ramos had grown up in Pomona, in a rough part of town. He'd gotten into trouble often, but it was never too serious. His father Enrique was a retired Texan SEAL who immigrated to California in hopes of finding a better life. He was fair but tough on his son, working hard to instill in him a sense of rigid discipline and respect. The whole neighborhood respected Enrique.

One time, the Sharkies were having a house party next door. They started making trouble, getting a little too rowdy. A fight broke out and spilled into Enrique's yard. He came outside to talk to them, trying to be cool. "Guys, you gotta break it up; this is my house. Why don't you take a few breaths and calm down. It's a nice day." He was just saying whatever he could to defuse the situation. One guy pulled out a .380 semiautomatic, pointed it at him sideways, which is something only amateurs do. Another one pulled a knife.

The older Sharkies still talk about it—how Enrique took care of them in less than thirty seconds. The guy with the knife ended up with a dislocated shoulder and a hand broken in three places. The one with the .380 wasn't as lucky. Enrique coldcocked him with one punch. The guy landed so hard on the driveway that he split his head open. From then on, the Sharkies didn't go anywhere near his street. Ramos witnessed that spectacle, saw his father's muscle memory spring into action a full decade after returning to civilian life, and vowed to change his ways.

But life had other plans. He met a girl from Texas, knocked her up, and ended up moving to the country his father had left. They kept in touch, but Enrique would never visit. "Fuck Texas," Enrique would say, whenever Ramos would ask him to come. "I almost lost my life fighting for them, and they gave me nothing in return."

Ramos fell in love with the country. He enrolled in vocational school, picked up several odd jobs here and there, but it was nowhere near enough to provide for a girlfriend and young daughter.

"I was on my way to trade school, you know. Woulda been an air conditioner repairman, something like that. Maybe after ten years, I woulda owned my own company, done all right. But no one would have given me respect, you know? I wanted fuckin' respect like my dad."

The Mandatory Enlistment Law was passed for all those twenty-five and under. Although he could have skirted it, Ramos joined just two weeks shy of turning twenty-six. He'd experienced an obscene amount of combat in a short period of time, was given an in-field promotion to sergeant for his astounding efforts.

At first his company assumed they were stationed in a hotbed. Then they thought, maybe he was a bad ass who went looking for trouble.

When he was transferred to the 51-7, where nothing had happened for months, the soldiers got wise. Misadventure found its way to the company with each new patrol. Everyone made sure to give him a wide berth and only stood close enough to mock him when they were back on base.

The 51-7 had a running bet with Ramos. Whenever something happened on his watch, he had to buy them all Pizza Hut, one of the few food treats in an otherwise MRE-filled wasteland. Ramos was $7,000 in the hole.

"Remember, guys: keep your eyes open and as far away from the magnet as possible," Alexander said.

"Least I'm not a fuckup like you," Ramos answered. "I'm your superior, so watch that gringo mouth."

Alexander hopped in the armored vehicle, lit one of his special cigarettes. The effect was immediate. As they drove toward Hammam al-Alil in the predawn hours, the unpaved road took on a burnt-sienna color, reminding him of the Carolina region of the Confederate States of America.

They were greeted by a group of villagers standing just outside Hammam al-Alil. Here, in the midst of a war zone, was a strange oasis of mud, grass, clear hot springs, and stinking sulfur pits. Inside one of the rooms was a sort of crumbling bathhouse. There was a large pool in the shape of a circle. An intricate set of green and blue tiles formed an outer ring. The sulfur pits were inside and outside the structures. They could see smoke billowing from one of the roofless buildings.

With the dreamfish now in full effect, Alexander's brain was busy filling in the details. He saw a man dressed like an ancient sultan standing in the middle of the spa. The man then turned into a Club Med cabana boy, who carried towels and a fancy fruit-laced cocktail. He shook the scene away and tried to focus.

Ramos spoke to the villagers in rapid Arabic. An elder pointed toward the smoking building, answering his questions in hushed tones. Young boys gathered next to him. All wore the same look of desperation and fear.

Ramos shifted his M4 carbine and turned back to the soldiers. "They got here an hour ago. They thought it was safe to open up. Then they said they saw a fireball come from inside there."

The village elder spoke again, his voice even more anxious. He ended by repeating the same word.

Sergeant Ramos nodded. "They believe it is something called *Anzû.*"

"And what the hell is that?"

"Apparently Anzû is a fire-breathing bird, like a cross between a dragon and a phoenix. And they're scared shitless of it, because it brings bad luck and destruction to all it visits."

Alexander watched the building shift shapes in front of him. The colors kept changing. He could hear a low growl coming from inside. He felt bile rise and collect in the back of his throat.

Ramos told the villagers to clear out as fast as they could. He gave them twenty minutes until he was sure they were at least a mile away. "A dragon—like hell it is. They're probably setting up camp there: keep the villagers away and sabotage the economy, too."

They approached with caution, each soldier taking a different location. Ramos walked with Alexander.

"Keep your distance, Magnet."

"Speak for yourself, junkie," he hissed. "I can smell you even through the sulfur."

They ran for cover against an outdoor shower, crouching to peer around the edge.

"See anything?" Ramos asked.

"No."

"Me neither."

They strained their ears, hearing only their breaths. The area was silent. Not even the wind blew. They were just about to move out when the sound of footsteps came from inside the farthest building to the right.

Ramos motioned for Alexander to head out. "Cover me."

He inched toward the smoking building, keeping clear of the entrance. Alexander followed after, making his way toward the boulders near the outside pits. A pool of sweat ran down his neck, collecting at the small of his back. The other soldiers moved on silent feet, as they investigated the other ends of the spa.

The first sulfur pit he came upon was strewn with garbage. Alexander wondered how anyone could believe the place was therapeutic. With every bubble that broke the surface came a sickening rotten egg stench that stung his nostrils.

He made eye contact with the other soldiers, making sure he knew their positions at all times and keeping his fear in check. It was OK to be on edge. But as he discovered during his prolonged episode where he'd lain in agony, the effects of dreamfish were more pronounced when one was afraid. Alexander breathed in and out in slow, steady breaths, making sure his heart rate stayed even. The rocks were ten feet away, just a few more steps to safety. Alexander stayed crouched, making himself as small a target as possible.

Something flickered in his left periphery. Without turning his head, he hit the ground just in time to miss the blast of gunfire. With excruciating heat from the springs now burning through his clothing, he returned fire in the direction of the enemy. He watched an enemy combatant's chest explode.

Then all hell broke loose. Ramos came running out of the smoking building, screaming for everyone to vacate. Alexander just managed to scramble to his feet in time to see the structure explode. Fear gripped him, sending the dreamfish into overdrive.

To his amazement and shock, the Anzû rose forth in one motion, its great mud-covered purple wings shattering the tiles with such force he had to shield his face from the burning debris.

Alexander tried to run, but his boots sank in the mud pit like it was quicksand. It didn't help that his body was heavy by the sludge already clinging to it. He lurched forward, managing to fall onto drier ground. Behind him, a rush of wind came as the other buildings exploded. There were now three Anzû shooting toward the sky.

The muscle memory of basic training kicked in. Alexander crawled toward the vehicles. The other soldiers were nowhere to be seen. The sound of scattered gunfire whizzed past him from behind, while in front, his brothers in arms fired well above. He wormed his way through the mud, hoping if he moved fast enough, the dragons would not tear his flesh to pieces.

Alexander whipped his head around to assess the situation. He saw no enemy combatants, heard no gunfire. He didn't dare look up in the sky, in case he saw the Anzû there, ready to swoop.

A commotion came from his front. Standing by the vehicle, the soldiers shouted frantically for him to hurry. Sensing his chance, Alexander got up and ran faster than he had in years, even though his boots were caked with layer upon layer of thick mud.

He was just ten yards from the armored vehicle when his foot touched something that made a metal clang. It lay hidden among the rocks. Sand and smoke filled his vision. A split second later, he was hurtling through the air in slow motion toward Ramos, wondering where the Anzû had flown to, asking why everything had gone silent.

Department of the Republic of Texas Army
Fifth Brigade Combat Team, Thirty-Sixth Armored Division
Forward Operating Base, Mosul, Iraq
APO BD 13956-2311

MEMORANDUM THROUGH Commander, Fifth Brigade Combat Team, Thirty-Sixth Armored Division APO BD 13956-2311

FOR Commander, Thirty-Sixth Armored Division, APO, BD, 13847

SUBJECT: Recommendation for an Honorable Discharge for Specialist Alexander, Braxton A.

Despite recent behavior displaying mental deterioration caused by rampant drug abuse and subordination causing deranking, Specialist Alexander was still a vital part of the 51-7 on his last mission. On Friday morning, 0935 hours, Alexander and squad were met with hostile fire in Hammam al-Alil sulfur springs, where insurgents had placed three large improvised explosive devices in three different buildings, set to go within seconds of each other, leaving four insurgents on duty. Alexander fought with courage, killing one of the four insurgents.

While retreating to their armored vehicle, Alexander stepped on a land mine, believed to be a leftover from the previous war, sustaining severe injuries. It is thanks to the bravery of his fellow soldiers and their training in tactical combat casualty care that Alexander survived at all.

Alexander has been airlifted to Landstuhl Medical Center in Germany. His prognosis is grim: second-degree burns, internal bleeding, amputation of both legs below the knee. Even if Alexander makes a full recovery, his mental state will most likely be a further hindrance to performing his duties to the best of his ability, even as a noncombatant. In the unlikely event of his survival, I am recommending honorable discharge, given his last performance as a soldier and reinstating of sergeant rank.

ATC, AR
Commanding

Chapter 2

Sgt. Biker unbuttoned his faded black leather vest, picked up the sledgehammer, and smashed the empty B & N hardware-store shelving along one side of the wall for all it was worth, which was ironic because it was not worth much at all. The other shelves he left intact for when the shipments arrived. With one set of shelving gone, they now had room for three pairs of bunk beds and the orange Smeg refrigerator he'd managed to get from Breeder in exchange for a litter of six healthy Maine Coons.

The Texans were crazy about Maine Coons, couldn't get enough of them, and would pay a pretty penny for kittens—rather, a pretty Texas penny, although he'd take any currency they offered. Whenever the army shipped out, the cats would go along, acting as mousers for whatever land they liberated, more often than not in the Middle East.

God bless the Christian Republic of Texas; long may she spend money on four-legged fur monsters. And for that matter, too, hats off to Breeder, who lived a stone's throw away in Mar Vista. There were so many cats in this part of California, thanks to that No Kill Shelter law no one bothered to repeal, that some parts of Los Angeles, like the Ballona Wetlands, had been taken over by the buggers. Biker knew how to trap the adults, care for the babies, tame the feral ones, and sell them to Breeder for his choice of currencies or, more often than not, trade them for whatever items he needed to reinforce and outfit his space.

The Smeg was in fine shape, big enough to keep food for the whole squad, maybe even two squads if they kept to canned goods. But it was also narrow enough that it wouldn't take up too much room.

Biker cleared the broken shelving, plugged in the refrigerator, and tossed in three cases of off-brand Mexican beer. It was just after eight in the morning. He pulled one out of the case, cracked it open, and drank it at room temperature.

The traffic on Washington Boulevard was already horrendous. A few months back, he'd commandeered the B & N hardware store and adjacent space, which over the years had been everything from a Swedish restaurant to a shared workspace for startup entrepreneurs to a store that sold electric bikes for $10,000 a pop before finally shutting down.

Biker wouldn't have been caught dead on one of those bougie bikes. Anyway, that was long ago. This stretch of Venice had lain fallow for quite a few years, and soon everything started rotting in the sunshine like fruit on the vine. He reasoned that taking over the space was doing the neighborhood a service, like gentrifying it. Biker brought with him able-bodied people to keep the place clean and free from crime. If sometimes he had to use a bit more force than was necessary, at least it got the word out loud and clear. The gangs soon slinked off to other corners of the city.

He sucked at the long-neck bottle and waited. The new recruit had missed the reconnaissance mission—second day in a row. She was young; he figured her to be in her early twenties. That might have been the problem. Finding kids that age with the discipline of real soldiers was getting tougher and tougher. Maybe she'd work out in the end, but it was doubtful.

He knew full well you couldn't treat a member of his crew like he'd been treated back in the day. They were too young. Too coddled. Hazing would only bring tears, and then she'd piss off back to Redondo or Calabasas or Laguna Niguel or wherever it was that her inexperienced ass came from. He could no longer afford to pick and choose. The time was getting nearer. He needed boots on the ground. And if they weren't up to snuff as soldiers, then at least they'd be decoys. He didn't even care if they bought the cause as long as they joined it and fought for it.

He saw her walking north toward him, carrying that yellow surfboard, still in a wetsuit, still barefoot. Biker smirked. How long ago was it that he and his banditos would steal down to Mexico under cover of night, guns on their hips, invisible as bats against a darkened sky? They'd hide in the villages, sneaking through the alleys for clandestine meetings with resistance members who planned to take Mexico from the inside, making sure it stayed Californian.

At first it was easy to run guns, and even easier to disrupt the checkpoints. They'd fire off a GTR-18 Smokey Sam surface-to-air missile provided by the folks at the Coronado base, and the border patrol and customs agents would run around like chickens with their heads cut off, afraid the end was in sight.

After a few months, they got wise and sent in reinforcements. Biker had no compunction about changing tactics with a few well-placed pipe bombs. After a dozen or so incidents and a half a dozen casualties, they had easy enough access with no one stopping them.

To think that all the while, the gringo tourists sipped their shitty cocktails in Ensenada, none the wiser. For all Biker knew, they were still there, chatting about nothing, with only a vague drunken realization that the change for their ceviche came in California dollars instead of pesos.

Biker and his gang of mercenaries had followed parts of the old dusty Baja 1000 route. He'd think of all those people who'd once raced here, the names of winners relegated to obscurity: James Garner, Steve McQueen—forgotten names.

At night, they'd ride in darkness with their headlights covered, being heard but not seen, instilling fear and gaining respect from the locals before the real armed forces rolled in. They called themselves Los Barrenderos, sweeping the streets in front and leaving a long slick trail of blood behind.

He was sure they could have taken more land, 100 percent certain of it. There was no need to stop with Baja, as important as that area was. But he was just a soldier, not a decision-maker. And when those Mexican *pendejos* went and sealed that border up tight, and Texas carved out another swath, it was game over. He rode back up the coast, back to an unrecognizable LA. It was as if while he was on the front lines of the war, the bottom had fallen out back home in Southern California.

The demarcation line was somewhere around San Luis Obispo. He'd seen it with his own eyes, as real and glaring as an exposed fault line. The North had the wealth, and the South had the most useless industry ever. Those Hollywood fuckers didn't even make movies for Californians anymore. They were more interested in selling schlock to developing nations with little grasp of the language but eager to spend their hard-earned cash to watch car chases and explosions or both.

Southern Californians lived like peasants beholden to their snobby northern population, who demanded everything from them and gave them nothing in return. How long could you keep a population down before it reared its ugly head and said enough is enough? They were a client state within their own country. He was one in a growing segment of people no longer anesthetized by the sun and organic foods or distracted by cheap entertainment. Every day, Biker watched a new horrendous film called reality. He was both actor and viewer. He saw it for what it was, and he had the sense to try and do something about it before it was too late. If it came down to it, he was born free and planned to die that way.

A hand banged on the glass window, snapping him back to present. She came in, laying her surfboard against the wall.

"You don't watch your feet, you'll get tetanus."

He guessed her hair was supposed to be blond. Years of surfing in the no-go zone had stained it puke green. Her bangs were faded pink, as if she'd tried to dye them and given up halfway through. He turned away as she walked to the bathroom, and he finished his beer in one long swallow. A few minutes later, she came out wearing dark jeans, a T-shirt, and a green military coat that was covered with patches.

"You should have seen the swell."

"And you should have been on reconnaissance."

She pouted, looking even younger than her age. Then, rebuke forgotten in an instant, her mood brightened. "Love the fridge. It's uh-maze-ing. What about the shipment? Any more info?"

"It'll come when it comes," he said.

She reached into the fridge, pulled out a beer, uncapped it with her teeth, and spit the cap on the floor. "You've been saying that since I arrived. What in the actual fuck?"

He pointed to a chair. She sat down, sulking.

"You've been here—what?—two and a half weeks? So far, you've done jack except eat my food and drink my beer."

She scoffed. "What is there to do? I already know where the enemy lives and works. I don't need to scope them out. I want action."

The others wouldn't be back until late that evening. They had hours to kill. "It'll come when it comes," Biker repeated. "Help me move this pile of wood."

She rolled her eyes. "Fine, Sgt. Biker. Sir, yes, sir." She straightened her jacket and stood in mock attention. "When am I going to get a name?"

Biker studied her. She had a black ace of spades tattoo on her neck just behind her right ear and a ring in her nose. Pale skin, acne scars on both cheeks. Five patches on her jacket: a rainbow, a star; one patch was just the words "Far Out," in purple and orange; another was a cartoon character he didn't recognize; and the last was an old red flag. He pointed to it.

"Know what that is?"

"Should I?"

"Hammer and sickle—industry and agriculture. It might not look like much, but a sickle's got a sharp blade. You don't look like much either, but you got a sharp mouth and are street smart when you aren't being stupid. So from now on, you're Private Sickle."

"That's rad." She marched in place. "I am Private Sickle. Sir, yes, sir."

He held up a hand as if to calm her. "Only if you keep your eyes and ears open and do as I say from now on. No more surfing till the job is done."

They threw the broken shelves away in the dumpster and fed the pair of Siamese he was fostering. They weren't quite old enough to sell to Breeder. Another few weeks would do it.

He took Sickle inside and taught her how to clean a gun. "I know you can shoot, but if you don't know how to clean, then it'll be useless when you need it most. This is true of all guns and rifles alike."

She watched with rapt attention the way a young daughter listens to her father read a bedtime story. He was surprised to see how fast she picked it up. Maybe there was hope for her after all.

"Seriously, when's the stuff going to arrive? And don't tell me, 'It'll come when it comes,'" she said. "You have to know something."

"All's I know is what they tell me. What I heard last was our shipment got diverted somewhere just outside Las Vegas."

"Oh," she said. "Well, that's not bad then. At least it's in California now. Right?"

"My thoughts exactly. But it still could be days, or it could be weeks till we get it. I just don't know, and I won't until they tell me. They call it 'a need-to-know basis.'"

Sickle repeated the phrase.

"And that's also why it shouldn't matter to you either—because your job isn't to ask questions. Your job is to take orders."

"So then what do you want me to do now, Sgt. Biker?"

"I wanted you to learn reconnaissance in case we start taking other areas. But since it's too late for that today, I'll teach you strategy. Then tonight you're on watch on the roof."

Biker went over to one of the cluttered shelves. After a minute of searching, he found what he was looking for. It was an old board game. He blew the dust off the top of it.

"For real? You want me to play a board game?"

"I told you already," he said. "Strategy."

"Yeah, but—"

"Would you rather learn out there when bullets are flying around you?"

"Hell no," she said. "But what the hell is Risk?"

"That's three times now: strategy."

She shrugged and sat back down. "If you say so."

Sickle watched Biker unfold the board game, which was a map of the world, and place it on the table between them. He could see her counting the number of countries under her breath.

She pointed to the board. "Whoa, hold up now," she said. "Western United States? Eastern United States? There are only two countries."

"Right."

"And they don't even have the right names. Is this like a fantasy game or something?"

Biker ignored the question. Instead he launched into a detailed instruction on how to play the game. Because they were only two players, they each selected an army. To make it interesting, Biker created a third neutral army that would act as a buffer between them. This army would be more of a neutral roadblock than an active participant. He then explained that wars aren't just fought between two sides.

"It would be easy if it were just us versus them. But it's usually us versus them with some other guys who are on our side but only up to a point. There are a lot of variables."

He tried to explain the concept. There were allied countries that didn't do much except pay lip service for political reasons. And there were countries that were hostile but hadn't declared war and just showboated for short-term gain. And finally, there were neutral countries that would do business with either side regardless of ideology. Often that kind of country thought they were being above it all, but in reality, they came out of it looking like assholes—like Switzerland and Nazi gold.

Sickle shook her head. "Dude, I have no idea what in the hell you are talking about. I thought you were teaching me strategy, not history."

Biker grabbed the dice and shook them in his giant fist. Everything about him was huge, from his forearms to his gray handlebar mustache to the black bandana on his head. He rolled the dice with such force they slid off the board and landed on the floor. Sickle scrambled after them.

"I know I'm not supposed to ask questions, but I've been meaning to ask you about your tattoo." She came back up, handing him the dice. "Who is that person on your arm?"

Biker glanced at the face with the pork-chop sideburns, shiny pompadour, and bee-stung lips singing into a microphone. A bright-colored light glinted off the wrap-around sunglasses, the same light that made the diamond-studded collar flash. "Why, little lady, uh, that's the King. Thank you very much."

Taking his beefy forearm in both of her tiny hands, Sickle gave the figure a good hard look. She then wrinkled her nose. "King of what? One of these countries on the board game?" She laughed, dismissing his arm with a throw. "This really takes the cake. Also, why in the hell did you thank me just now?"

Biker opened his mouth to answer, but she waved him off. "Never mind. I forgot; I'm not supposed to ask questions. Just teach me how to play this game. I'll need to learn all about strategy before we get out on the field. Who knows—maybe by the time the shipment comes, I'll be an expert."

They played for a few hours. He beat her three times in a row. Then she beat him twice. Biker let her win the last game when her frustration got so great she threatened to cry if she lost. Not that Sickle was bad at strategy—she was just inconsistent. Sometimes she'd surprise him; other times she was careless, and he'd anticipate her every move. When they called it a day, Sickle pestered him with questions about geography, history, and the world in general.

He stood up to stretch his joints. "All I know about the world is what I've seen with my own eyes. All I know about history is that it's in the distant past. And borders are ephemeral. You're lucky if you can control the immediate space around you. Speaking of which, let's get something to eat and get ready for the evening watch."

Sickle stretched her skinny legs. "Did I do OK for my first lesson in strategy, Biker?"

His smile was brief. "Seen worse."

They locked the front door, pulled the metal gate across the front, and walked a few blocks to Boris, the Russian place, for dinner. Most restaurants in LA came and went, but Boris was so far from anything approaching trendy that it had been a mainstay for decades. The restaurant was always either near empty or packed with Russians. The past few times Biker had tried to enter, he'd been met with a polite but firm refusal from the woman who ran the place.

"We are closed. Come back tomorrow, yes?"

In each case, the same three men would glare at him from their table at the back. He assumed the place was a front but had yet to discover the truth. If they sold arms, they might be useful.

The woman greeted them with politeness this time, her eyes turning distant when they came across the Soviet flag on Sickle's coat.

He ordered stroganoff to share. The TMZ channel was on the flat-screen TV above the bar. A startled-looking pop singer at a European airport was answering questions about her choice to not wear underwear as some kind of protest.

"Ugh," Sickle groaned, "I can't stand her. She hasn't had a hit in like five years."

Biker glanced around to look at the screen. "No idea who she is. But I know the airport."

"Oh yeah?"

"Orly, in Paris. They discovered a firebomb in the terminal a few months back. Managed to disable it just in time."

"And the worst part is she changes her hair with every album. It's not making your music any better, girlfriend. Give it up." And then she added, "Hey, you know those commercials where people are always testing their DNA to find out where they come from?"

"Do I look like I watch TV?"

"OK, so listen. There are these commercials that promise to tell you where you came from if you send them your DNA. Like you can find out you're from—I dunno—Germany or something like that."

Biker waved the woman over and asked for vodka. She brought him the bottle and two glasses. "Why in the hell would anyone want to do that? First of all, you don't know who is behind it. Who is taking your DNA? Is it the government? And if so, which government? Second of all, what does it even mean to be German?"

She shrugged. "Beats me. I didn't even know where it was until you pointed it out on the map."

They spent two hours in the restaurant, leaving to get home before the sun set. Biker had a few generators, so they were good for power. The streetlights were another matter. Most of Southern California suffered from rolling blackouts. Power grids hadn't been updated in years. The ones they'd lost in the previous war had not yet been rebuilt. It was just another unfilled promise from the Northern Californians.

They let themselves in, pulling the metal gate closed behind them.

"Where is the rest of the crew?" Sickle asked.

Biker reached in his vest, pulled out his burner phone, and dialed a number.

"Go ahead. Right. OK. Sounds good.

"Ran out of gas," he told Sickle. "Managed to get enough gallons for a full tank from some sympathizers in Boyle Heights, but it's past curfew.

They're going to take their chances in the eastern zone, then come back at dawn."

"Oh shit, that's not good. What if they're caught?"

"We've got people in the eastern zone. They'll be fine for one night." He reached into the Smeg and pulled out four beers. He handed them to Sickle. Then he grabbed his rifle and handgun. As an afterthought, he asked her to grab two sleeping bags, too.

"We'll take shifts. The place is more secure than anything else, but you just never know."

He'd outfitted the roof with automatic searchlights and multiple layers of barbed wire around the building's perimeter. This left enough room to shoot if necessary. So far, it hadn't been.

They sat on folding chairs in silence. Every so often, someone on a bicycle with regulation glowing wheels rode east.

Sickle aimed her rifle at one of them, following the rider's path but never shooting. She was careful only to speak when they were out of eyesight. "Why are those fuckers allowed out?"

"For the same reason they only pay fifteen percent in taxes," Biker said. "They're from the North. Complain too loud and they'll find a reason to report you. Next thing you know, you're out of a job, if you were even lucky enough to have one in the first place."

"Fuck those guys," she said. "Biker?"

"Yep."

"The shipment's going to come soon, right?"

"Soon."

Chapter 3

"Good morning, ladies and gentleman all across this great land of Texas. You are listening to the *Luther Holderman Show*. It's great to be with you for four wonderful hours, broadcasting live from our nation's great capital city, Austin. And I tell you what, folks, there is nothing like a beautiful October morning in Austin.

"Now, we'll get to your calls after my opening monologue. And for those of you already on hold, I'm seeing a lot of great topics of discussion, which are also on my to-do list. I don't even need to tell y'all the one-eight-hundred number. It's been in your brain for the past decade. By the way, thanks for making WLOB the number-one talk-radio station in the country for the seventh year running.

"OK, so as I said, on my to-do list we've got a brand-new trade plan between Texas and the United States of America. A lot of y'all are complaining about it already, saying, 'Luther, this is a raw deal for us.' And I understand where you're coming from. Why should we give 'em a break? I mean, we've got all the resources they do and more: we've got oil; we've got water; we've got timber up in the Yukon. We're the biggest nation on the continent. Why should we shortchange ourselves? Let me just say: I…hear…you. I get it—really. I understand where you are coming from. But as your highly accomplished and intelligent host, I see things from an aerial view.

"Look, the reason you tune in to this show is for in-depth analysis, right? We're not gonna just regurgitate talking points all the time, and we don't go in for conspiracies either, by the way. Leave that to the losers on the other side of the continent—that's their business. On my show, we give it to you measured and straight.

"So why on God's green earth would we want to make new trade deals with the States? Well, it's simple, folks: diplomacy. The fact is the States are the second most powerful nation after us. Who else would be? Quebec? Cascadia? Give…me…a…break.

"The Confederate States are great. I love those guys. And you know that I, your amazing host, have a home down in the Bahamas. I even have an affiliate studio down there where I can broadcast. But they'd be the first to tell you, with the hurricanes they've been having this season, it's really rough economically right now. They are really hurting. And the restructure and rebuilding efforts are gonna take months. Speaking of, you remember how Hurricane Billy hit us last year? The Confederate States were the first after the Cajun Navy to send troops and help us shoot looters on sight. But even more spectacular from those guys: when they got everything up and running again, they spent their hard-earned tourist dollars visiting us, so we have to repay them when they're up and running, too. Be sure to visit the Confederate States on your next vacation.

"My point is they're not in a place to help us with the war efforts in the Middle East, and I get that. You heard the president today say he would help the Confederate States by sending troops if need be. And the United States pledged the same for the CSA. And so did Deseret.

"So what about Deseret? You probably think: they're a prosperous country; why aren't they supporting us? They *are* supporting us—more than you know.

"I have some friends in our fine government, names I can't share with you, golf buddies, but they are telling me that behind the scenes, Deseret is a prime mover in helping shape diplomacy in countries we're liberating in the Middle East and in North Africa even as we speak. You have to hand it to them. They really are grand statesmen. You heard the president last week talk about how much he loves their ambassador—what's his name?

"Hey, Spencer, what is his name? My producer Spencer will know. Ah, that's right—Ambassador Gregg Tennis. He really is a fine man.

"But let's face it, folks: the Deserets are a majority Mormon country.

Now just wait! Don't take that out of context! You just know the media will jump all over that—you know, jump down my throat, especially over in California. So let me explain what I mean before you go there.

"I am not—repeat, *not*—knocking the Mormons at all. Deseret is a fine country, I have friends there, and I go skiing in Park City every winter when I choose not to golf in the Bahamas. I really don't care what kind of religion they have, folks. That's what makes me a true believer in liberty. It doesn't matter what you believe as long as you believe in something, is what I always say.

"But by and large and practically speaking, a lot of Mormons are pacifists. And that's a noble principle to adhere to—it really is. The world needs fewer wars. That's something all of us can agree one no matter where we're from or what our political belief system is, right, left, or center.

"However, it's just not realistic in these times, being a pacifist. I mean, how could it be? I'm a God-fearing man, understand, and I mean this with all respect: you're just not gonna end the Middle Eastern wars or any conflicts we're currently involved in; you're just not gonna bring Texan democracy and our values to the rest of the world if you don't fight for it.

"We've got some great allies assisting us, as I said. And Deseret is providing valuable diplomatic assistance. And as for God, listen—fold your hands and pray all you want to if it gives you comfort and makes you happy. But after you're done praying, you have to get your hands dirty. Because wars are won by showing the enemy how mighty you are, with soldiers who believe in the cause and know why they are fighting, and that is to free people who are oppressed who look to Texas as a shining light of freedom. The folks back home here can pray to keep everybody safe, but at the end of the day, wars are won by putting boots on the ground. Everyone knows this.

"Now, I know you lefties out there will say like you always do, 'Oh yeah, Luther? Well, how come *you* didn't join when you had the chance? What kind of hypocrite are *you?*'

"Those of you loyal listeners out there—you already know. But for those who are new to the program, let me state again for the one millionth time: I would have absolutely joined up if I could have, and I was standing in the recruitment center in my skivvies in front of the doctor getting my physical all set to join and fully believing I *would* join, but I got rejected because of the sciatic-nerve spasms. That's right. It came as a result of that hernia I had when I went out alligator hunting and tried to haul in that two-hundred-pound gator on my own. Even to this day, on cold winter mornings, I feel it in my spine down to my ankles. At least I have the alligator boots to prove what I did. Still got 'em, still wear 'em. But I tell ya, if I knew then what I know now…If I had known that going out that day would have stopped me in my tracks and put an end to my plans of joining the finest army in the world, I would have stayed home and watched football instead.

"But thankfully, as with all great people in the world, they don't become victims of their own situation. They get out there, and they pull their boots up, and they say, 'Nothing's going to keep me down.' And so I started my career in radio in a little tiny outpost in Kansas, twenty-five years ago. And now a quarter of a century later, I'm broadcasting across the country from Yukon down to the Mexican border. I even hear they listen to me in Mexico, too. Luther, *el hombre grande*, eh?

"My point is we've got the best army in the world because they're good at choosing only the crème de la crème when it comes to recruits. They need people at the peak of their physical shape, and they're tough, and they don't let just anyone in, least of all someone with flat feet or sciatic-nerve issues.

"Well, I'll tell you why. The Texan army knows you win a war by marching. And God bless those men and women who are serving in the Middle East, Africa, Asia, and in all those bases here and abroad. They're doing yeoman's work for sure. But there's just no way you can march when you're in constant pain, and they know that.

"They also know that foot pain is the leading cause of a bad night's sleep, too. It makes sense, right? Maybe you have a job where you're on your feet all day, or you have to walk a lot; even if you sit all day long at work like me, if you don't have the right kinda footwear, your feet hurt, and then when it's time for bed, you get in there and toss and turn because, dang it, your feet are swollen and they hurt like hell.

"Thank God for Foot Mattress. Our newest sponsor, by the way, so thank you for that. Foot Mattress is one of those ingenious ideas that makes me wish I came up with it. It's such a simple idea.

"You call them up, and they send you a kit. You stand on these two pads in your bare feet, and the pads scan your soles, like an MRI. They determine the issues you have, whether it's your spine or your sciatica or your posture or incorrect shoes or one of a thousand other potential issues. And then they give you a digital readout and tell you the problem or problems you have. You take that to your doctor, and he works on your issues internally. Meanwhile Foot Mattress gets busy making your customized space-aged adjustable foam pillows. They send them to you within two business days. And I have to say, they really impressed me with their quality as well as speed. So you get 'em, and you place 'em at the end of the mattress where you put your feet. I haven't slept like that in years, folks.

"They guarantee you'll notice a huge difference within the first week, or they will give you your money back, minus the cost of shipping. Can't beat it, one hundred percent organic and made in Texas. Try Foot Mattress today.

"All right, before we head into commercial break, I have time to take a call. Up first on the *Luther Holderman Show* is Daisy, who is calling from California. Now, should I assume you're a lefty, Daisy?"

"No, I consider myself an independent thinker, which is why you'd have to be crazy to advocate war so far away and intervention in the Middle East when—"

"Sorry to cut you off, but are you from Northern or Southern California, Daisy?"

"I'd rather not say."

"I see. The reason I ask is, you know, California has its own issues—would you agree that's a fair point?"

"Every country does."

"False equivalences aside, I'm speaking specifically of California. From what I understand, the South is still reeling and trying to rebuild. They're like the Confederates, only instead of being hit by a hurricane, it's your own government that's laying waste to them. Unemployment is twenty-five percent in some parts of the South. More than half the population lives below the poverty level. It's no wonder people are leaving there and coming here in droves."

"You know, Luther, it's hilarious that you have the nerve to call yourself objective. The amount of progress we've made would astound you, but you don't realize it because you're still sticking to the same old narrative from twenty-five years ago, when you started your broadcast."

"I just saw a report on KPOC, a news station out of the great city of San Diego. The reporter showed parts of the Coachella Valley out by the Salton Sea that still don't have running water after—what—six months?"

"The environment is to blame, you see—"

"Do we have that clip to play, Spencer? Well, he'll find it, and we'll play it in the next block. My point, Daisy, is that this isn't old news. It's the *same* news. This isn't me making something up. This is news from California showing real economic depression. The idea that you're going to judge us for trying to bring the world a better way of life is preposterous. Honestly, before you throw stones, you should take a look at your own glass house. Sure, you can blame the so-called environmental impacts, but you know what? Texas has a desert, too, but you don't see that happening here. Same with Deseret. But hey, maybe if you keep raising taxes and putting up progressive leaders like you always do, then things will change, right? Thanks for the call, Daisy. We'll be right back on the *Luther Holderman Show*."

Chapter 4

He'd seen the birdlike man a dozen times or more. In and of itself, this wasn't surprising; the Mad Hatter had plenty of regulars. What had once been a seedy biker bar had gentrified along with the rest of the neighborhood. First came the yuppies on their custom Harleys, the ones so big they might as well have been cars. Then mothers, children, families, and retirees followed.

The owners were all too happy to expand. First they built out a large covered patio with matching white plastic tables and chairs. Then they added a separate dining room away from the bar. Next came a second bar up front for the college kids to watch their football games. This pleased the die-hard locals who kept to the back bar by the pool table, which was where Alexander was sitting when he saw the birdlike man walk in at three fifteen on the nose, always fifteen minutes after he'd sat down to order and nurse his one beer.

Gone were the days of drug abuse, anxiety, and depression. With moderation (he still drank to dull the pain) came clarity and the notion that he didn't want to be another suicide statistic, offing himself one night only to lay dead for weeks or months in a forgotten corner until a furious landlord found his mummified body.

That's not to say he wasn't drinking to dull the pain and hush the inner demons when they'd appear. Alexander was aware of the situation and kept an eye on it. He knew the slope was slippery. Constant boredom plus a decent disability check and pension every month equaled a tempting invitation to walk into the fog and stay there licking his mental wounds forever.

Returning soldiers who gave in to one light vice would often then turn back to the harder stuff. From there it was just a matter of time before they ended up living on the streets, out of their heads. He was determined to avoid that scenario. He drank with discipline.

Alexander treated the transition to civilian life and the new challenges that came with it as a mission to accomplish; this constituted an approach that helped keep him centered. As a civilian and free man, he had more self-control than at any time in his life. Perhaps he'd gotten something out of the army after all.

But if his training had not abandoned him, neither had the lingering paranoia that had found a home in his brain fever since his dreamfish days. He regarded every new person and new situation as a potential threat, until proven otherwise. It took him months just to trust Nancy, the Mad Hatter's bartender. She was used to dealing with bikers and vets; she had the patience of a saint, the mouth of a devil, and packed a mean punch.

"You doin' OK, hon?"

Alexander nodded but stayed silent. The birdlike man sat at a table underneath the candy-apple-red 1968 Corvette that hung from the ceiling upside down. The Mad Hatter displayed cars and motorcycles as its main theme. In addition to the Corvette, the place also had a few motorcycles mounted around the original space just under the ceiling and license plates from states that no longer existed.

The lunchtime crowd had gone hours before. Alexander sipped his beer and glanced at the birdlike man, who seemed to be watching him without making it obvious. Early fifties, gray close-cropped hair—a soldier of some kind, maybe even an officer.

The stranger always wore the same tailor-made charcoal-gray suit, like a uniform, very unusual for this kind of place. Even the groups that met here on Sundays after church didn't dress that well.

Was this man really watching him? If so, why? After he'd returned from Iraq, Alexander checked in with the authorities as instructed. There was no need for a parole officer; they'd considered his debts to society more than paid. He was assigned a member of the civilian transition team from the Department of Veterans Affairs. This person located a great apartment at a veteran's rate, set up a new bank account for his benefits, and helped him get a disabled driver's license. After that, his only duty, if one could even call it that, was to report twice a week to the VA hospital for physical rehabilitation. He was also given the option of counseling if he so wished, which he did not.

"No TV on this side—that's a good thing. It's quieter. Man doesn't need to drink with distractions."

Alexander turned to see the birdlike man was smiling.

"Mind if I join you?"

"Depends on what you want," Alexander said.

The birdlike man held up his hands in defense. "Nothing, son. Just felt like buying a fellow soldier a beer."

As if by reflex, Alexander sat up straight. "One's my limit. Thanks all the same."

The birdlike man nodded. He put his hand on a barstool but didn't sit. "Good man. Not everyone has self-control. It's the first thing you see to go on a soldier when they return. That and they get a beer gut. Most of 'em shave it off after a year or two when they remember you don't need to eat four thousand calories a day when you're sitting around with your thumb up your ass. Sergeant Braxton Alexander, am I right?"

Alexander didn't answer.

"Seen you come in here a lot," the birdlike man said.

"So?"

Another smile—approachable but guarded. "A few months ago you needed two crutches. Then one. Now that limp's close to gone, too—remarkably fast progress."

"How would you know?"

"Oh, it's my business to know. You see, son, I'm part of an organization that works with vets. Just because you're no longer in active duty doesn't mean you can't still be part of the effort."

Alexander sniffed. "Effort? That's rich. Don't tell me—you served over there and are one of the few who still believe in that shit."

The birdlike man waved the thought away. "You misunderstand me, son. We have nothing to do with Iraq, Kandahar, or Western Sahara for that matter. Our ops are strictly continental. I'm what you call a scout. Our organization is always looking for good men and women."

"To do what exactly?"

The birdlike man shrugged. "You name it. And you name where. We've got jobs at home in Texas, jobs in the other countries. We need people."

Alexander sipped his beer. "Boots on the ground."

"Exactly."

He swiveled in his chair to face the birdlike man. "Yeah, well, let me tell you something, scout." He pulled up his pant legs, revealing the two metal prosthetic legs. "My boots never left Iraq. I paid the price twice already—three times if you count my psyche. If you think I'm ever going back in the field, you're out of your fucking mind."

The birdlike man stared at the prosthetics. "Standard issue—not bad but not top-of-the-line, either. We can get you much better ones. We're talking technology and mobility beyond anything the army can afford to provide." He raised his eyes to look at Alexander. "Son, we're not part of the armed forces. No one would ever put you in a combat situation. For all I care, you could get fat sitting in front of a computer eight hours a day—and get rich doing it, too. All you have to do is come work for us."

He reached into his pocket, pulled out a card, and put it on the table. Then, almost as an afterthought, he took out his wallet and dropped a hundred-Texas-dollar bill on the bar. "Nancy, this soldier's drink is on me. Keep the change."

Alexander waited until the man left to pick up the card. There was no name on it, just an address and telephone number and a logo: TexIntelSecuriCorp.

Two weeks later, Alexander sat in his beat-up blue pickup truck, holding the business card, trying to come up with a reason not to walk inside their office. His army benefits covered basic needs, as well as medical expenses, but left no wiggle room if something unexpected happened. What had the birdlike man said? He could become rich just sitting in front of a computer. He wondered what the man's definition of "rich" was and what he'd have to give up to achieve it.

The TexIntelSecuriCorp offices were on an access road, parallel to the highway. The neighboring buildings in the office park were a strange mishmash of retail and services: a horizontal office now turned into an unconventional-looking Baptist church, a gourmet restaurant that only opened for dinner, a Spanish-speaking day-care center, a small retail store that sold yarn and knitting needles, and what was called an airport hotel, even though the airport was more than fifteen miles away.

At the center of this office park, sticking out like an imposing fifty-five-story thumb made from steel and glass, was TexIntelSecuriCorp. Alexander must have driven by the building hundreds of times without knowing what it was. In the evenings when the sun beat its rays against the windows, they turned metallic sepia, making it look like a gigantic lottery scratch-off card.

The lobby was bright and modern and devoid of human life except for one security guard who sat behind a desk, staring at a computer screen. Alexander walked over to the touch-screen directory. Even though the building displayed the name of the company in block letters, there were many other businesses inside: lawyers, dentists, accountants, and the like.

He touched the screen, scrolling with his finger until he found TexIntelSecuriCorp. The company took up the top six floors of the building. Without a name to go on, Alexander realized he was at a loss.

"Help you?"

He turned to the security guard. "I'm here to see someone from TexIntelSecuriCorp. But I'm not sure who."

"Name?"

"Like I said, I don't know who it was."

"I meant your name."

Alexander supplied it and waited while the security guard made a telephone call.

"He'll be down in five minutes. Take a seat over there." The guard pointed to an off-white modern leather sofa.

Five minutes later, the birdlike man walked over to Alexander, hand outstretched.

"Glad you could come by," he said. "I'll skip the tour until after we've spoken at length."

They took the elevator to the fifty-fifth floor. The doors opened, revealing the same sterile decor as in the lobby. The birdlike man led

Alexander to a meeting room, ushered him inside, and told him to make himself comfortable.

Alexander sat facing a painting of a man dressed as a cowboy, wearing a broad hat and pale pink neckerchief. The cowboy sat on a horse with a gun in his holster and a rifle in his hand, pointed upward to the sky. In the background a craggy mountain range shone in purple and gold. Despite the size of the mountains, it was the man who looked larger than life.

"A bit too western for my tastes, but I have an affinity for him."

"He doesn't look familiar."

The man with the birdlike face nodded. "He was an actor, eons ago. I don't think his fame rose to even cult status. John something-or-other. Anyway, thanks for coming."

"What now?"

The birdlike man sat down in front of a folder, checked its contents, and met Alexander's gaze. "We'd like to offer you a job. But first we need to determine what kind of job is right for you."

Alexander nodded to the folder. "You've read my file and seen my disability. Not sure how many options there are."

"You'd be surprised."

"Oh?"

The birdlike man stood up, went over to a console, and punched a button. A projection screen lowered itself. "I want to give you a series of tests."

"To see if I'm crazy, right?"

"On the contrary, son, I want to make sure you weren't brainwashed by the army. Discipline is good. Blind faith is not. I'm just going to administer a short test to make sure. All you need to do is watch the screen while we monitor your reactions. Is this something you are OK with?"

Alexander looked around the room, wondering who "we" was. Then he saw a mirror and assumed it was two-way. He shrugged. "I guess so."

The lights dimmed. Alexander was shown a series of opposing images: war and marriage, death and joy, work and play. The images soon got more abstract, showing people he didn't recognize, unfamiliar faces in familiar scenarios: a scientist standing by test tubes; a man dressed as a general, sitting in an old Jeep; another man, also wearing a military uniform but looking more like a South American dictator. Then the images became more unusual: a musician on stage, cutting himself with glass; an actor in a theater, also on stage, holding a skull in his hand. The series continued for a full twenty minutes. When the presentation ended, the lights came back on, and the screen closed itself.

"Did you recognize any of those historical moments?"

"Not a one," Alexander said.

"And the people?"

"Not by name."

"Can you clarify?"

"I can tell from context what the professions were, a scientist or army personnel, but if they're supposed to be people from history, I didn't know any of them."

A buzzing sound came from a monitor on the table. The birdlike man went over to the source of the sound, punched a button, and waited for a printout.

"You weren't supposed to recognize any of those people. We were trying to gauge, first of all, your level of objectivity. Are you so thoroughly clouded by the values of the Great Country of Texas that you can't think for yourself, or can you put those values aside to make objective decisions on what is best for Texas?"

Alexander laughed. "I could have answered that without having to take a test. The answer is no, I'm not clouded by anything. Texas sent me to the army to avoid punishment. I didn't join because of patriotism or sense of duty. My file should have told you that."

The birdlike man nodded. "This is a more detailed process than finding out whether or not you'll fight to uphold Texan values. What we do is more complicated than that. We're fighting to preserve our way of life—that's a given. We have different motives, and we go about it differently."

"In what way?"

Alexander's transparent curiosity was not lost on the birdlike man. He sat down and smiled. "Let me answer that question with a question, son. What do you know about California?"

Three hours later, Alexander left the TexIntelSecuriCorp offices. The following Monday, he would begin a two-week vetting in earnest, which the birdlike man insisted was necessary before he could be gainfully employed and receive his mission.

"Although I have to say, 'mission' is a word we do not like to use," he said. "We prefer 'assignment.' It's less lofty that way. Besides, 'mission' sounds like there's a specific beginning, middle, and end, whereas this is different—much more case specific. You'll see what I mean, assuming you pass the vetting process."

In a conspiratorial tone, the birdlike man also told him that the reason they made potential candidates wait until the following week was to make sure candidates cleared their system.

"Drug test: we're not against drugs, per se," the birdlike man insisted, "only the detrimental ones. Again, this will all be covered during your vetting, but just keep your nose clean until then."

Alexander thought it seemed like a lot to go through for a desk job, but again, he was reminded that was only one option. He could go into the field on any manner of assignments. He cut the birdlike man off before he was told that it would all be covered during the vetting process again.

"Fair enough," he answered. "Just sign this contract. You agree to our terms. Namely, you won't speak to anyone about this. And you won't hold it against us if you aren't hired. You will receive compensation for these two weeks either way."

"How much compensation are we talking about?"

"Fifteen thousand dollars."

"And if I get hired?"

The birdlike man thought. "I'd have to ask HR for a hard number but at least two hundred thousand—plus bonuses."

Alexander drove home, thinking about all the ways he'd be able to spend that kind of money. For starters, he could buy a new pickup truck. Then he could get a house, too, but nothing big or fancy, just a little corner of the world to call his own. He'd been poor all his life and couldn't imagine having material goods. He was never one for sports cars or luxury clothing. Greed wouldn't turn him ugly.

On the way home, he made a vow. If he passed the vetting process, he'd do more than keep his nose clean. He'd keep his head down and get to work and really make something of himself. The army had tried and failed to reform him. Now he'd do it on his own.

The following Monday, Alexander arrived at TexIntelSecuriCorp wearing a new button-down shirt, dark jeans, and black dress boots, trying to split the difference between civilian and military outfits.

He started by meeting twenty people the birdlike man introduced as the Leadership Team. They were all top managers of various departments. A few were in charge of intelligence; another group headed up cybersecurity. One person was in charge of what they called extracurricular activities. In addition there were people who controlled finance, logistics, and communications, which included, among other areas, maintaining a social-media presence and spreading propaganda and disinformation.

They gave him psychological tests. They took blood, urine, and hair samples. They showed him strange films, tested his foreign language skills, and questioned him about politics.

California came up as a frequent topic of conversation. Alexander could not quite understand why. Beyond what he heard on the news, he knew next to nothing about the place, except that it was on the coast. He'd never had the money or desire to visit and never met anyone from there. He didn't know Los Angeles from San Francisco and had trouble pointing them out on a blank map, let alone describing with any accuracy what the terrain was like. He was surprised to learn that within that country there were deserts, snow-capped mountains, temperate areas, valleys, and hills. California was almost as diverse as Texas.

Midway through the second week, it was still unclear to Alexander whether he was going to get the job. On one level, the employees were still guarded with him. But on another, it felt like he was already an employee going through orientation. The birdlike man never left his side, always asking him if he understood what was going on or needed clarifications, encouraging him to ask questions even if they might decide not to answer. He spent a good part of each day sitting through formal presentations about TexIntelSecuriCorp. Why would they bother if they hadn't made up their minds to hire him?

For the past five years, he learned, the company had operated with tacit support from the Texas government, who funded them like an NGO, although the corporation also received private donations and was profitable in its own right. As an NGO, TexIntelSecuriCorp was prohibited from hiring government employees, but that was not to say the corporation didn't have its own employees working in the government.

"Have to make sure we know what's really going on," the birdlike man said. "Things change minute by minute."

They gave him a crash course on the history of the country of California, brought him up to speed with their current state of affairs, and explained the difference between the North and South, making sure he understood the unique characteristics in each region's culture as well as the role of the country on the geopolitical stage. Over the past few years, the South had ramped up its attempts to secede. Each attempt was quelled. What always followed were severe penalties from the capital in Sacramento, which only strengthened the southern resolve. The groundswell of support continued to grow.

During one such course, Alexander raised his hand. "How come this is the first I'm hearing of any of this? You'd think Hollywood would have made a hundred movies about it by now, right?"

"They're not allowed to," the birdlike man said. "The North controls the film bureau. They have final say over which movies get made and which get censored. They have the narrative on lock."

"With all the support, why don't they secede legally? Through a vote?"

The birdlike man laughed. "You're talking about democracy, son. Never happen in California. It's not only a point of pride on the North's part, either. They can't afford to lose the South and see any attempts to break away as a threat to their security. There's oil and natural gas down there. But there's a bigger reason, too."

"What's that?" Alexander asked.

"The North has to prevent the South's efforts to separate and gain a foothold on the global stage. Since they quelled the last rebellion, any attempts to rebuild have been met with routine disruption, bureaucratic slowdowns, tax levies, and even physical intimidation."

Alexander pondered this. "The whole situation sounds like a powder keg."

The birdlike man stood in front of the large conference-room windows looking down upon the eight-lane highway that led as far east as the US border, as far west as the Texan side of Joshua Tree.

"Got that right, son—it's going to explode one way or another. Best we can do is help keep it contained."

At the end of the week, they presented him with a contract. Alexander accepted the job. They also brought out a chocolate cake and gave him a slice. His salary was Texan $220,000 a year plus expenses and bonuses. The figure amounted to five times more than he'd ever made before.

The leader of intelligence gave him full clearance to all the information they had on California. The more he read, the more it made sense why Texas would want to take advantage of the inevitable civil war. Alexander could see both immediate and longer-term benefits.

Even though Texas was the largest country on the North American continent, they only had one port in the southwest part of the country, and that was at Rocky Point on the eastern side of Baja in the Aztlan region.

Mexico and California had successfully kept Texas boxed in at Rocky Point, so both countries could negotiate lower tariffs. The ships would arrive and end up getting stuck, forced to unload their cargo onto trucks to complete the journey. By the time they arrived in Northern California, produce was rotten, and goods were overdue.

"But it's a different story now," the birdlike man said. "Southern California's still reeling from the failed rebellion. Had to come to us, hat in hand for help. We can produce enough guns for the civil war in one week if we wanted to, and they know it. We said yes, of course."

"In exchange for what?"

"Control of ports in Ensenada and San Diego. At first they balked. But we got them to change their minds."

"How?"

The birdlike man laughed. "There are two kinds of tactics that unions in the United States will use to get more for their workers. One is an outright strike. The other way is a slowdown. That's what we're doing. Since they wouldn't give up the ports, the delivery's coming by land."

"Let me guess," Alexander said. "It's not going as fast as they hoped."

The birdlike man nodded. "And by the way, Mexico doesn't want

Southern California winning the war because they'll lose the power to negotiate when we get the ports. They're keeping their mouths shut right now. But rule number one is you never underestimate Mexico."

The birdlike man took Alexander to lunch in the expansive cafeteria on the fifty-fifth floor of TexIntelSecuriCorp. It was known for being one of the best restaurants in town, made all the more exclusive because only employees could dine there.

They sat by the window and ordered steaks with chimichurri and fried potatoes.

"Wanted to give you the last fine view of Texas you'll get for a while. Leadership agreed. We're putting you in the field."

The birdlike man explained that they'd rather do that than stick Alexander behind a computer; he was better suited to act as a liaison as an official member of TexIntelSecuriCorp. "They won't trust you at first, of course. But if you show your operational experience, it will go a long way in making them think you're officially there to help."

"What am I unofficially there to do?"

"Just start by keeping your eyes and ears open. Rumor is they are planning something big and are organized like never before. Get in good with the main group. Make them feel like Texas is supportive. But don't show your face too much. When shit blows up, you don't want to get caught standing next to the hand grenade."

The birdlike man said the rest of the Leadership Team would provide him with the details, including the route to take, an address where he'd live once he got there, and the name of a commander to try and embed with at all costs.

"One more thing." He produced a slim electronic device the size of a cigar box. "You'll need this to file your reports."

Alexander opened the device. It looked like a glorified pager with a screen and small but full keyboard.

"Type just like you would on a computer. The device instantly translates your words into code. It's encrypted on screen, when you send it. When we download the message, the encryption changes to a completely different set of code. Try it."

Alexander tapped to turn it on. The screen was black with a green cursor prompt. He typed "The quick brown fox jumps over the lazy dog." Before his eyes, the words changed to "The fab four, La Bamba, Happy birthday, Mister President."

"All you do is hit send," the birdlike man said. "That's it."

"Just out of curiosity, are those words supposed to mean anything?"

The birdlike man laughed. "Just bits of esoteric nonsense. The Mexicans patented this invention. They call it El Rompecabezas. We're paying through the nose for the right to use it." He pushed away his plate. "Gotta get back to work. Take the weekend and relax before you get started. Might as well let you know now, your route passes through Las Vegas. Be sure to stop there for a day or two. Let the South sweat a little while longer."

Chapter 5

"Listener-supported KLAW presents: the *True Progress Show*. Each week for three hours, we discuss real issues that Californians are facing and use civil conversation to push for social and economic change. I'm your host, Ramona Rainbow Markham.

"Judging by the number of people already on hold, everyone's got a lot to discuss today. We will get to your calls. But first, I have a special guest with me this morning. He's the head of the Northern California Progressive Unionist party, Professor Nathan Fellows. Nathan, it's great to have you back."

"Thank you for having me, Ramona. Always a pleasure."

"As we head into the regional primaries, the NCPU has really worked hard to get out the vote this year. I can't turn a corner without seeing a red-shirted volunteer in my neighborhood."

"Absolutely. But what you are seeing in terms of door-to-door canvasing now is just one end result of a concerted effort that started about three years ago. We gathered tons of data to really uncover the pressure points in Northern California and craft messaging that would resonate not just with our core base in San Francisco but also with more rural folks who live on the borders of Cascadia and Deseret.

"And all of that research went into the Let's Get Going campaign."

"Correct. But it's not just an empty slogan. All of us here in Northern California have work to do. It's a collective effort. So part of it is saying, 'Hey, enough cheap talk, you know. Let's get going.' But it's also meant with a sense of optimism and excitement. Like when you were a kid and wanted to go to the beach on a summer day and you'd bug your parents to hurry, you know? Let's get going!'"

"But in this case, the parents, so to speak, are our leaders in Sacramento."

"Our elected officials need to get on this for the greater good. They're getting lost in the endless rabbit holes of think tanks, and while I have nothing against that in theory, speaking as a professor, you really do need to start implementing ideas at some point. Otherwise it's just theoretical ideas and wasted money."

"I have read the NCPU's manifesto, and I must say it's tantalizing. But it's also quite radical, even for the most forward-thinking area of the country, if I'm being honest. You're calling for a ban over the next five years of all vehicles that aren't self-driving, pushing for a basic guaranteed income of one hundred thousand a year and a ninety-two percent tax rate for the top earners. What realistically are the chances that anyone in Sacramento would vote for a tax rate that high?"

"Actually, our internal polling indicates fifty-three percent of likely voters in San Francisco are in favor of a guaranteed income. Before I became an economics professor, I was the head of the Electrical Workers Union, so I know firsthand how hard it is to live here. I don't know about you, but I don't want to live in a society where the people at the top who already have more than their fair share don't take care of others. They have a moral obligation."

"But surely people will bristle at a ninety-two percent tax rate proposal—"

"First of all, that's phased in over a decade. The top earners will still have plenty of money to buy their yachts and build sixty-thousand-square-foot fortified mansions. But I'd rather shift the focus to the real benefits here. The fact is my proposals will help all of Northern California. This is a proposal for all of us: rich, poor, and middle class."

"Right, I just can't imagine anyone in Sacramento would risk his or her career to vote in something like this. What would you say to convince them?"

"What I would say, Ramona, is, I would ask them, 'Do you want to end up on the wrong side of history? Because that's where you'll end up.'"

"Let's take a call. Richard in Solvang, hi; you're on the *True Progress Show*."

"Thanks for taking my call. Professor Fellows, as a resident of Southern California, I can't help but notice your proposal seems to stop somewhere around San Louis Obispo. Is there a reason you're only focusing on Northern California when the bottom half of the country has been so devastated by the actions in Sacramento?"

"Well, Richard, I guess you might have missed Ramona's opener, where she stated I am running for the regional primaries so my focus is on—"

"With all due respect, Professor Fellows, don't insult my intelligence. Everyone knows the Northern California primaries are just a stepping stone for the national elections."

"Sir, I would ask you not to question my commitment. Remember, I started as an electrical—"

"Yeah, we know. Twenty-five years ago you were a union head for two whole years; then you quickly parlayed that into a teaching job and then got tenure, and now you're angling for a career politician gig."

"Richard, you're violating the rules of the *True Progress Show*. We'll have to cut you off if you engage in hate speech."

"Hate speech? Ramona, it's hardly hate speech. Most Northern Californian politicians don't even finish a full term before they vacate to run for federal office. We've had ample time to see this in action, as you've been the majority ruling party for decades now."

"Frankly, that sounds like a Southern California problem to me, sir. Perhaps if you ran better candidates, you'd win more elections."

"Professor Fellows, we must bring this discourse back to civil levels."

"Ah yes, the standard answer—it's our candidates that are the problem. You claim to be so progressive and fight for justice, Professor, yet half of the country remains completely neglected. You only want to take care of your own while we are really suffering down here."

"Now, that's an unfair statement. I will grant you, Richard, there is a lot of work to do. But from my point of view, Northern California will be in a much better position to help Southern California when our own house is in order."

"Sure, sure."

"I have said many times that we are more than willing to work with Southern California to improve conditions there. Watch any of my lectures on YouTube, and see for yourself."

"Despite his problematic speech, Richard does bring up good points, Professor Fellows. If, as you say, Let's Get Going is more than a slogan, what would you propose Southern California does to improve its quality of life?"

"Great question, Ramona. Here's what I would say: all politics is local. So I would begin by doing what we did up here. Start the Southern California Progressive Unionist party on a grassroots level. Change won't ever come unless you work for it. So my advice to folks like Richard is this: be that community organizer. Get on the grassroots level. Knock on doors. Take your destiny into your own hands. Remember, I started as the head of the Electrical Workers Union. If I can do it, anyone can. "

"Powerful words indeed, Nathan. Thanks for sharing your insight."

"Thank you for having me."

"You're listening to the *True Progress Show* on KLAW. Remember, you won't hear such spirited discussions anywhere else because we are truly independent. Shows like this come to you commercial free. And that is only made possible through the generous support from companies and individuals like the Arthur K. Abramowitz Trust, the Northern Californian Center, Alphabet-Google, Yelp, Amazon, Apple, Uber, Microsoft, and from loyal listeners like you. I'm Ramona Rainbow Markham."

Chapter 6

It took Alexander a few days to get to Las Vegas. He drove in an unhurried pace, stopping when he got tired to sleep in roadside motor inns. The route was circuitous; he went north through Norman and Wichita before heading west, past Dodge City and Durango. He skirted the Deseret border, choosing to drive through the eerie, violent tumbleweeds that blew across the highways in Aztlan.

He pulled into Las Vegas on the fourth evening. TexIntelSecuriCorp had booked him a room at the Hotel Bionic, a robot-themed resort and casino that specialized in laser shows. In some dark way, it amused Alexander that his prosthetic legs might get him mistaken for an employee.

Alexander gave the lifelike android valet his car keys, smiled for the drone at the front reception desk that took his photo and created an ID in a matter of seconds, and told the man dressed as a cyborg to take his bags up to his room without him. He was in need of dinner and a strong drink to untie the knots in his back.

Before he'd left, the birdlike man had made good on his word and provided him with prosthetic legs that were the cutting edge of mobility. He couldn't believe how well they worked.

Out of all the challenges that came with his disability, movement was not one of them. Alexander found that sitting for long periods of time caused the most discomfort. Part of it was psychological. It would have been natural to get out and stretch one's legs after a long drive. Now he only felt his thighs manipulating the legs, while, at the same time, the strange sensation of having two phantom limbs. The feelings canceled each other out, leaving him bewildered.

He strolled through the lobby, doing his best to avoid getting sucked into the casino's black hole. He consulted a directory, at a loss of where to eat.

A robotic voice spoke into his left ear. "Help you find something, sir?"

He turned around, surprised to find a floating electric eyeball winking at him in a way that could be described as cheerful.

"Er, yes," he responded, "I'm hungry, but I don't know where I want to eat."

"I can help with that," the floating electric eyeball said. "Hotel Bionic has four restaurants to choose from. The Motherboard is a great spot for families. If you like craft cocktails and tapas, you'll want to head over to Servo. The Lithium Lounge features our most audacious dishes. And finally for a no-expenses-spared meal of a lifetime, ABSO has the best tasting menu in the city if not the entire country."

"Thanks. I think I'll go to Servo."

The floating electric eyeball winked again. "When would you like to dine?"

"As soon as possible." And as an afterthought, he added, "It's just me."

A small circle closed in the center of the eyeball, like a pupil contracted by light. A bright but harmless laser appeared, scanning Alexander's retinas. "Excellent, Mr. Braxton Alexander, I have you down for a table of one in five minutes. Would you like me to escort you?"

"That won't be necessary."

"As you like. Just follow the red carpet counterclockwise, and you'll arrive at your destination in two minutes."

It was just after ten thirty when he entered the restaurant, surprised at how crowded it was. A real man dressed in a metallic tuxedo led him to a small table and presented him with a menu that had an embossed circuit-board illustration on the front of it.

Alexander held up a hand to silence the waiter's reeling off of the nightly specials and said, "Just bring me the first thing you mentioned and a double scotch on the rocks."

He was on his second drink and feeling it when the half roast chicken with new potatoes arrived. He wolfed it down. Then he waved the server over for the bill.

"We scanned your retina already, sir. The bill's been charged to your room."

"Fine, whatever."

Alexander left the restaurant, walking with deliberate steps. His mood had soured, but he could not say why. By all rights he should have been happy. A job with a six-figure salary and a move to a better climate was nothing to get upset about. He'd gone from wasted soldier to working professional. Yet he was uneasy and ill-tempered nonetheless.

On legs that became unsteady, he walked through the resort, heading nowhere in particular. He didn't know which was worse—the constant surveillance from robots and security cameras on the walls and ceiling or the tourists who plunked their hard-earned dollars down in a desperate chance to win against a house that always beat them, oblivious to the fact that every move they made was scrutinized. Was this what he'd spent years fighting to protect?

Civilian life might have gotten financially better, but he was still a soldier taking orders. It was all happening too fast. What did he really know about TexIntelSecuriCorp? They had deep pockets, acted as an unofficial arm of the government. They were playing chess with human lives.

What if it was all a trap somehow?

He walked past a gaggle of old ladies with hair the color of Q-tips, sitting at pachinko machines and coin pushers. The metallic clicks and clacks pricked at his ears, echoing in his skull until the sound reminded him of bullet spray. The noise made him shrink. He wanted to hurry away from it, but the flashes of purple and pink light coming from the games rooted him to the spot like a catatonic patient. His eyes darted from side to side, looking for visual respite: a blank wall, a neutral color, something, anything that resembled nothing.

The smell of heavy smoke from Confederate Cuban cigars stung his nostrils. The noises grew louder. Alexander's heart pounded in his chest. He wondered if this was the onset of a flashback.

A scream came from behind him, one he recognized with relief as being joyous. As if the spell had been broken, he turned around to see a man on his haunches, shoveling chips into an overflowing bucket. The man, still chomping on his cigar, turned to Alexander.

"I won!"

A robot with a vacuum attachment rolled over. "Allow me, sir." The vacuum sucked up the coins, making sure to capture them all, including the ones in the bucket. Alexander watched as a red counter appeared on the robot's chest.

"Congratulations," it said with what seemed like genuine excitement. "As you can see, sir, I have kept an accurate tally of your winnings. If you'll just follow me to the cashier…"

The man stood up and hurried after the robot.

"He'll be back here in an hour thinking he can double it, but he'll end up losing it all. Just watch."

"I'd rather not." Alexander turned to find the source of the voice. It belonged to a woman who wore nothing but an aqua and silver body suit. Her face was painted with the same colors.

"You don't seem like you belong here."

Alexander agreed. The woman's voice had an accent he couldn't place. She also sounded drunk.

"You live here, in this town?"

"Just passing through," he answered. "Moving west."

"Ah, you are lucky. No one in his right mind would want to live here. But maybe you have guessed I am not in my right mind." Her breath smelled like whiskey.

"That makes two of us."

The woman nodded. "I am Marie-Eve. I am from Quebec. I just finished my show, and I am drunk already. Maybe it could be OK if you join me for one more."

It wasn't a question so much as a statement. Before he could answer, she took his hand, leading him away like he was a child who'd done something wrong. They walked toward a wall that was covered with the same circuit-board motif as the restaurant's menu. She squinted at it and then moved two steps to the right.

She rapped on the wall, which turned out to be a door. When it opened a crack, she barked something in French. She yanked him through the door, letting it shut behind them with a bang.

The woman spoke without looking at him. "We will not go out there to the tourist bars. I will take you to the green room. It should be empty now. There won't be another show until three this morning, but I am done for today."

They turned left and then right and then went up a flight of stairs. He took pains to keep up with her stride. She pushed through a double set of doors revealing the back of a giant stage.

"I am here working for Cirque Du Soleil for three years now. I am an acrobat and dancer. Right now, to me, we are doing the worst show ever, called Roboto. It's about the birth of the robotic being. Complete and total *merde,* but the tourists don't know any better. They don't even know there's a storyline."

They crossed the stage from left to right, until they reached another set of doors. This led to a dressing room with costumes thrown everywhere. And finally, they reached a single door that led to a room with a few couches, a television, a refrigerator, and a well-stocked bar.

"You will make me a drink," Marie-Eve said. Again, it wasn't a question but a statement. "Whiskey straight."

Alexander did as he was told. He poured vodka into a tumbler for himself.

"You said you will soon be moving west, eh? Where?"

"Los Angeles."

Her eyes appraised him. "Hm. Well, you are not moving there for love."

"Work," he said.

Marie-Eve shrugged. "Either way, it must be so nice to leave. I hate it here. I wish I could return to Quebec, but Cirque doesn't give you a choice. You go where you are needed. And it's not like there's another company to join. There aren't many opportunities for me." She sipped her drink and then pointed it at him, as if seeing him for the first time. "Ah, but you are a soldier, no? I can tell by the way you hold yourself."

"I'm retired," Alexander said.

"Better for you," she said, raising her glass. "What should I say, huh? Thank you for keeping us safe?"

"Please don't," he said. "Do you know how many times I hear that a day? It stops having meaning."

"Maybe as many times as someone tries to grab my ass every day," she said. "And that stops having meaning, too."

She changed the subject and told him about the Front du Libération du Québec, the paramilitary group who terrorized the country in the 1960s and early '70s.

"My mother told me back then even one pipe bomb in a mailbox was enough to keep people on edge and make them stay at home. Now it is not so much the same. Thousands die here and there, but there's always a crowd to see the Cirque, even with uprisings in California, so close to here. But at least you served."

Alexander looked around the green room, noting with a sense of relief that there seemed to be no security cameras there.

"I never kept anyone safe, not back here and not over there. In the army you're told you're doing the right thing and fighting the enemy. Truth is, the people we have to fear the most are the leaders of the armed services. They brainwash the soldiers and make the worst decisions when the war draws to a close."

Marie-Eve laughed. "But of course. And they fill your mind with the idea you are fighting for what is right. But this is just a romantic notion." She finished her drink and got up to make another. She pointed to Alexander's glass. He nodded.

"Do you know? I am most afraid of the Mormons in Deseret."

Alexander laughed. "You're afraid of a nonviolent, nondrinking, nonswearing people. Makes total sense."

Marie-Eve frowned. "You think I am joking? They have this little desert oasis of sun and fun and excitement completely surrounded. What will happen if they decide they want to take over Las Vegas?"

Alexander stopped smiling. "There is no way they'd ever invade Texas," he said. "Deseret would cease to exist in about ten minutes."

"Perhaps yes, perhaps no," she said. "But I tell you: if it happened, I would not be surprised."

She handed him his drink, fixing her eyes on his. "Your name?"

"Braxton Alexander."

"Rank?"

"Sergeant."

"Serial number?"

"Classified."

She laughed. "Do you know, I don't often talk to people unless I am forced to. Coworkers, mostly. But I am glad I talked to you tonight. You will be in LA tomorrow?"

"Probably, if all goes well."

"And I will be there next month." She brightened. "For vacation. I have many friends there. And I would like one more." She found a piece of paper, wrote down her number, and handed it to him. "Call me in a month."

He took the number but didn't say anything.

She looked at him. "Go, before I change my mind and keep your here," Marie-Eve said, shooing him out of the room like a cat.

Alexander took the elevator to his room and crawled into bed without turning on the lights or shutting the blinds. The sunshine woke him at nine the next morning. Rather than endure the throngs of casino goers, he phoned down for eggs and bacon.

He got into his pickup truck just after noon, heading due south toward Henderson. Although the area once known as Area 51 was due north of Las Vegas, this strange part of the country was dotted with alien lore from the ridiculous to the sublime as far south as the Mojave. Though the conspiracies had long since been debunked, a local economy still thrived on selling figurines, novelties, and alien-themed food, like Space Pies and Astro Teriyaki Jerky.

Marie-Eve was nice, which seemed to Alexander an odd thing to think. He knew nothing about her, didn't even know what her skin looked like underneath the paint. But something about her frankness seemed real and refreshing. For her, Las Vegas didn't represent a glitzy getaway or the place to take a chance at becoming a millionaire. She was there for the work and the work alone. He imagined she kept to the confines of the stage and the green room, only visiting the casino area as a way to remind her of what she wasn't. He could not see her venturing out on the Strip to barhop.

Even under the paint, he could see the lines on her face were pronounced, as if somehow both had experienced the harshness of battle—hers on stage, or rather, backstage, where groping hands from drunken gamblers and coworkers took their chances as if she, too, were a game.

He remembered what she'd said about having friends in the city. The more calculating soldier part of him filed this detail away for the future. She might know someone important who could be of use. Then again, she could just be a harmless woman full of French Canadian bluster, all talk and no teeth. Still, it never hurt to stay in touch.

TexIntelSecuriCorp had an apartment secured for him on the border of Santa Monica and Venice, within easy drive of the group he was supposed to meet, yet not so close as to cause suspicion. He'd take it slow, making sure their guard was down before he made a move to help under the guise of being a hired gun.

He stopped for lunch at a diner called Sputnik that featured a menu with enough UFO puns to make him cringe. He ordered the U-F-Oh-So-Delicious Reuben with a side of Freaky-Deaky-Fries and a Little Green Milkshake. To his surprise, the food was excellent.

He paid for his meal, asking the surly man behind the counter if he'd ever seen any aliens.

"You're kidding me, right?"

"Of course."

"I was gonna say. You didn't look like a tourist."

Four hours later, he pulled into the driveway of his duplex apartment on Rose Avenue, back throbbing from the drive and feeling very much like an alien.

Chapter 7

The packing material was strewn about the hardware store floor. Ten minutes before, Sickle had broken open the crate with a crowbar, removed the AR-15s, and laid them on the tarp. She counted them out loud and turned to Biker with exasperation.

"Twelve? That's it?"

"We've been over this. We're one small group out of many in Los Angeles County. We all got the same amount, which means a couple hundred guns. How many did you think Texas would send?"

She picked up a weapon, weighing it in her hands.

"Clean the place up," he ordered.

"Yes, Sarge," she said, giving him a flippant salute.

"Tell me, Sickle. Why are you here? I mean, why are you really here?"

She grabbed a broom and swept with slow, carful movements. "You think because I'm young I don't have a good reason. Or because I'm a woman?"

"Didn't say that. Thing about it though, young people let their emotions get in the way. The worst kind of soldier is an idealist. Know why?"

She shrugged and kept sweeping.

"Because idealists are willing to die. Anyone who's willing to die usually does. You have to want to live at all costs for what's right, not die for it."

Sickle stopped sweeping. "I'm not willing to die for any cause, so you can stop worrying about that."

"So why fight them?"

"They treat us like we're backward, exploit us for our oil and agriculture, tax the shit out of us, and if we speak out against them, they fine us for violating speech laws. I'm not interested in speaking truth to power. I want to cut power off at the fucking knees."

The knocking was loud and sudden. Biker motioned for Sickle to cover the guns with the tarp. He grabbed his revolver and hid it behind his back as he walked to the door. He didn't recognize the man who stood facing him.

"What do you want?"

The man spoke with a drawl. "Sorry to disturb you, sir. I'm a delegate from Texas. They sent me to make sure your shipment arrived—and to offer assistance."

Biker glanced over his shoulder. Sickle was sweeping, the guns out of sight. He tucked his revolver into his belt and opened the door. He stood in front of it, barring entry.

"Sure took them long enough to arrive."

"Well, sir, I am sorry about that. I'm not in charge of shipping."

"What are you in charge of?"

Without answering, the man handed Biker a business card. "Name is Braxton Alexander. The great country of Texas sent me to help."

Biker felt Sickle appear behind him. He stepped back to let Alexander in, shutting and locking the door behind him. "I'm Sergeant Biker. This is Private Sickle. Help how?"

"Scouting, logistics, coordination, tactical mission tasks—you name it. Everything but firing the actual weapons."

Sickle folded her arms. "Why? Are you chicken shit?"

"No, idiot, because it's a violation of the Texan constitution," Biker said.

Alexander smiled. "It'd be different if we'd signed a protection pact with you southern folks, or even if I were sent here unofficially, but that's not the case. My job's to check in and see if you have what you need."

"I can't speak for the other groups out there."

"Oh? Well now, that's funny because I was told you were the leader of the groups."

Instead of responding, Biker said, "We have what we need."

Alexander nodded. "How many are in your outfit, and where and when do you plan to strike?"

Biker shook his head. "Listen, Mr. Alexander, I don't know you from a hole in the wall."

"I respect that, but you need to understand, we didn't arm you out of the goodness of our hearts. We have an interest in your success." Alexander looked at Sickle. "So far I see one old man in a leather vest and a skinny chick with pink hair who looks like she's sixteen, and I have to say, if this is the best you have in your outfit, you might as well surrender now."

Biker showed Alexander the pistol, gesturing toward the window with it. "The rest are out gathering supplies. You want to look 'em over, come by at the end of the week or so. But first, you and me—we're going to get to know each other."

Alexander sat down on a chair, crossing his legs to reveal a flash of metal prosthesis at the ankle. "Go for it. Want to hear about my combat experience as a veteran of three tours of duty in the Mid-East wars? Oh but, that's easy enough for you to look up. What else do you want to know?"

"Which department do you work for?"

"The Foreign Relations Office," he said. "Also easy enough to confirm just by calling. Office number is on the card. What about you, little lady? What can I answer for you?"

Sickle didn't say anything.

"How about this," Alexander continued. "We delivered a dozen Bushmasters with bump stocks to you and enough ammunition to keep each of them going for two full hours. I believe that's true of something like eighteen other groups. Now, how would I know that if I wasn't legit?"

"It doesn't prove anything either way. I'm more interested in whose side you're on."

"I told you, Texas has an interest."

"It's one thing for a country to send arms. It's another thing altogether for them to send a man to help."

"And just one man, too," Sickle snorted.

"You'd have to ask my superior on why they do what they do," Alexander answered. "We hate Northern California as much as you do.

As for me, all I can say is once a soldier, always a soldier. Now instead of wasting time, why don't you tell me what else you need, so I can get it?"

Biker looked at Sickle. "You really want to help, get us gas."

"Gas?"

Biker nodded. "We're under a strict ration here in LA. You've got a Texan driver's license, right? The ration order doesn't apply to you. Your best bet's the Northern Block, around Hollywood."

"Done," Alexander said. His smile was not returned. "Guess I'll come back on Saturday with the gas and meet the rest of the crew."

After he left, Sickle screamed in frustration. "I can't fucking believe he called me a kid. Who the hell is he to judge our chances, Biker? He doesn't know how many are on our side."

"I told you not to get emotional."

"But he insulted us."

"Texans are like that."

Sickle bit her lip. "OK, OK." She went back over to the tarp and unwrapped it.

"I'll check all these, make sure they're clean and working."

"Good," he said.

"Biker? Why did you lie about the gas? He goes up to the Northern Block, he might end up dead."

"I want to see how he handles himself. If he survives, we'll know he's on the level."

"But you don't think so," she said.

Biker looked at the card Alexander had given him. His name was in gold lettering. There were two phone numbers, one for his cell phone and the other for the office. No address.

"Just seemed a bit too much of a coincidence, his showing up less than an hour after we received the shipments."

Sickle thought about it. "You think he's a spy or something?"

"I don't know."

"I guess anyone can fake a Texan accent," she said. And then with a horrible Texan accent, she said, "Y'all want me to do anything about it?"

"Keep an eye on him. Find out where he lives, who he talks to, what he does. I want to know if he really is a friendly representative or if he's full of it. And if he is full of it, you tell me and I'll handle it."

"Aye, aye," she said. "Can I borrow the moped?"

"Yeah, but remember the charge'll only get you two hours of driving. After that you'll be walking it back. And take the helmet, so he doesn't see you coming."

Chapter 8

Alexander drove back the way he came, passing the palm trees yellowed with rot, half-rusted cars, taco stands, and donut shops. Los Angeles smelled like sulfur, but he kept the windows rolled down, trying to drum up a breeze in the stifling heat.

Something about the old biker piqued his interest. He had the air of legionnaire who'd seen his share of combat. Was there an organization funding the rebellion? If so, the organization didn't have a lot of money or influence. Otherwise, they'd have no trouble getting their own weapons and recruiting others, for that matter. Regardless, it was something he had to consider. Nothing could be ruled out at this point.

Alexander wondered if Biker would check the cover story he'd supplied. The birdlike man had warned him Southern Californians were mistrustful. But who wasn't? For years, Sacramento had treated them with disdain. A capital city hundreds of miles away that claimed they had their best interests at heart had systematically pushed them to the bottom rung of the ladder. Of course they'd view anyone who wanted to help with suspicion. Alexander's own experience taught him that for every grateful civilian, there were two who would put a bullet in his brain if given half the chance.

He turned right on Rose Avenue, passing by a homeless encampment that had overtaken a long-since abandoned golf course. There must have been a hundred tents and makeshift shacks packed together, a minicity within a city. On the other side of the street, the houses were fortified with walls that were eight feet high, some with barbed wire. If this was the result of Northern Californian policy, it was no wonder the South would do anything to change it. Texas wasn't perfect, far from it, but it was a testament to the government that a safety net was provided for all but the unincorporated and semiautonomous regions, like Aztlan and the Acadian region, who took care of their own without federal assistance.

Alexander pulled into his duplex. A homeless man with a scraggly beard scrambled over to the gate, stopping at a respectful distance.

"Hey, man. You want some flower? Best shit around."

Alexander shook his head. "I've had my fill of weird drugs."

The homeless man shook his head. "Nothing weird about this—it's pure flower."

Alexander looked at the man, holding in his dirty hands a baggie filled with green leaves. "No, I'm telling you: I did my share of drugs, and I'm not going back."

"This is the way forward." The homeless man tried to hand him the baggie. "Here, look. This isn't a drug. It's flower. I mean, I just smoked it. You see anything weird about me? Am I acting funny to you?"

Alexander turned to enter his duplex. "Sorry."

The man tossed the baggie. It landed at his feet. "Case you change your mind. Try it. You'll see I'm being straight with you."

He went inside, leaving the baggie on the ground. There was no central air-conditioning inside his place, but the open windows created a fresh cross breeze. Alexander removed the Rompecabezas from his suitcase and typed up his first report.

He typed with two fingers, making sure there were no spelling errors, as he didn't see a delete button. When he finished, Alexander watched in fascination as the words changed into their special enigmatic code.

His first brief report read, "Day 1: Have arrived in Los Angeles. Made contact with two resistance members. One a mercenary, the other a young girl. Shipment received. They don't trust me. They'll most likely call for confirmation. Will send another communiqué when there are developments."

It changed to: *The Jeffersons. You're soaking in it. Be Bop Baby. Donald Duck. The Persistence of Memory. To be, or not to be. John Lennon…shot twice in the back…dead on arrival.*

Alexander hit send and closed the Rompecabezas. He looked outside the front window just in time to see a black moped pulling away.

A few days later, Alexander went to look for gas in the Northern Block. The baggie was still in the driveway. He picked it up and shoved it in his pocket.

He knew very little about Los Angeles except for the jokes they told on Texan sitcoms and late-night talk shows. Airheads, surfers, wannabe actors, or a combination of the three populated the sunbaked city.

Driving through the sprawl, he saw a different reality that made him realize his own current neighborhood was by no means unique. Giant mansions threatened to encroach on tiny tin-roof shacks. For every pristine six-bedroom mansion with swimming pools and a battalion of landscapers, he saw miniature palaces for the downtrodden. Unrestored structures were half eaten by termites and always with bars on windows, as if anything in there would be worth stealing. In Los Angeles, he figured, not even life was worth taking.

The sidewalk blocks all teemed with beggars, who often made camp outside exclusive condominiums complete with private rooftop fruit gardens and security guards in the front entrance. It was as if the city had never learned the concept of middle and working classes. There were only these two extremes, more often than not in the exact same spot.

The only thing worse than the drastic economic differences were the speed with which things seemed to have happened. Neighborhoods that must have been breathtaking at one point were now covered with garbage. He drove past a residential street where stray dogs roamed, and people who lived hand to mouth sat stunned and dirty in the sunshine, their only abundance being poverty and the natural beauty of the landscape that surrounded them.

He drove north, aghast at the seeming casual obliviousness with which the privileged went about their business. He reached West Hollywood. The neighborhood had also fallen on hard times. A boutique hotel that looked like it had been constructed just a few years ago was already in a state of decomposition: paint faded, windows broken. Drug addicts and drunks shuffled inside. Male, female, and transvestite prostitutes jockeyed for space on the corner.

He continued north, noting a sign on a hill. A proud landmark of the neighborhood was now battered, crumbling, and vandalized. Most of the letters were missing, stolen to sell for scrap, most likely. Alexander laughed out loud when he realized the only letters left proclaimed he was driving through "HO."

It took a full hour of driving until he found what he was looking for. On the corner of Santa Monica and Vine was a graffiti-covered gas station fortified to look like a bunker. It was the first he'd seen that looked open and claimed to have gas.

He pulled up, got out of his truck, and went around to the pump, carrying three ten-gallon gas cans. He had just lifted the pump's handle when Alexander heard the unmistakable sound of a gun cocking.

"What the fuck you think you're doing?"

He turned to see an attendant with a purple Mohawk and facial piercings standing three feet away from him. The man held a small pistol in his hand, aimed at Alexander's stomach.

"Well, I planned on getting gas." He put the pump back on the handle.

The attendant waved him away from the pump. "That's not how it works, motherfucker."

Alexander raised his hands but kept within close range, knowing with experience that the closer you were to an enemy, the easier he was to disarm. And while the attendant looked like he wouldn't think twice about shooting, his gun hand was shaking. Drugs, he thought. Or nerves. Or both.

"Tell me how it works."

"You need a ration card," the attendant said. "And I need to see the money—in your hands. Then I fill your cans up. You don't touch the pump. Where the fuck you think this is—Beverly Hills?"

"I don't know where that is. I'm new in town," Alexander said.

The punk stepped closer. "Well then, you don't get shit. And if you don't get in your truck and get out of here, in ten seconds you're a dead man." He glanced at the license plate.

"I knew you Texan rednecks were stupid, but I didn't think you were this stupid."

The punk stuck his fingers in his mouth, making a loud shrill whistle.

As if on cue, two more gas-station attendants ambled out of the store. Like the first, they were pierced and covered in tattoos. They wore steel-toed combat boots. And all of them carried the same kind of pistol.

"This right-wing piece of shit just rolled his pickup truck into Hollywood—to get gas."

The other two laughed.

"Man's new in town. And what does he do? Drive into Hollywood of all places." The first attendant shook his head in mock sadness. "Y'all might just be the dumbest redneck I ever did done meet. Say your prayers, boy."

The group laughed. While pretending to act scared, Alexander turned sideways, making himself a smaller target. The first attendant took a step toward him. They were less than two feet apart now.

"Thanks a lot, Sergeant Biker."

Before the first attendant could respond, Alexander kicked upward, knocking the gun from the man's hand. He then lunged for the man's face, ripping a piercing off with each hand, taking skin with it. The man yelped in pain. Alexander punched him hard in the sternum, leaving him doubled over in pain.

The other two fired and missed. He dove for the gun and ducked behind the truck for cover. The remaining attendants continued firing, but their aim was poor. Fearing they'd hit a pump by mistake, Alexander shot twice, hitting them each in the forehead. They fell at the same time.

He ducked behind his truck, waiting to see if anyone else would come out of the gas station. When no one did, he proceeded to fill up three cans. The first attendant lay wheezing for breath, face blinded by blood. For a brief moment, Alexander wondered if he should kill the attendant.

No, he thought, let him live to think twice about messing with Texas. It was only when Alexander had left the neighborhood did he realize his hands were shaking and covered with blood.

Chapter 9

Alexander took La Cienega Boulevard to Olympic, eyes scanning the rearview mirror the entire time for police. TexIntelSecuriCorp hadn't briefed him on what to do if he'd gotten into that kind of scrape. While he doubted the punk he'd left half alive would call the police, he might have friends who were all too eager to track him down. By the time he got to Santa Monica with no incidents, Alexander figured he was in the clear. He might not have been welcome in Hollywood, but the rest of LA seemed a lot safer.

He drove back to Venice and found the bar nearest to his duplex. It was dark and uninviting, smelled like stale beer, peanuts, and mentholated cigarettes. Before the door shut behind him, Alexander caught a glimpse of his hands in the sunlight. He went straight to the bathroom and washed the sticky blood under scalding hot water until they felt clean. His nerves were jangled; his insides felt raw.

He ordered a shot of vodka, downed it, and ordered another. At that time of day, there were only two other customers. One looked like he hadn't left the bar in years and sat half slumped underneath the television. Alexander imagined there was moss underneath his chair.

By contrast, the second customer looked like it was her first time in a bar of any kind, let alone a dive bar. She sat sipping a beer. The television illuminated the pink strands in her otherwise green-blond hair. She was staring at him.

"Look who it is—the long, tall Texan with the metal legs."

"In the flesh," he said. "What are you doing here, Sickle?"

"Oh, me? Just hanging out. Have any luck getting gas?"

Alexander motioned for another drink. The bartender was more interested in the TV show.

"Question: what is flower?"

Sickle smiled. "Why? You want to try it?"

"A homeless fella tried to sell me some. When I declined, he gave it to me."

She shook her head in disbelief. "You serious?"

"Sure am. He didn't seem stoned but told me he just smoked it. Seemed straight as an arrow to me."

"I would hope so," she said.

He reached in his pocket, inching the baggie out so only she could see.

"Oh, that's it all right. Even in this light, I can tell it's the real deal. You haven't heard of it?"

"We don't have it in Texas that I know of."

"Well you guys are backward," she teased. "You should try it. Honestly, it's not like pot."

"Famous last words."

"No, man, listen. It was a strain of marijuana the Mexicans discovered. Then they genetically engineered it, so it would make you smarter."

"Come on."

"I'm serious. They took the stoner out and put the Mensa in."

"Have you had it before?"

"Of course," she said. "The more you smoke it, the smarter you get. Smart doesn't even do it justice. Lasts a heck of a long time, too. I smoked it once a few months ago, and I felt supersmart for weeks. But each time you smoke it you stay a little smarter. It's like getting an education."

"If you say so."

She finished her beer. "I do. If you want, I'll smoke it with you to show you there's no fear or harm."

"Flower."

"Yep. Or Chocolate—that's what the Mexicans call it: choco-latte," she said in a heavy accent.

"Is it legal here?"

"Sort of. We're better off going to your place. People find out you have it, they either think you're rich or that you're a dealer who has other stuff. It's not cheap."

Alexander finished his drink, leaving money on the counter for both of them. The bartender never took her eyes off the TV.

Sickle put on her helmet and hopped on her moped. "I'll follow you."

He should have known. Had Sickle tailed him to the Northern Sector, too? Considering the danger, he didn't think Biker would risk it. He pulled into the driveway and motioned her to do the same. They went inside, and he told her to make herself at home. He made sure the Rompecabezas was locked in his suitcase where he left it and then fetched two beers from the fridge.

She had a small glass pipe and a lighter lying on the table. He put a beer and the baggie in front of her.

Alexander frowned. He'd gone down enough drug-fueled rabbit holes to last a lifetime and a half and really wasn't interested in returning to that life—not when he'd worked so hard to clean himself up and especially not now that he was employed.

But if Sickle knew what she was talking about, it could be beneficial. If nothing else, he'd get on her good side by sharing and try to win her confidence. And if it turned out to be a trick, he figured nothing could be worse than dreamfish.

Sickle packed the pipe. "I'll go first, and then we'll wait a few, so you can see what happens." She smiled. "Promise: nothing'll happen."

"Fair enough."

"Here's to clarity." She toasted him with the pipe, lit it, and drew the smoke deep into her lungs. "You got a radio around here?"

When he shook his head, she opened her backpack and pulled out a portable one. The sound that came from the speakers was louder than he expected. Sickle turned the small dial until she found a college radio station. The DJ mumbled about some new band he'd seen the night before in the Southern Sector that was a mix of *norteño* and metal. To Alexander's relief, the DJ played something other than what he described.

They sat in silence, listening to the music. Three songs went by before she passed him the pipe.

"Start with one hit."

He took it, lit it, and inhaled. The effect was instantaneous—as if hidden tunnels in his brain were revealed. It was at once profound and mundane. It was nothing like the carnival light show of LSD, and it didn't take him on a spiritual journey into the self like ayahuasca, and he did not descend into the pits of hell like he did with dreamfish.

He heard the song coming from the radio. Having never once picked up an instrument or studied music, he knew it was in a septuple meter and that this was unusual for rock 'n' roll. He closed his eyes and pictured the sheet music, knowing with certainty he could play it on any instrument he chose. He let that train of thought go, noting with a strange deal of pride that his mental capacity felt like it was growing, somehow.

Sickle watched him with curiosity. "So?"

"Feels like my IQ jumped fifty points. Otherwise the same."

She laughed. "Told you."

They talked for hours. He let her do most of the talking, listening as she told him everything he'd need to know about Los Angeles, confirming suspicions and filling in the details.

The city was ungovernable, the economy in a state of near total collapse. For every respectable-looking street with decent people, there was one next to it under gang control. Whole neighborhoods, like Hollywood, were considered no-go zones, just like the most toxic parts of the Pacific Ocean.

A black market was extensive and profitable, keeping Southern California afloat. The best that local politicians could do to try and govern was divide the city into sectors that were easier to manage, at least in theory. This proved not to be the case, however, and only sewed more division among the population already at each other's throats.

As always, only the richest parts were safe. Beverly Hills and Bel-Air were safe, same with Manhattan Beach. Venice and Mar Vista were borderline areas.

Six months ago a citywide curfew was imposed in order to control crime. But this was easy enough to ignore if you lived in the richest neighborhoods or knew how to avoid detection.

While Southern California in general faced a lot of issues, Los Angeles seemed incapable of dealing with the basics of government, including solving the dire problems the city faced.

"It's now at the point of absurdity," Sickle said. "There are currently six no-go zones here, either because of crime, toxic levels of poison, or disease."

Alexander shook his head in disbelief. "Disease?"

Sickle nodded. "From the homeless encampments like the one across from you. One downtown had a tuberculosis outbreak a few weeks back. There's a growing hepatitis A problem in Newport Beach. The Northern California representatives just turn a blind eye to it. And that's pretty fucked up considering their federal building downtown is surrounded by it."

"I saw bombed-out villages in Iraq that were healthier."

"Now you're starting to understand what we've been living under." She looked at her watch. "I should get going."

He stood up and walked her to the door. "Thanks."

"For what? It was your flower, not mine."

They made plans to meet on Sunday at the hardware store. He watched as she left his driveway, heading west toward her own area.

If Sickle had known he was being set up, she'd kept it to herself. He hadn't pressed the issue, figuring she'd clam up if he did. Alexander brought out the Rompecabezas and fired off another note to TexIntelSecuriCorp, describing the state of the city and the location of the federal building.

He suspected that was going to be their target. He told them he planned on doing a reconnaissance mission to check the building out for himself. In the meantime, however, he would take things slow. After some deliberation, Alexander decided not to tell them about flower. He didn't want them feeling like he was compromising himself by using the drug even though it would be necessary to maintain his undercover guise and win them over.

He pressed send. Two minutes later, he received a message that read: *Watusi, Stuffed Crust Pizza, Slinky, Here's Johnny, Who shot JR?*

When he decoded the message, the words changed to "Biker is a former mercenary. Federal building already ID'd as a potential target. Find out for sure and when."

Chapter 10

He gave Biker the three full gas cans with the same casualness as if he'd picked up groceries from the corner store. Though his face never betrayed it, Biker's demeanor changed after that. Still, he held all the cards and used this to his advantage. Alexander could only wait until Biker was ready to share their plans. Maybe the flower really did make people smarter. He was sure Sickle knew nothing of importance, but he spent the next few weeks palling around with her, doing odd jobs, even helping bottle-feed Biker's kittens.

He fell into an uneasy routine, spending most days at the hardware store and evenings at home. Although introductions were perfunctory if they came at all, Alexander managed to meet the rest of the resistance members. They appeared at the store alone or in pairs. They came from all walks of life: rich and poor and middle class, black, Asian, Hispanic, and white. All of them but Biker and Sickle were in their mid-thirties.

They were all called by an alias, as per Biker's instructions. He also explained they were kept split up so as not to cause alarm in the neighborhood. A group of twenty people arriving every day at the same time might catch the eye of the locals, who might call the police, or the neighborhood heavies, who were much more effective at dealing with issues because they had no compunction about using brute force when it came to dealing with troublemakers.

Biker said he would summon them all only once, the night before they planned their assault, thus minimizing the chances of getting caught. Alexander also suspected a further rationale was to make sure that if by some slim chance there were a whistleblower in their midst, there'd be no chance of being called out. Biker took every precaution imaginable and kept everyone in the dark.

One day while Sickle was out picking up kitty litter, Alexander asked Biker how he chose the soldiers.

"New recruits seek me out through the underground, or they get referred by another division that is full up. I decide pretty much on the spot if they're gonna work out or not. If I like 'em, they live with me for a time until they get cleared. If not, I send 'em away."

"Sickle's your newest?"

"That's right. I know she's young, but she's good to go into the field. She's a street kid," he said. "Seen some shit, been in fights, knows her way around a weapon. What I'm saying is there's not one ounce of gullibility left in her. At the same time, she's vulnerable. I wanted to rescue her, keep my eyes on her, and make sure she's not running around with the wrong crowd. There's a lot of fucked-up predators out there, and here she's safe—I make sure of that. Anyone laid a hand on her, I'd chop that hand off. Besides, she's good with the cats."

"Because that's a requirement? Being good with cats?"

Biker told him about the side business. "She's increased profits twenty percent."

One afternoon, Alexander found a working pay phone and dug out Marie-Eve's number.

"Monsieur Braxton. I wondered if I would hear from you," she said. "You've seen how fucked up LA is by now, no?"

"That's one way of putting it."

"Parts of the city get worse every time I come, but there are parts that stay beautiful. I hope you are free tonight."

"I will do my best to make myself free," he said.

"Good, because I am going to a party in beautiful Bel Air, and you must come as well. There will be some very interesting friends of mine there, and I feel you must meet them."

"Sounds good."

She gave him the address, telling him to arrive no earlier than eight thirty, or she would not be there. "Without me, you won't be able to get in, believe me."

He hung up, wishing he'd thought to ask if there was a dress code. He went back to his duplex, rummaged through his suitcase, and found his only acceptable dress shirt and tie. It would have to do.

Right before he left, Alexander rolled a makeshift joint and smoked a small amount of flower, wondering how long he could keep the stash before it ran out and hoping it would allow him to make a good impression on Marie-Eve and her very interesting friends.

He found the address an hour later, pulling to the front of a very large estate, where a valet handed him a yellow ticket and looked at his pickup truck with distaste before driving it away. A butler in a formal tuxedo stood ramrod in front of the door.

"Yes?"

"Marie-Eve invited me."

The butler stood aside. "Very good, sir. Ms. Charmont has just arrived."

The entrance to the mansion was stunning in its opulence. A giant modern chandelier in the shape of an orb hung from the ceiling. The floors were Italian marble. The grand staircase had red and gold carpeting. Alexander didn't know much about art but assumed the portraits hanging on the walls were priceless originals.

He stood at the top of the stairs, scanning the room until he saw Marie-Eve surrounded by a group of men. It took him a moment to recognize her without body paint: light tan, high cheekbones. The only wrinkles were two laugh lines that complemented her face. She was wearing a red suit and wide-brimmed hat that gave off an air of irreverent sophistication.

Upon seeing him, she broke away from the group. "Monsieur Alexander, so lovely to see you," she exclaimed in delight. "And looking smart in your shirt and tie. Come, I must introduce you to some important people and also some very dear friends of mine. I think you will very much like them. They are different from these hangers-on."

She took his arm, leading him past the throngs of guests, most of them chatting in small groups. There must have been two hundred people there, not counting the servants who brought out catered food and champagne cocktails and removed empty glasses and plates with silent discretion.

A giant of a man sat in front of a Noguchi table, drinking something from a Tom Collins glass. His face brightened when he saw Marie-Eve approaching.

"Ah, I was hoping you'd be here." His accent was thick.

"May I present to you, Braxton Alexander. This is my good friend Paulo Aveleyra."

"May I say, senor, that you carry yourself like a soldier."

"That's because I used to be one."

"You see, Marie-Eve? This nose always smells authority." Paulo nodded. "It's OK; I still welcome you—provided you aren't on official business."

"I'm only here for fun and games," Alexander said.

"And you will find both in abundance here. We spare no expense."

"Is it yours?"

Paulo laughed. "No, it was a figure of speech only. I'd never leave my beloved Jalisco. Besides, I have too much to do in Mexico."

"Do you work for the government?"

"Hardly, senor. I spend my days making sure the Mexican Intelligence leaves the people I do work for alone." Paulo winked.

"Ah," Alexander said, "say no more."

"You might as well hear it from me before you hear it elsewhere. I work for Los Tigres Traficantes. We are the largest producer of chocolate in western Mexico and the largest supplier to California among other countries. Speaking of, you don't sound like you are from here."

"I'm from Texas."

Paulo's eyes shined. "Ah, now that is a coconut we still have not cracked open. Can you imagine? The largest country on the continent would be a—how do you say?—feather in our cap. So many people there, just waiting to become smarter—and so many people who need to, if you don't mind my saying so."

Marie-Eve wrinkled her nose. "No politics. Besides, a drug is a drug."

Paulo scoffed. "This might have been true at one point, but no longer, my lady friend. Even our own government sees the benefits. We lead the world in education and reform. This is hardly a dirty stick of *la cucaracha*, eh? Why, just look at what it has done for us. While your side of the continent is busying itself with endless skirmishes and political infighting, we have consolidated our strengths. But never mind, tonight is no night for bragging. Tell me, Marie-Eve, have you taken Senor Alexander to meet the little fellows of the house?"

"Not yet, we're just on our way."

With a slight bow, Paulo presented him with a card. "Should you come to Mexico, I will show you around. Or if you are in need of assistance, let me promise you that any friend of Marie-Eve is a friend of mine." He shook Alexander's hand with a vicelike grip.

They walked into another large room past a man who sat at a black grand piano, entertaining three women who wore long black gowns and satin gloves up to their elbows. Then they moved past the sofas where people lounged and through the open glass balcony doors, weaving past the kidney-shaped pool until at last they reached a large cabana lit only by citronella candles.

Marie-Eve clapped to get everyone's attention. "My lovelies, I am pleased to introduce you to someone who lifted my spirits when I was having an off night in the doldrums of Vegas: Monsieur Braxton Alexander."

He saw the two lanky blond women curled up on the chaise lounges first. They were languid and elegant in a way that only people who are accustomed to having lots of money are. Then he saw the two gray aliens seated in between them, looking like real-life cartoons.

Alexander's stomach churned. His racing pulse beat against his temples. He stared at their faces, which were content, if not beatific, wondering if he was having a flashback. Marie-Eve gave his arm a reassuring squeeze.

Braxton swallowed. "Nice to meet everyone."

The aliens managed to nod in unison without moving their heads.

They one on the right spoke first. "How very nice to meet you, sir. These beautiful ladies are Yelena and Yulia. Neither speaks much English, I'm afraid, nor French for that matter, although that is surprising considering most Old World Europeans know at least a bit of French. *Mais, c'est la vie.* Or perhaps since we are in California, I should say *c'est la guerre* instead."

The two women sat unperturbed, cradling their champagne flutes, lost in their own worlds.

"Oh, Joe, your bon mots are tiresome," the alien on the left said.

"Don't mind my friend here. He is sometimes known on occasion to mistake corrosiveness for gay repartee. I simply can't take him anywhere." He extended his stubby, rubbery hand. "Braxton Alexander, it is very nice to meet you. My name is Shoeless Joe Jackson."

"Any friend of Marie-Eve's is a friend of ours," the other alien said. "I'm Catfish Hunter." He then spoke in fluent Russian to the women. They shrugged like twins, drained their glasses, picked up their clutches, and left without saying another word.

"I told them to mingle. They're both beautiful women and very nice when you get to know them."

"Just not very conversational, even in the mother tongue," Shoeless Joe said. "At least when it comes to words," he said, flashing a devilish smile.

They both patted the chaise lounges, beckoning Marie-Eve and Alexander to sit.

"What do you say?" Catfish said. "Girl, boy, boy, boy?"

Marie-Eve declined. "Cheeky. It is I who must mingle now. One of the Cirque owners is here, and it is bad form if we are not seen together."

Shoeless Joe stood, taking her hand. He was no more than four feet tall. "Darling, you know what they say: to whom much is given…"

"It's OK; we have much to discuss with your friend," Catfish said. "Now then, Marie-Eve tells us you came here all the way from Texas? Are you here for business or pleasure? Assuming one can even have a pleasurable experience in Southern California anymore."

Alexander took in the lush greenery, adorned with solar-powered golden lights casting a warm glow across the lawn. "Oh, I don't know. I've been to worse parties."

The aliens laughed.

"Whose place is this anyway?"

"Ours," Catfish said. "Well, not *ours* in that sense. We're not coupled, as it were."

"Lord no, it's strictly friendship with us," Shoeless Joe said. "This isn't our primary home anyway."

The sound of laughter came from poolside. Alexander turned around to see the two Russian women, now topless, jumping into the pool. Several men followed suit, disrobing with abandon. The aliens watched with scant interest, as if it were a background image on TV.

"Both of us live on a NEA, if you would," Catfish said. "Near Earth asteroid," he added.

Shoeless Joe caught a servant's eye, showed him his empty glass, and held up three fingers, which was easy enough since the aliens only had three fingers on each hand. The servant nodded and returned with three fresh drinks, leaving with the empty glasses.

"It's all rather very amusing," he began. "We represent two rival mining companies. Both sent us to the same NEA a lot closer to Earth than most humans would guess."

"As competitors, we're not really supposed to fraternize," Catfish said. "It is quote, frowned upon, unquote. But being so far from home and our main bosses, we figured, what's the harm? A few years later and now we're positively thick as thieves."

"When this place came up for sale, we decided to go halfsies on it," Shoeless Joe said. "Now, I know what you must be thinking: why not get a bigger place than this?"

"Truth is we did consider getting an even bigger monstrosity," Catfish said. "But we're only here a few times a month. Anything more is extra upkeep and an added expense."

"I can imagine," Braxton said.

Catfish laughed. "The Texan soldier can imagine what it's like to choose a twelve-bedroom chateau instead of a twenty-bedroom manse. I just bet you can—especially now that you're employed with the best of the best."

When Braxton didn't respond, Shoeless Joe leaned closer, speaking in a stage whisper that was at once conspiratorial and comical. "What if I told you, my dear boy, that we know who you work for? Wouldn't surprise me if you were here on official business."

"Don't think we didn't notice how you evaded our business-or-pleasure question with such dexterity," Catfish said. "Seems like someone's getting smarter."

Shoeless Joe continued in the same whisper, enjoying every moment. "You see, we know you're on the flower, sir."

Braxton felt his face get hot.

"Oh, please don't worry," Shoeless Joe said. "We won't breathe a word. Besides, we're partakers, too. And we've got plenty to spare. You see, we've also got this lovely hacienda in Mexico."

"We'll make sure you don't leave empty-handed tonight," Catfish said. "And mum's the word, sir. Do you know—for some reason Marie-Eve's against it?"

As if they'd conjured her, Marie-Eve strode back to the cabana. "Against what? I only caught the tail end of your conversation. But I assume once again, you are making fun of me, you two clowns."

Catfish pouted. "Why, never in a million years."

"As a matter of fact, we were sharing with your friend our thoughts on California's ensuing civil war, which you are not for." Shoeless Joe winked at Braxton.

"I am not for war in general," she said. "I saw how futile it was in my own country. And I can only assume that a former soldier like Braxton would feel the same. Ah, but either way," Marie-Eve said, putting a hand to her chest. "Should it really be our concern? We are not from here. We are outsiders, no? We are not judge or jury."

Catfish nodded in agreement. "To a certain extent, you are right. Unless there was a way we could somehow work together in benevolent fashion. 'We come in peace' and all that."

Alexander wanted to hold his tongue but found he couldn't. "Doesn't it bother any of you at all? Half of this country is in decay. For every beautiful house like yours, there are hundreds held up with duct tape. I see ruins everywhere."

Catfish had a faraway look in his eyes. He put his hand up, as if to paint the scenery. "Corrosive beauty, the grandness of decay, a tragicomedy set against swaying palm trees, the feeling of glorious decadence, pretty ugliness, up close and personal, pockmarks and all," he sighed. "It's like living in an Otto Dix painting."

Marie-Eve sipped her cocktail. "Even I feel some compassion for these poor people, and I am not from here. Is empathy not part of your genetic makeup?"

Braxton watched Shoeless Joe's eyes soften and fade at the sound of her contempt. "But you misunderstand, *petit chou*. We don't take pleasure in the misfortune of others. But it is inevitable. Sorry if I sound fatalist. Of course I want the best for all."

Catfish's eyes also softened. "But he's right, you know. We don't enjoy watching others suffer, far from it. But when Rome is inevitably burning, one must admit the sound of the fiddle makes for a nice soundtrack."

They fell silent, watching the revelry. Marie-Eve finished her drink. "I suppose in some way we are all just spectators—like watching a game of chess."

"Or better yet, baseball." Shoeless tapped Braxton's knee. "Tell me, are you a fan of baseball?"

"Not really."

"No? What a pity. We love listening to it."

"Listening to it? You don't watch?"

Shoeless Joe shook his head back and forth. "Today's games simply don't have the same excitement. It's not like the golden age." He mimicked hitting an invisible baseball glove with his fist.

Catfish smiled. "Your radio broadcasts came to our planet years ago, bringing us such joy: the shot heard round the world, the house that Ruth built. It's no exaggeration to say baseball fundamentally changed our culture."

Marie-Eve rolled her eyes. "*Tabarnak.* They'll be talking baseball for days now."

Shoeless Joe laughed. "It's not our fault your Expos folded." When she threatened to smack him, he held up his arms in playful defense. "Forgive us, you're right. Besides I want to hear what the soldier has to say about the oncoming civil war. What do you think?"

"I'm not informed enough on the subject," Braxton said.

Catfish wagged a knowing finger at him. "You're deflecting again, Mr. Smarty."

"Please," Marie-Eve said, "must we? This is a party, no?"

"My dear, you are absolutely right," Shoeless Joe said. "Braxton, I suspect you *do* have some thoughts on the subject. Hopefully we will discuss them at another point in time. Oh dearie me, look at the time."

The two aliens stood and shook Alexander's hand. "We like to listen to the games on the same day as you would have heard them on Earth. Tonight's an exciting one, too. Bob Feller is pitching a no-hitter."

Almost as an afterthought, Catfish reached into his body and pulled out a mobile phone. His stubby fingers tapped at it for a few seconds. "I'm just letting the valet know to fix you up a package. It'll be in your car."

"A package from the, uh, florist," Shoeless Joe said. "Sometimes, I amuse myself."

Braxton watched the two disappear through the crowd, pausing now and then to shake hands or blow kisses and chat with the Russian women, who were still in the pool and did not seem inclined to leave. Instead of walking back inside, they glided over to a dark corner of the lawn. Alexander watched them shinny up a palm tree with ease. After a moment he saw two small bright circles of light ascend from the tree and head into the sky.

"So," Alexander said, craning his head upward, "how in the hell did you come to know them?"

Marie-Eve shrugged. "Same as everyone—they came to a Cirque show. Walked backstage right past everyone just to compliment me. Security probably thought they were in costume. The funny part is they're the only people to do so who didn't try to grope me. They actually meant their compliments. Do you want to get out of here?"

"Please." Before they left the party, Marie-Eve liberated two bottles of wine, a bunch of grapes, a sheath of crackers, and a wheel of brie. She directed him to the motel just off Pico, not far from where he lived.

He retrieved his pickup truck and followed her instructions, pulling into a jungle-themed motel that featured an animatronic woman and man in loincloths, whose waving hands beckoned the weary traveler into a dense tropical paradise, long since neglected on the outside. He thought perhaps she felt more comfortable in familiar surroundings, however kitschy they might appear.

"It doesn't look like much, but the rooms are amazing; you will see," she said.

They walked through the stone cave structure, passing through the motion detector that set off the sounds of dinosaurs and tribal drums, walking by two other bungalows until they reached the third.

Her place was a multiroom suite, with a large living room, kitchenette, and king-sized bed. There was also a fireplace and back porch complete with an earthenware fireplace.

She threw the cheese in the fridge, opened the wine, and tuned the stereo until she found a station that played soft instrumental music. The room was cool and pleasant. They sipped their wine and savored the type of silence that comes as a respite after leaving a loud party.

"Do you think there's really going to be a war here?" she asked.

"I think so," he said. "This place feels like a pot about to boil over. If the rest of Southern California is the same, then it's only a matter of time."

She shuddered. "I don't understand Catfish and Shoeless Joe. The resistance members in the South and Northern Californian leaders are like toys to them, to keep them amused and distracted. How can they see it like that?"

"At least they're realistic about it. Back home, Texans write inspiring songs about the Middle East wars we fight and still fight, even though there's no real way to win and we don't get anything out of it even if we do win. They're blinded by the old 'might makes right' mantra."

She took their glasses and placed them on the coffee table. "Braxton Alexander, I have a command for you."

"Oh? And what's that?"

"Turn off the lights," she said. "That's an order."

She came into his arms. Each kiss drew them deeper. They felt a hunger neither had known was possible. After a time, she forced herself to break away. She stood in front of him, panting. With eyes locked on his, she took off her pants. She then raised her foot and placed it on his knee.

He felt the coldness of steel and knew before he even looked. The metal reflected in the light of the moon.

"Two years ago, I fell from the trapeze," she said. "They gave me a choice. I could learn how to perform like this, learn all over again, or take a year of compensation. I chose to keep performing."

It was odd, how moved he felt. He stroked and kissed it as if it were real. He then stood up and undressed, revealing his own condition.

"I've got you beat."

She said nothing and drew him close once again.

A few hours later, still lying in bed, he said, "Someday, Marie-Eve, I hope I'll get to see you perform."

She turned to him in mock anger. "Someday? And what do you call last night? A rehearsal?"

Chapter 11

"Welcome to another brand-new edition of *The Outer Reaches*, the largest and fastest growing program in the overnight block of AM radio. I'm Frank Sandoval, broadcasting live from midnight to four a.m. DST; that's Deseret Standard Time. If you're new and just found us, welcome to the only program that searches for wisdom on an otherwise desolated planet.

"Before we get into the show, you'll notice the opening song has changed. That's because it is a New Era. You can feel it, right? I think we all can. Even the most closed-minded among us know that the times are no longer the same. As the ancient Greek philosopher Heraclitus said, you can't step into the same river twice. But if you really think about it, you know, things change so quickly that you can't even step into the same river once.

"Anyway. Last week, Dee Dee and I were having dinner at the ranch, and we were talking about the New Era. And she said to me, 'Hey, what you really need is a new theme to go along with the New Era.'

"Now, I don't like to talk about my private life very often because, as you know, in my line of work, a few baddies out there would love nothing more than to make me disappear. This is also why we keep moving compounds and why I never disclose my true location. However, I want to pull the curtain back tonight just a crack to let a little light in the room, because I am so proud of Dee Dee. She's a very talented musician and has had a very successful career as a producer and songwriter. I wish I could tell you what she's done, but believe me, if you knew her real name, you'd say, 'Wow, I know those songs.' Well, what you are listening to at this very moment is her latest composition, called appropriately enough, 'New Era.'

"Tonight, we have a very special guest who has been on this show only once before—hard to believe but it's true. He's a pilot who has flown every aircraft imaginable in every capacity: from production test flying to commercial airliners, fighter jets during wars, secret government missions, to—oh, yeah—landing on the moon. He even helped design the first flight-simulator video game that became the gold standard in training for all air forces on the continent. And, ladies and gentlemen, he's acted as a stunt coordinator for movies, so he's a hotshot and a celebrity, too.

"Should I go on? He holds the *Guinness Book of World Records* record for the most flights, with forty-four thousand hours of flight time under his belt. To put that into perspective, we're talking more than five years he's spent in the air. This captain has flown around the world more times than any human being alive or dead. And before retiring last year to spend time with his wife and children, he helped launch Deseret's newest and most clandestine air-force test site in a remote location. It is my pleasure to welcome back Charlie Wade.

"So exciting to have you on the program once again."

"Thanks. It's been a few years, right?"

"I think so. But let's be honest, you were still the most fun at parties then, too."

"I don't know, Frank. From what I hear, your show has grown exponentially, too."

"First time you were on, we'd just started in syndication. Now we are heard around the continent on three hundred stations. Sorry, I meant three hundred and two stations! Welcome aboard, Cincinnati and Las Tunas, which is our third city to broadcast out of the Confederate United States."

"Congratulations."

"Charlie, have you've been taking it easy since you retired last year?"

"Hardly. I think in some ways the real work is now beginning."

"Well, in the midst of all this flying for commercial airliners and two World War efforts—I should add you were a decorated hero too, so thank you for serving—it's amazing to me that for the first half of your stellar career you never once encountered a UFO. And then in the second half, boy, did they start to appear with more and more frequency."

"Oh yes. You know Moore's law, right? This is proof. It got to the point where my last year of flying felt like I had escorts all the time."

"It's really good I have you for the whole show, Charlie, because I want to pick your brain about all this. Ufology is still a study in its infancy; is that fair to say?"

"Well, modern ufology certainly is. And it's not one that is being accepted by the mainstream scientists; that is without a doubt. People are still adamant about declaring it a pseudoscience. I get called names, you know: crackpot, kook, whatever. People say things like, 'Oh, you know, he's working with the government to spread disinformation among the gullible to protect the real research that's happening.'"

"And you categorically deny this."

"Frank, the government doesn't need to spread disinformation to the public. We have one of the most transparent administrations ever elected. But I am giving you and your listeners my word. UFOs exist. Aliens exist. I've encountered both with my own eyes—so many times. And not just in the sky, either. The whole reason the government asked me to help launch Fort McMullin in Deseret was because they needed a depot for the craft we've salvaged."

"And you have nothing to gain from lying."

"No. Remember, I'm retired. I'm no longer on the payroll. And I'm not out here to just sell books. I have integrity. And as far as I'm concerned, when it comes to UFOs and aliens, that part of the science is settled."

"But if I'm understanding you, some parts are far from settled."

"Absolutely. Vast amounts. Look, I'm just one pilot. Even working as a consultant with the government in my current capacity, I will say this is tip-of-the-iceberg stuff. There are things we definitely know, but there are plenty of other things we don't."

"Your latest book, *Look to the Sky*, is unprecedented in that you were given complete access to Deseret military areas that were highly restricted until then. You were actually allowed to see classified documents and interview some former employees who were in charge of investigating the very first downed spacecraft. To say it is an in-depth study is understatement."

"Thank you."

"But you also make some controversial statements. Like for instance, there is zero proof of alien abduction."

"Correct. There are people with so-called repressed memories who make these claims, but they are all unfounded. It's wishful thinking at best, and at worst these people need psychiatric help."

"That's a bold statement, sir."

"Not particularly, Frank, I've seen these, uh, abductees up close. I've conducted interviews with them on behalf of the Deseret Intelligence and National Science Administrations, as well as in, shall we say, more informal and less official settings when they're not as on guard or careful with their word choices. I can say with one hundred percent accuracy that the grays don't do it and would never do it. It's not in their nature. And they have assured me the same is true of the greens."

"Oh, now this is interesting, what you just said. Our listeners are all familiar with the term 'the grays,' which of course is the way we've been describing the aliens since they first landed here and were recovered at Roswell. It's well known they have gray skin. But I've never heard the term 'greens' before. Are you really saying there are some with green skin?"

"Absolutely."

"What kind of green?"

"I would describe it as being a sort of parakeet."

"Parakeet—sort of a yellowish green, then."

"Yes, like that. We first encountered them in the Deseret summer, when they were molting."

"Sorry, did you say molting?"

"Yes, that's where the confusion originally came from. You see, when it's molting season, their skin goes through multiple color changes. The first recovered alien and subsequent sightings were all gray. But it was only recently I saw the green ones."

"And the parakeet color results after they have finished molting."

"Of course. How else would you explain it?"

"Well, I'm looking to you for explanations. You're the expert. Does this mean there are two alien races?"

"No doubt about it. One finishes molting and keeps their gray color; the other is green."

"This is incredibly riveting: two races. But I suppose I should back up for a second and ask you something. If they aren't abducting people, then what are they doing here?"

"As far as I can tell, they're only here part of the time. They come and go."

"So when they're here—"

"I would say, they are hanging out like the rest of us."

"Two alien races—both are visiting our planet, both coming and going. Wonder where they go when they aren't here? Any idea, Charlie?"

"My working theory is that they are traveling between dimensions."

"Interdimensional travel. Huh."

"Yes. Mind you, this is all speculation on my part at this point, and further investigation is necessary to prove it, but my theory on why they are traveling between dimensions is because they are looking for something important."

"Like perhaps a resource? As in, if we ran out of water, we'd search for water?"

"No, I doubt that. Think about it, Frank. They have spacecraft that is far more advanced than ours. They can reach our planet from wherever they came from, light-years away. They have technology we can only study at this point. It's way beyond our comprehension. What kind of resources could they possibly need?"

"Fair point."

"Also, in the interviews I've conducted, they are highly intelligent life forms that have been mistaken by humans as being nefarious when in fact they could not care less about us."

"Fascinating. So you believe they aren't looking to abduct us, and they aren't out for resources."

"No. However, I must stress that, on that second matter, I haven't asked them about it directly. As you know, my retirement from flying and from working with the government was somewhat—"

"Acrimonious?"

"That might be a bit harsh, Frank. In fact, I resent that. Let's just say, the air force felt before I did that it was time to move on. My point is that I've not had contact with the grays or greens in almost a year. My research still continues unabated, however, just without the deep pockets of the military to assist."

"Naturally. And through your independent studies, you've come to the conclusion that the aliens are traveling between dimensions, but they aren't looking for resources."

"Yes."

"Because as you say, they are too far advanced."

"Correct."

"Well, Charlie, do you have any idea what they are doing at all?"

"As I said, this is a theory only. But I think when you and your listeners hear my answer, you'll all have one of those collective 'why-didn't-I-think-of-that' moments."

"Should we wait until the next break to pick it up, or do you have time to tell us now?"

"Oh, I'd rather tell you now, and then we can explore this topic further after the break, as there is much to explore here."

"Go ahead; don't keep us in suspense, Charlie."

"OK, as far as my research goes, all signs are pointing to the same place. The aliens are traveling between two dimensions because they are in search of something important to them."

"And that is?"

"Hidden treasure."

"Wow. You have heard it here first, ladies and gentlemen: hidden treasure. It is now twelve forty-five in my great corner of Deseret. Sometimes I sit here and think, 'Gee, what a vast, unknowable universe we're in. It boggles the mind.' Maybe right now you're working the night shift. Or you're lying in bed. Or you're out driving under a trillion stars. Either way, you're in that rare quiet time where it's just you and your thoughts and my voice. It's that moment of reflection, when all of us come to the very same profound conclusion. Regardless of who we are or what we believe, in our heart of hearts we know that we're just one tiny speck in this giant, unfathomable universe.

"It's all so fleeting, our sense of knowledge. Is it not? One moment we think we have a grasp of our own planet, but then an expert guest on a radio show drops an eye-opener on you about other beings that live here and travel between dimensions. If that's not enough to keep you awake at night, what else will?

"Thankfully I do know one other eye-opener, and that's Espresso Ronzio. The good people of Ronzio harvest their beans in Chiapas, Mexico, right on the Guatemalan border, and only roast in small batches in a time-honored way. I'm having an Americano even as we speak, and I have to say, their roast is unmatched because it's never bitter. That's right, no lemon peel needed. Right now, listeners of *The Outer Reaches* save twenty percent on each pound of whole bean coffee when you go to their website and use the code 'Outer Limits.' So do yourself a favor. Stay open-minded, stay alert, and drink Ronzio.

"I'm Frank Sandoval. We'll be right back after these messages."

Chapter 12

Alexander woke just after four in the morning. The room was hot, and the sheets, soaked with sweat. He didn't need to open his eyes to know he was alone. He reached out an arm to confirm the emptiness on the other side. Her side was cold, but the room still smelled of sex.

He switched on the light and found the note on the nightstand.

Cher Braxton Alexander: I must go rejoin the Cirque. The room is paid for until next Sunday. Enjoy if you like. You were lovely.

Alexander opened the refrigerator, ate the cheese and crackers for breakfast, and then stood under a very cold shower until his teeth chattered. He remembered to bring in the gift from Shoeless Joe and Catfish Hunter. He sat in the dark of early morning and smoked.

When he left, he made sure the Do Not Disturb sign was on the door. He didn't think there was a reason to return, but one never knew. Braxton backed out without turning on his headlights and drove down the silent streets until he reached his duplex. No one stirred in the encampments next door.

Inside, he found the Rompecabezas and sent a detailed report. Far from being concise, it was a rambling free-association piece; he would go off on tangents whenever one would occur to him, offering his opinion as well as vague speculation. He told them about Los Tigres, the aliens, and Sergeant Biker; he theorized as to what other targets they planned to assault, as well as how they might carry out their plan. By the time he pressed the send button, his wrists were hurting. Three minutes later, he received a short response: "Steer clear of anyone working for Los Tigres. We do not have operatives in their outfit as of yet. Aliens are known to us already and have been valuable source of intel. We have positive confirmation from other operatives that California Department of Homeland Security building is target. Scout the premises, and report back to us. Find out date of attack. Strong-arm Sgt. Biker if necessary. Exact coordinates to target will follow shortly."

Alexander got back in his truck and slammed the door.

"Need-to-know basis, my ass," he said out loud.

It didn't matter how much he was paid or what they promised. He was still just a grunt—put in the field to confirm things they already knew.

He didn't take the highway, driving on backstreets and side streets instead. It would be dark for another hour or so. At this time it wouldn't take long to get downtown, no more than forty minutes. He had plenty of gas. The air was cool and fresh for once. At that time, during the dwindling hours between late night and early morning, it seemed as if all of Los Angeles was in a blackout. For all he knew, it was.

He saw no cars on the street, not even police cruisers. Thinking about it, he hadn't seen any police cars at all. They couldn't all be undercover. Alexander kept a steady pace as he drove down the streets so as not to arouse suspicion, never driving too slow or speeding.

What did TexIntelSecuriCorp mean when they said they knew the aliens? Were they informants? Undercover agents? Neither reason seemed plausible, because if it were true, it would suggest Texas was powerful enough to have influence on other planets, not just with other countries. And if that were the case, how was it they had not infiltrated Mexico?

Downtown Los Angeles was just as neglected and full of downtrodden people as the rest of the city. The skyscrapers once meant to look futuristic now seemed out-of-date and forgotten. Entire blocks of condemned apartments, pawnshops, and diners long since closed left him feeling like he was driving through an abandoned set of a post-apocalyptic movie.

Signs of life were few and far between: here, an alley cat; there, someone passed out facedown on the sidewalk.

A garbage truck upended a Dumpster, sending inhabitants scrambling and screaming. The response came from the driver, who gave zero fucks. "You know not to sleep in there on Mondays. Ain't my problem."

In the midst of all the grime was the strangest of all sights: a large group of joggers wearing glow-in-the-dark orange jerseys and running shorts. Alexander watched them tiptoe around or jump over sleeping drunks and junkies and race past end-of-the-line prostitutes, who called out to them by name.

He drove over the LA River into the Eastern Sector, found an empty space by a sprawling cemetery. A man emerged from the shadows, approaching him before the key was even out of the ignition. He spoke in Spanish using slang Alexander was not familiar with. When he answered in English, the man's face broke out in a broad smile.

"Hey, man, you're a little far from home."

"So?"

"Tell me what you want; I help you find it."

Alexander put his hand on the door handle. "What I want is to get out of my car."

"Sure," the man said and kept smiling, "you pay me, and I'll watch your car. Ten dollars."

From the illuminated headlights, he could see the man wore cowboy boots decorated with elaborate beads in the shape of an animal. Boots like that were expensive. Alexander could just make out the shape of a switchblade in the man's inner pocket.

"Five," he said and got out of the car.

The man looked him up and down, weighing his chances. After a moment's hesitation, he shrugged. "*No hay bronca.*"

Alexander handed him the money and started walking without looking back. No sense in causing a disturbance here, not over a few dollars and not while he was on their turf.

Just like Iraq, he thought. Everyone quotes a higher price than they will settle for because they know they'll end up paying a higher price in the end if they aren't careful.

It took him thirty minutes to get to the California Department of Homeland Security building. By then the sun was up, and that part of downtown was looking less destitute. People in suits carried briefcases. A man stood on the corner, yelling into an earpiece while eating a pastry. A pink and yellow food truck selling egg sandwiches was parked just off a small square. Dozens lined up, waiting their turns to order.

He walked on parallel streets in order to scope out the building without getting too close. On the opposite side of the place was a multilevel outdoor mall with shops that catered to the local clientele: passports-while-you-wait stores, notaries for hire, translation services, predatory law firms, a drug store, and cheap fast-food joints.

The shopping mall could make a good vantage point, same with the park, although neither location provided much cover. There were much taller buildings surrounding the Homeland Security building on all sides. The majority were offices, but some were luxury high-rise condominiums. Even a cursory look proved the neighboring buildings would be all but impossible to break into. He could forget about descent from a neighboring rooftop as that would be impossible.

Alexander knew the buildings were earthquake-proof, including California Homeland Security. This meant they were impervious to all but the most powerful explosives. Unless Biker and his squad had such capabilities, it started to seem like a lost cause.

Trying to act casual, Alexander crossed over to the park, scanning the side of the building. A large open-air patio wrapped around it, but it was only accessible from the downstairs front entrance. The back was not any less secure, with one set of metal double doors he presumed would only open in the advent of a delivery or an emergency. Completing the perimeter only left him feeling surer of the plan's folly.

He walked up the giant set of four steep steps that led to the line of people waiting to go through the metal detector. No, it couldn't be done, unless somehow they managed to breach this entrance. He had no idea how many guards were in there, although as often was the case, the number was almost always less than one would expect.

"Help you?"

Alexander found himself outside the front entrance, face-to-face with a guard who carried an H&K MP5 submachine gun. Looking for an out, he spotted a woman with a large cup in her hand, heading into the building.

"Why, sir, I was just trying to figure out where that lady got her coffee from. I wouldn't mind a grande-sized buzz myself."

Without looking at her, the man said, "She didn't get it in here; I can say that much."

"I see."

"Try the food truck across the way there," he said and pointed in the direction of the park with his gun.

"Thank you very much, sir. I do appreciate that," Alexander said in his best drawl.

"Uh-huh."

Alexander spent another half hour exploring the area, looking to see if there was anything that might be used to advantage: a fire escape, a window that could open with ease, a door for the mailman that was easily accessible, a corner shop, or a disabled entrance. The search was fruitless.

Then he remembered the woman with the coffee. She'd shown her badge to a different guard, who stepped aside to let her in without having to wait in line or use the metal detectors. If they could procure enough badges, they might be able to get through the lobby undetected. Depending on Biker's plans, it wouldn't even take the whole crew. Sometimes the best battles were fought with the fewest foot soldiers.

Alexander drove to the hardware store and banged on the door until Biker opened it. There were twenty men and women in the room. All were dressed in black from head to toe. They were all busy cleaning and loading their guns. Sickle came to the front door to join Biker.

"Been trying to reach you for a few days," she said. "Your phone break?"

"I just got back from the Homeland Security building," Alexander said.

"Well, shit," she said. "They finally told you—'bout time, too."

"What are you talking about?"

"We were told not to say anything until they gave the go-ahead," Biker said.

"Can you speak in plain English?"

Biker smirked. "When you showed up, I had my doubts. Your story sounded like horseshit to me. You smelled like a soldier. So why would they send a soldier to make sure the guns arrived and nothing else. What did you call it? Observing but not helping? And you just happen to arrive on the same day as the guns?"

"It was kinda a coincidence," Sickle said.

"So when you left a card and told us to double-check, I did just that and called TexIntelSecuriCorp, just to make sure you were on the level. Funny thing about that: they said you were still being vetted and asked me to help. Told me, 'Give 'im a mission; see how he does.' So I sent you to the one place in Los Angeles they hate Texans the most to see if you'd survive." He adopted a redneck southern accent. "And hey golly, you did."

Alexander just stood there in shock. The pieces fell together before him. From the start, the birdlike man seemed a little too kind and a little too persuasive: sending him off to do their bidding, giving him orders without revealing their true intentions. Him: a lowlife with no legs. They'd promised him riches, made it sound easy. But at the same time, they'd made it sound oh so important. Your country still needs you. But it was all a pack of lies.

Texas never needed Alexander: not when they sent him to the Middle East, not when they sent him to California—not now, not ever. He'd gone where they'd sent him and done what they'd told him.

The only real decision he'd ever made for himself was to enlist instead of go to the pipeline chain gang. Ironic that the only choice he'd made was the one that turned him into a pawn from that moment onward. But it was worse than even that. Even a pawn has the potential to defeat a king and win the war. Alexander never felt like he wielded that power. He didn't even know where to stand on the battlefield.

"That's right, soldier boy," Biker said. "All that business about being an observer without helping was made up. They just wanted to make sure you didn't fuck things up like you did in Iraq."

Alexander lunged at his throat, tightening his fingers around Biker's windpipe. The others rushed in to break it up. In the chaos, Sickle screamed. Someone punched his jaw, while a flurry of hands pulled him away. Two men finally shoved him against a wall, pinning his shoulders with such force his vision blurred.

Biker rubbed his throat, motioning for the others to let him go. "They don't award medals for having a wounded ego. Put it away, Alexander. You completed one mission, and TexIntelSecuriCorp has authorized the rest. Now the real work begins. And I'll be damned if you're going to stand by while we do the fighting. You've been given the all clear, and you're gonna help us win this bitch."

Chapter 13

They spent the day going over the plans of attack, looking at a large aerial photograph of the building and its surroundings. The building had been chosen for several reasons.

Just a few months before, the president of California, George Jordan, had passed what he described as an emergency measure barring Southern Californians from being employed by Homeland Security, citing their failed coup attempt as justification. The president was careful to stress that the measure was temporary and would be rescinded if Southern Californian leaders stopped encouraging or enabling revolutionary behavior.

Through Biker's network of moles, they'd learned that this was the beginning of a much larger effort to purge the southerners from government participation all together. Hitting the Homeland Security building would therefore send a powerful message.

Beyond mere symbolism there were practical reasons, too. As Alexander already noted and Biker confirmed, the building only had two exits, despite its size. There were the main glass doors in front and one emergency exit at the back that was only open during fire drills. There was also very little in the way of security. Although there were CCTV cameras, just six armed guards were on duty at all times. Four kept to the front of the lobby, ensuring people went through the metal detectors one at a time and checking IDs thoroughly.

Early on, they had considered forging the badges. But only lawyers, high-profile administrators, and security guards were issued them. And among those groups, not even one person was allowed to carry concealed guns. The guards would surely know each person by name and face. A stranger showing up with a badge, however convincing the forgery, wouldn't fail to arouse suspicion.

Instead, their plan to take the building was as simple as it was brutal. Descend on the building during the morning to neutralize the guards and post soldiers in front to take care of outside authorities. They'd move in waves to keep up the bombardment.

"Obviously they're not going to come out and say it, but the Los Angeles County Police are on our side," Biker said. "They have orders in place to stand down. The Northern Californian SWAT or National Guard teams are the ones we'll have to deal with. But we'll attack during rush hour. At that time of morning, downtown LA is gridlocked even on a holiday. Figure a minimum of fifteen minutes before they can reach us. We'll have control by then."

On neighboring streets they had vans containing fertilizer, propane, and gasoline parked and ready to mobilize. A nail bomb was placed in the adjacent park. These were set to detonate at five-minute intervals to sow confusion as much as terror.

Alexander frowned. "There'll be hundreds in that building. No way in hell you can take all of them hostage."

"We're not planning to," Biker said. "We're only interested in the chief of Californian Homeland Security, and we know exactly where he'll be at that time. We have his daily agenda. Once he's secured, a fire team will take over the PA system. People will stay right where they are, or we'll start shooting anyone who moves."

"You know, all the planning in the world doesn't matter when things don't go as planned," Alexander said.

"We have the element of surprise on our favor. And we've trained for months now. There are close to a dozen groups around the city coordinating as we speak. We're prepared to go it alone and go it as a solid unit. We're doing this shit tomorrow morning, and we're as prepared as we'll ever be. As for you, I want you in the back by the emergency exit."

Alexander shook his head. "You don't get to order me around."

"Your bosses say otherwise."

"Fuck them, too. Besides, I've got to patch the gaping hole in your plan."

"Gaping hole where?" Biker asked.

Alexander pointed to the open-air mall. "Right there, genius."

The group kept low the rest of the day, moving like silent ants throughout the store. They ate canned chili and drank beers until the sun set. Sickle, Biker, and Alexander went up on the roof to keep watch and sleep in shifts.

They made plans to leave before dawn. Biker volunteered to drive the two to their rendezvous point and then park in an adjacent lot on his own. The more invisible he could stay, the better.

Sickle stood at the roof's edge, smoking a flower joint, scanning the streets for signs of life and finding none.

"Biker said after this was all over I could surf in the no-go zone again. You ever surf?"

"Do I look like a surfer to you?"

She didn't answer, keeping her eyes on the streets. After several minutes, she sighed and stepped back to face him. "You must have felt this before, right? The night before a battle." She tried to pass him the joint, but he waved her off.

"Yes, I have," he answered.

"Any words of wisdom?"

"Try not to get shot."

"Come on," she said. "I'm serious."

All the prebattle pep talks from commanding officers he'd ever heard were clichés, nothing more than talking points about strength in numbers, God, fighting the good fight, being a prevailing light against the darkness of evil—nice-sounding words that did very little in the face of true battle. The soldiers who hid Bible's in their breast pockets and prayed the Ninety-First Psalm were better off than anyone believing the hollow words from a commanding officer. He saw something in Sickle's eyes that registered as fear. She needed some form of comfort. He put his arm around her shoulder.

"Don't worry about being scared, Sickle. There'd be something wrong with you if you weren't scared. Once you're in it, the adrenaline and muscle memory will take over. You'll mostly be on autopilot. Every second you stay alive tomorrow means you're one second closer to freedom."

They stayed awake all night, watching the North Star and Venus poke through the hazy sky. There were no sounds to speak of. No cars drove by. Sickle shivered in her army jacket. At four, they went downstairs.

Biker ordered the group to leave in ten-minute intervals, driving their cars with the headlights off and with no sudden acceleration. When the last car pulled away, Biker locked the hardware store, as well as the metal gate, and threw Alexander the keys.

"If I don't make it, do me a favor. Come back and wipe the place down. I told the others to keep their gloves on, but you never know."

Alexander nodded but said nothing. He started his pickup truck and headed out with Sickle sitting in the middle and Biker riding shotgun. He could feel her tense thigh pressing against his.

The guns were wrapped in cloth to keep from rattling. They'd given him a Zastava M91 with a scope that Biker had zeroed, along with two spare magazines and a SIG Sauer for closer-range shooting.

At that time of day, the traffic was light. Alexander kept to the speed limit as he took I-10 east. The other cars in the outfit had enough of a head start that he never caught up with them.

He dropped them on Broadway in front of the former Hall of Justice building, now a place for squatters, artists, and drug addicts. They walked with the cloth-wrapped guns tucked under their arms. No one said a word.

Alexander pulled away from the curb, took a left at the intersection, and drove for four blocks until he found a spot in a parking lot off of Figueroa Street, noting that he could pay for the spot at a machine, rather than through an attendant.

He tucked the SIG Sauer in his belt, concealed it with a cardigan. The M91 was disassembled and kept in a large briefcase. To anyone who might have seen him, Alexander looked like just another white-collar worker, heading to some nondescript job.

He walked up First Street and then took a left on Temple until he reached the mall. While the downstairs cafes and restaurants were open, no other store would be for a few hours. He also knew there was a vacant storefront on the second floor that overlooked the Homeland Security building, with windows taped over and a sign that read, "Pardon Our Appearance, Reopening This Winter," in large letters.

He took the stairs, found the store front, and tried the door. He was not at all surprised when it opened. The floor was covered with tarp; the walls, not yet plastered. He went behind the counter and looked out the window at the Homeland Security building. Even at this hour, people were in line, waiting for the building to open. He checked his watch. It was seven thirty.

In the darkness of the room, he opened the briefcase and assembled the M91. Without being able to fire, he couldn't be sure if the calibration was still correct. He looked through the scope at one of the guards. He then spent some time scouting the rest of the building. The open-air floor had no joggers at that time of day. The only employees in the offices he could see into were maintenance workers, who dusted, emptied trash, watered plants, or brewed coffee. The sight of coffee dripping into industrial-sized carafes made his mouth water. He wished he'd stopped at the store below for a cup. But he dismissed the thought as soon as it entered his head. The last thing he wanted was a witness with a good description of him.

A pang of paranoia struck Alexander. What if Biker had lied to him? The birdlike man from TexIntelSecuriCorp had explained the assignment in complete detail. He was not to take up arms. He was only to offer noncombative assistance if requested or needed. He'd been through rigorous training before he left. Would the company really send him into harm's way or let the Southern California rebels put him in the field as well?

It didn't seem likely. No, Alexander thought, it was more feasible that the whole thing was a set-up. If the coup failed, then somehow Alexander (and Southern California) would get the blame.

On the other hand, what did he really know about TexIntelSecuriCorp? He'd taken everything the birdlike man said at face value, taken him for a service member without questioning it, accepted the salary without asking what price he'd have to pay for doing so.

In that light, it was just as likely that Biker was telling the truth and the company was lying. He was bought and paid for. If the rules were changed without anyone telling him, it was just too bad.

They carried no walkie-talkies, arguing that if one person were apprehended, it would be a dead giveaway that others were involved. Instead, they planned on communicating in small groups only. Biker had wanted him stationed at the building's back entrance. What did Alexander's refusal mean for the team? There was no objection to it, quite the opposite. Biker saw the logic in his reasoning. If no one was stationed in the mall, then anyone could attack. With his position, he could shoot from the rear.

The thoughts tumbled and crashed into each other. He felt used but didn't know by whom. Or was it just plain paranoia? If, as Sickle had said, flower made the person who used it smarter, Alexander saw no evidence of it at that moment. Perhaps it was she who'd set him up.

He rubbed his eyes, trying to clear away the thoughts. Alexander glanced at his watch: 7:55 a.m. Zero hour was 8:00 a.m. He wiped the sweat from his hands, picked up the rifle once again. He was just about to look into the scope when he heard the first explosion.

He saw the smoke in the park to his left. A homeless man whose clothes were on fire ran toward the mall's fountain. Looking through the scope, he saw the line of people by the food truck rooted to the spot, transfixed at the scene. The guards in the Homeland Security building shifted back and forth, unsure whether to leave their posts.

Alexander watched one guard claw at her two-way radio, trying to pry it loose from her belt. He saw the first wave of the resistance running toward the building before she did. Five seconds later, she was hit. The bullet must have hit an artery. Blood spurted against the glass as she fell.

The second guard managed to shoot twice before he was killed. Though the shots were wild, one hit a resistance member, whose forward progress was brought to a halt. Even though the member fell facedown, he could tell from the shape and size that it was Sickle. A flash of greenish yellow hair peeking through the black hoodie confirmed the suspicion. Every second she lived was another second toward freedom. She hadn't lasted more than sixty seconds.

The second wave attempted to enter but seemed to make no progress. Alexander could see there were more than the six guards Biker had claimed, three or four times as many. He watched as each resistance member fell like black-clad dominoes.

A second bomb went off to Alexander's right. As if somehow marking the start of a change of orders, the entire army rushed the building's entrance at once, instead of going group by group. Some threw hand grenades, while others used suppressive fire to cause confusion. As soon as the last insurgent reached the building, the vans pulled in to barricade the front.

With thick smoke now coming from the lobby and people running in all directions, it was impossible to know where to shoot. Alexander just stood, rooted to the spot, viewing the scene through the rifle's scope as if through a camera. The insurgents had entered the building. Perhaps they'd taken out all the guards. He had no way of knowing.

Two wounded innocent bystanders ran toward the mall, covered in blood, their mouths contorted in screams he could not hear. Soon the sound of sirens came. The ambulances and police cars were stuck on the off ramp. Just as Biker had said, they were boxed in by the rush-hour traffic. Even when they managed to exit the off ramp, there was confusion as to where they were supposed to go. With the remaining bombs detonated, downtown Los Angeles was in shambles.

Three giant armored trucks with extended battering rams barreled toward the building from the west side of the street. The first two swept away the vans like they were toy cars. And then, as if they were at the end of a roller-coaster ride, the doors of the third armored truck opened all at once, and soldiers poured out. He had no idea how many there were, perhaps thirty. The other trucks opened, and a similar number rushed out. With the casualties the resistance had already suffered, Alexander knew they were in for a slaughter.

He broke down the rifle, put it back in the briefcase, and exited the storefront. The mall was empty. He spotted the emergency stairs in the back and took them to the ground floor. He waited to see if he could hear anything coming from the other side of the emergency door: a soldier, a siren. All he heard was silence.

He waited a full minute and then opened the door. It led out to a street that to the entire world looked like a regular street on a regular day.

He walked until he could find a street that wasn't blocked and, when he found one, took the quickest route to his pickup truck.

TexIntelSecuriCorp had sent him to assist and observe. And what Alexander had observed through the scope of a rifle was the death of a young girl he hardly knew and the death of an independent Southern California, a dream that would never return.

Chapter 14

"Hello, everyone; we are back. This is Byrum Saam and Mel Allen here in Chicago's Comiskey Park. We're in the last half of the ninth inning with the White Sox now up to bat. This has really been a heck of a ballgame."

"It sure has been, By. I don't know if the Dodgers were just worn out from traveling here from Los Angeles, but it's like they didn't show up until the fifth inning today. But now it seems like they found their footing, and it's culminated in a heck of a play in the eighth that stopped the tying run right at the plate."

"I'll tell you, with such great pinch hitting, defense, and pitching, the Dodgers are definitely in lock step, absolutely. This is the kind of game that fans travel thousands of miles to see, and they've definitely gotten one today, boy."

"Speaking of travel, you know, they've chartered half a dozen planes to fly the teams, their families, and the sportswriters to Los Angeles for Sunday's game. I hear they're expecting more than ninety thousand at that game. And of course, we'll be there, too."

"OK, first baseman Norm Cash is now up to bat, leading off against Larry Sherry. He swings and fouls. Cash hit two forty this season. Aparicio is up next, and after him, it's Nellie Fox. Sherry throws and it's inside: one ball, one strike for Cash. Here comes a curve ball, and it's up and straight into the dugout: one and two."

"You can't get better baseball than this: World Series, game two, the Dodgers down by one. If you had asked me earlier in the season, I would not have expected either of these teams to be here, but it just goes to show—"

"And Cash swings. There's the ball heading straight to Hammers, who throws it to Sherry, and that's all for Cash. Now, Aparicio is up. He had a heck of a day: first a double, then a single. He swings and misses: strike one."

"The Dodgers pitching has really been—"

"Oh, there's a hit, straight to Willis, and Aparicio is out: two down. And now, Nelson Fox is up. Sherry throws, Fox hits, it's out toward second base. Charlie Neal throws, and that is it. Folks, the Los Angeles Dodgers have come out and won game two of the 1959 World Series."

"This was just a heck of a game: a Charlie Neal homer in the fifth, two all in the seventh, and then Neal scores again."

"First time the Dodgers were ahead, all game."

"That's right, Mel. And then Sherry ends on a perfect ninth. Now, we'll give you the rest of the highlights shortly, but first, I have a question for you. When you're washing your hair, do you find that your shampoo just stays around unless you keep rinsing and rinsing? That's because a lot of shampoos on the market today leave a sticky residue that just makes your hair sag. But thankfully that's not the case with White Rain. It's the only shampoo that rinses out the first time and leaves your hair feeling clean and fresh. Women will love it. And gentlemen will too. So trade in your shampoo for something better: White Rain."

Chapter 15

The pickup truck shook from the force of armored trucks thundering past in the opposite direction. An attack drone loomed in the sky like a large metal wasp. A second rose and hovered, suspended, before following in its wake.

The highway was an obstacle course of car crashes. A jack-knifed truck lay across three lanes. Emergency workers parked in rows along one shoulder, covering bodies with blankets. Wounded passengers staggered toward a makeshift triage where others were standing or lying, brown with dried blood, black with dirt, pale with shock.

The pickup truck moved at a snail's pace, winding and weaving through the wreckage and debris. Through the window, Alexander could see fire and smoke from a lower floor of the Homeland Security building. Whether it was the result of the resistance or the federal response, he could not say.

Just twenty feet ahead, he saw a policeman dressed in riot gear flagging him down. He shoved the suitcase under the seat but kept the handgun in his jacket, hoping he wouldn't have to use it. He slowed to a stop and kept his hands on the wheel.

He could feel the officer's gaze piercing him through the visor. The policeman came up to the driver's side window, tapping on it with a bludgeon.

Alexander rolled it down, asking what was going on with as much innocence in his voice as he could muster.

Instead of answering, the policeman opened the door. "We need your truck to help with the wounded. Get the fuck out."

"Officer, I'm a veteran of the Texan army. Used to be a driver and a medic. Let me help."

The officer waved him out of the car. "First time in my life I'm glad to see a Texan. Help me load them up. I'll escort you to Cedars-Sinai."

Alexander rushed over to the triage. It was all he could do to take in the scene. A woman with blood-streaked arms cradled a lifeless toddler who couldn't have been more than three years old. A man lay with his left leg contorted in a strange shape. The EMT workers loaded people into scoop stretchers, their faces blank.

"Help me grab them," the policeman said.

They spent the next ten minutes loading the wounded into the truck. The policeman tried to force the woman to give up the toddler, which only caused her to scream louder in hysterics. Alexander fought the urge to shoot him.

Instead he said softly, "It's OK; let her keep the baby. There's room enough in the cabin."

The policeman nodded, got in his vehicle, and took off with lights flashing and sirens blazing. Alexander floored the truck to keep up, winding through the chaos that stretched for miles in either direction.

The woman sat holding the toddler, color drained from her face. When she spoke, her voice was emotionless. "We were going to spend the day at the Natural History Museum. They had a live butterfly exhibit. He'd never seen them in real life and now…" She didn't finish the sentence. Her eyes were wet when she turned to face him. "Do you know what's going on?"

"Something happened at the federal building. Looked like explosions, maybe bombs. I don't know what it was," he said. "I was driving and got caught up in it, just like you."

"One minute there, the next minute gone," she said, her voice stilted and distant, as if talking to someone who was no longer there. "He's cold. And so am I."

They pulled into Cedars-Sinai emergency entrance and were greeted by a rush of nurses, doctors, and orderlies. He left the woman alone in the car while they helped unload the people from the bed of the truck.

One person had died along the way, shards of glass all over his face, head cracked open, the face twisted in frozen agony. The policeman said the man had gone through the windshield of his sports car with such force that the airbag had failed to deploy in time, something that occurred with more frequency than most people realized.

A nurse whispered to the mother in Alexander's truck, trying to soothe her. It took a minute for her to find a vein for the hypodermic needle to go through. The mother passed out in an instant, her arms still cradling the toddler.

"They cleared the worst of the highway. The rest are coming through. Thanks."

Alexander could only nod in silence at the policeman as he got back into the truck.

"I guess Texas is where all the real heroes come from," the policeman said.

But Alexander didn't hear him. He was already on the street.

Just a few minutes later, he pulled over to vomit, choking on the bile as it filled his nostrils. When nothing was left, he continued to drive. He decided to go back to Marie-Eve's motel, thinking it would be safer there.

He brought in the briefcase, the Rompecabezas, and the box of flower. The room was just as he'd left it. The faint fragrance of Marie-Eve still lingered. Alexander wished he could hold her, talk to her, let their bodies intertwine—anything to erase the memories of the morning.

Since becoming an adult, Alexander had witnessed a lot of things he wished he could forget. But there was no unseeing what was seen. The real tragedy was that almost every mission was doomed to fail. He knew this was true of military and civilian life. Even disobeying orders wouldn't change the outcome of history.

He sat on the sofa where he'd first kissed Marie-Eve and wept for the woman with her toddler, for Sickle and Biker and Southern California, the place that was not his home and never would be. But that was true of Texas, too.

Was he doomed to live a soldier's life of temporary stops along the way before he, too, would end up a casualty of war? Or could he break free? He ached for reprieve and salvation. But where would it come from, and what hero would come to save him?

He wiped his eyes and stood up. He went to the bathroom to rinse out his mouth, absurdly angry for a moment that Marie-Eve had not left a toothbrush or toothpaste. He was gripped with an urgent need to sleep, to descend into darkness. He undressed, got into bed, and slept a dreamless sleep, not waking until noon the next day.

The hunger pangs woke him. He hadn't eaten in two days and felt weak and lightheaded. He left the motel and walked down the street to a pizza place. He ordered an extra-large pepperoni to go, slipping into the next-door bodega to buy toothpaste, a toothbrush, and a twelve pack of beer.

Back in the motel, he wolfed down the first slice and almost choked on the second. He opened a beer and turned on the TV, more for background noise than anything else. He thought about writing a report for TexIntelSecuriCorp but dismissed the idea as soon as it entered his head.

Instead, he dug in his pants pocket and found the card that Paulo Aveleÿra had given him, picked up the phone near the couch, and dialed.

"Hello; who is this?"

"Alexander."

"Who?"

"Braxton Alexander. We met at a party a while back?"

"Ah," the voice said with recognition, "Marie-Eve's friend. You're the soldier."

"Former soldier."

"Of course. And speaking of, I guess you heard about what happened downtown, right? Terrible." His voice was thick with irony.

"Yes, it certainly was," Alexander said.

"Guess you are glad now that your soldier days are behind you, eh?" Paulo laughed. "But tell me, what can I do for you, my friend? Surely you aren't out of chocolate by now."

"No," Alexander said. "Truth is, I need a change of scenery. I'm looking for work."

"Leaving TexIntelSecuriCorp so soon?" When Alexander didn't answer, Paulo laughed. "Now I wonder, why would that be?"

"I hear Mexico is quite advanced."

"This is correct on all levels, *mi amigo*. Socially, we've eliminated poverty. Everyone has basic income. Scientifically, more patents have been registered to us than any other country. Economically, we have the sixth largest economy in the world; I think we're just behind Texas, right?"

"I wouldn't know."

"And what's more, far from those European socialist democracies that breed complacency and mediocrity, Mexico is very productive. Even as we speak, I am inspecting a new strain of chocolate the labs have developed that is not only easier to grow but is suitable for children under twelve. Once the self-driving fleet is ready, it'll also bring the cost down."

"That's really remarkable."

"It's our own little Walden," he said. "Everyone wants to move here now; it's true. But you see, we have a strict immigration policy with the rest of the continent."

"Oh."

"*Lo siento, amigo.* Nothing personal against you, I promise. But after years of making us sneak into your own shitty countries and pick your stupid grapes and lettuce for a pittance, we are now in—what shall we call it?—a state of reciprocity. Not even Marie-Eve could get work unless the Cirque opened a permanent company here, and even then the amount of red tape would keep them in limbo for years."

"I can't blame you one bit."

"Still, it's reasonable to want to leave Los Angeles. Southern California is a sinking ship. But I'm willing to bet TexIntelSecuriCorp has another, uh, assignment for you, elsewhere. Don't run out on them just yet. If nothing else, you can make a pile of change from them, no?"

Paulo laughed and rang off without saying good-bye.

Alexander picked up another slice of pizza and turned up the volume on the TV. On the screen was a large table where some men in suits sat. He read with alarm the news scrolling on the lower third of the screen. In three minutes he was caught up on everything he'd missed since the previous day. As he suspected, the rebellion had failed. Two hundred resistance members had been killed in all, with a further two hundred innocent victims also killed as a result of bombs that exploded outside and inside the building. It was only due to chance that the explosions hadn't been more catastrophic.

There were more casualties reported on the highways. Overnight, the Northern California Special Forces raided multiple areas in Southern California, rounding up dozens of sympathizers, participants, and family members, executing most on sight. Los Angeles was under a strict curfew. The more Alexander read, the angrier he felt.

An announcer broke in.

"And now, the delegation of mediators between North and South California have arrived. We are ready to begin."

Alexander's mouth dropped when he saw the two aliens walk into the room, wearing three-piece suits, making no attempts to conceal their features. They took their places in the center of the table, flanked by the Northern and Southern California representatives.

Shoeless Joe cleared his throat and addressed the crowd of seated reporters. Gone was his jaunty playfulness, replaced with a grave, somber tone that was eerie.

"Ladies and gentlemen, I will try to answer questions at the end, but I do have a prepared statement to read, and I think it will go easier if you'll allow me to read it first. This is a joint announcement on behalf of Shoeless Joe, which is me, and my colleague, Catfish Hunter."

He fished in his breast pocket for a piece of paper he unfolded with care. He also unfolded a pair of bifocals and put them on before reading.

"Two days ago, a group in Los Angeles representing a Southern Californian insurgency attempted to overthrow the Northern Californian government by taking hostage the head of Homeland Security. In the ensuing hours, many lives were lost. However, it must be stressed that due to the efficiency and restraint of the SWAT teams, the loss of life was not nearly as great as it could have been."

Shoeless Joe glanced at Catfish before continuing.

"As this is the second attempt by the Southern Californians to rebel and force independence, and this particular instance has escalated in violence and scope, Northern California is treating this as an act of aggression.

And while they are not prepared to call this a declaration of war, they have taken steps to implement martial law until some degree of diplomacy can be reinstated.

"Under martial law, the ordinary rights of Southern Californians are stripped, including the right to vote and travel freely, and anyone suspected of attempting to overthrow the government will be arrested and sent to internment camps in Bakersfield.

"The president has asked myself and my colleague to act as diplomatic mediators to try and assist in the restoration of order and come to an agreement that both sides will find acceptable. I must stress again that Northern California does not want to respond to this act of aggression by declaring war; nor do they want to call our effort on their behalf any sort of brokering of a treaty.

"Semantics aside, we have spent the last twenty-four hours negotiating with both heads of the Northern and Southern Californian regions to agree to a cease-fire, hopefully a permanent one. As a result, we have also brought in outside help. I would now like to turn this over to Ms. Monica Ferrero, the Texas ambassador to the Republic of California. Ms. Ferrero?"

He passed her a microphone. She was dressed in a dark navy business suit. Her black hair was pulled back in a severe ponytail. She was quite plump, but her features were soft and inviting.

"Thank you both for your efforts. I must first start by saying our hearts go out to everyone involved in this tragedy, and we pray for the lives lost and the innocent families and loved ones who have suffered throughout this ordeal.

"It is not the role of the Christian Republic of Texas to take sides or hold one group accountable over the other. However, we want to ensure that the relationship between our two countries remains as strong as ever, regardless of y'all's situation. And by the way, I should say that this entire statement is fully endorsed by the president of Texas.

"Now, as I said, we do not want to put ourselves in a position where we are choosing sides or to make it seem as if we are in any way influencing your domestic politics. What that being said, I met with both delegates, and both are of the same opinion that Southern California is in desperate need of humanitarian aid.

"I am pleased to report that with the blessing of the president of the Republic of California, who regrettably could not attend today's meeting, Texas is sending humanitarian aid to the South. It was only six weeks ago that Southern California had granted us unofficial custody of their ports in Ensenada and San Diego for trade purposes. Now those city ports will be under our charge for as long as the humanitarian efforts are needed. And the president has ensured us that we are also welcome to dock in San Pedro as well.

"Of course, we understand this is only a temporary measure due to the nature of such an emergency. But Texas has the largest fleet in the world, and this will be the largest humanitarian operation mounted in recent years on the continent, at least as far as we know. We will be bringing badly needed medicine, potable water, and resources to some of the people down there who need it most and who haven't had access to it since—well…If you like, we can take questions, but please state your name and which newspaper you work for first."

A sound came from Alexander's left, startling him. He dug under his jacket to find the Rompecabezas vibrating and flashing yellow. He flicked it open with his thumbnail. The code read:

Hee Haw. Travis Bickle. Cabbage Patch Dolls. Jake and Elwood.

When the message decrypted, it read, "Mission accomplished. Great work. Report to the office next week."

Part 2

Chapter 16

"You're listening to KZSC, eighty-eight point one on the radio dial, or online if that's your thing. Whatever. This is *Asleep at the Wheel* with your host DJ Harley. And we just finished an exclusive live performance with the doom thrash band Malström, who was nice enough to come down to the studio to support our annual fund-raiser. They were super rad, too. In honor of Malström, I've changed the name to fund-*razor*, as in the slash-yourself kind. Good stuff, I know. Now, I know two of the three band members have to go to class, but Rory Storm, the lead singer and bassist, is going to stick around; is that right?"

"That's right, Harley."

"Great. 'Cause like, I was really like, wanting to ask you a couple of questions."

"Go for it."

"So, Malström—what kind of name is that?"

"Well, it's Swedish for 'maelstrom.'"

"Cool. I mean, just the name itself sounds so metal."

"Yeah, but it wasn't just chosen because of the sound. It represents our philosophy. We're living in a violent, chaotic time, right, so we're creating the soundtrack to it."

"Right. So, when you were setting up, you told me you almost didn't make it here because you were almost arrested. Can you talk about that?"

"Yeah, it's not the first time; it won't be the last. I was protesting the California government's treatment of the Southern Californians."

"So, can you enlighten me and the audience about this? Because most people up here are feeling like at this point whatever grievances they have are kind of overshadowed because of, like, their act of terrorism."

"That's exactly why I'm protesting. We view the insurgency down there differently. They're being systematically oppressed. How do you want them to respond?"

"Yeah, it's, like, really awful."

"And I'm not ashamed to say I'd fight on their side, too. Our fucking government has it coming. Wait—can I say that word?"

"No, ha-ha, not really."

"See, it's just one more form of oppression. At the end of the day, I'm an activist, right? I would consider that my real job. Malström is just how we get bail money."

"But Northern California is, like, superprogressive. How do you identify politically?"

"Everyone in the band espouses individualist anarchism."

"You're anarchists?"

"Not as cut-and-dried as that, and when people hear that word, they think of those idiots who dress all in black and beat people up for saying something they don't agree with, and that's the antithesis of what we believe."

"So what do you believe?"

"It would take days to explain it all. But for the sake of argument, let's start with our government, our wonderful government that's busy taking away the rights of the Southern Californians. Who gave them the power to assign any of us rights, let alone take them away?"

"I hear that in the lyrics to songs like 'My Rights Are My Rights.'"

"Right, and songs like 'Thoreau-a-Go-Go.' We always say, our sound grabs you by the throat, but our lyrics grab you by the brain."

"So true. Yeah, I don't know anything about Thoreau. But it seems deep. So, I did want to ask about the song you ended your set with today. What's it called?"

"CVB."

"Oh. Yeah, I couldn't really catch all the words. But it sounded like you were saying 'Strength through division,' right?"

"Yeah, here's the lyrics: Strength through division is what we all need.

I am not establishment. I am CVB. No one cares about your, um, 'effing' think piece. No one cares about your wish for peace. The only way to make a dent is fight until you're spent. Strength through division is what we all need. I am not establishment. I am CVB."

"Real cool. So, like, I have to ask a question, though. What is CVB?"

"That's a great question, actually. I don't know."

"Ha-ha, really? You just made it up?"

"Not exactly. Um, we saw it spray-painted in a tunnel up in San Jose. I don't know what it stands for, if anything, but maybe it's a tag? Our drummer, Sick Pig, knows every graffiti artist in the area but had never seen that one."

"So it's random."

"Oh, totally. We just thought it sounded like some shadowy organization."

"Nice. I like the fact it rhymes. It's so cool. It's, like, funny how certain letters just rhyme, you know?"

"Yeah. It's funny."

"Cool. This is DJ Harley and Rory Storm of Malström. Thanks for hanging."

"Absolutely."

"In a few minutes, my girl DJ Becky's gonna join me, so it'll be double girl power, but we're gonna go from my show, *Asleep at the Wheel*, to her show, *The Directory of Illusions*, which is more chillwave and darkwave. You're listening to KZSC, eighty-eight point one on the radio dial, or online or even through our app, which I forgot to mention during the last break.

"And now I want to remind you too that we are doing our annual fund-raiser, or fund-razor as I call it, to come up with the goods to pay for the license next year. If you go to our site, you'll see a bunch of premiums you can get for your pledge. Like we have this really nice water bottle that I know for a fact will also fit an entire bottle of wine into it, so it's great if you go to the beach or camping or just need to get through class or something. There's also a hoodie with the eighty-eight-point-one logo on it. And we're doing some different stuff this year, too. Totally. Your awesome DJs, like myself, are contributing one-off items, too. Like, if you pledge twenty-five dollars, I'll make a special painting just for you. I plan on doing, like, fifteen of them over the winter break, so by the time we charge you for your pledge early next year, they'll already be in the mail. And, guys, you can go to my home page or Facebook page or Etsy store to get a feel for what I do. But if I do say so myself, it's pretty rad, ha-ha."

Chapter 17

The birdlike man was on the phone when Alexander walked into the room. Without stopping his conversation, he gave Alexander the thumbs-up sign and pointed to a chair.

"Is that so? Interesting. Yes, I'll tell him. He just arrived. OK, I'll let him know. Bye."

The birdlike man hung up the phone and rubbed his hands together. "I just knew when I first scouted you the results would pay off in a big way, son. We sent you in, and you ended up giving us more than we could have bargained for, yes, sir."

"I didn't do anything," Alexander protested.

"Humility—I like it."

"They gave me weapons, they said I could fight, and I didn't fire a shot. I walked away from it."

The birdlike man nodded. "Precisely what I'm saying. You walked away and made Texas proud." When this received no response, he frowned. "Seems like no one's told you anything?"

"Because no one has. All that came through on that crypto machine was 'Great work' and 'See you Wednesday.' I haven't been told shit."

"Shit. My apologies. Something must have gotten lost in the shuffle. Those damn machines, you know. The bottom line: your decision to disobey their orders has put Texas in an even better position than we'd hoped. And just to clear the air, the order for you to fight came from Biker, not us. I've been nothing but transparent with you. I made you a promise you wouldn't be put in battle, and I meant it."

"So Biker had no authorization from you."

"None whatsoever," the birdlike man said.

The birdlike man's eyes rested on a thick folder on the corner of his desk. Then, as if making up his mind, he said to Alexander, "Son, I'm about to do something I've never done in my entire years of service before today. I'm going to break all kinds of protocol—because I believe you have a right to know what really transpired. Have a look through that. I'll pour us both a stiff drink."

Alexander hefted the folder and made himself comfortable. The birdlike man placed a tumbler of whiskey in front of him. Alexander ignored it and started reading. From the very first page, what he read astonished him.

The Southern California revolt and involvement from Texas had more to do with the Middle East than Alexander ever could have fathomed. Five years before the judge gave him a choice to join the military or the oil penal colony, the Middle Eastern war began when an unknown tribe from Iraq flew a plane over Chicago and dropped a twenty-one-thousand-pound bomb on the city, killing 13 percent of the city's population in the process.

Texas and its allies, the Confederate States of America and the United States of America, sent troops to the Middle East, while Deseret provided medicine and other supplies. Despite their mutual defense pact, California declined to send troops or even aid, leaving the relationship between the two countries tense.

But after a few icy years, a pro-Texan faction in Southern California became emboldened to challenge the legitimacy of the government for its actions. This gave rise to the secessionist paramilitary group known as the Sons of the New Golden West. The group took root in Pasadena but grew to include factions in Riverside, San Bernardino, and as far south as San Diego.

This gave rise to what the report called the First Rebellion. While the details in the report were scant, the First Rebellion lasted three weeks during which time Southern California declared itself a country with a seat of government in Pasadena. They even hoisted a makeshift flag above their new parliament house. Texas was ready to welcome their new ally, even going so far as to make plans to send an envoy.

Their victory was short-lived. The North sent in troops and the navy to quell the rebellion. The leaders were arrested and put in solitary confinement. The rest were sent into exile in Hawaii or imprisoned up north.

Two years passed. The South had fallen into complete decline. They received no economic help from the North. Proposition 5259, which stipulated all persons living south of San Louis Obispo were subjected to further limitations on their constitutional rights, was the final straw.

The Sons of the New West, once thought to be eradicated, rose again. Hardly a unified group at first, they'd made several clumsy attempts to better their part of the country. First they tried legal channels, via a grassroots movement, electing local and regional politicians who promised to peacefully push for legislation. But the politicians were either completely neutered or had no intention of giving up what little power they had. So once again, the group turned militant, took up arms, and looked for a leader to achieve their goals.

Alexander turned the page, seeing a photo of Sgt. Biker in the top corner.

"He used to be a mercenary. Didn't care who he killed or which side as long as he got paid. Then for reasons we don't know, he found his inner patriot later in life. Picked his motley crew by hand and trained them all to be smart and ruthless. We're certain some Hollywood bigwigs funded him but have never gotten names. Biker was convinced this was their now-or-never moment. Planned to go out kicking and screaming—which is what he did, poor bastard."

"He and everyone else who rushed in there."

The birdlike man shrugged. "We knew they were never a real threat to the Northerners. Even with our help, it was always going to be David versus Goliath. At best, we hoped they'd at least send a real message. Couldn't even get that right."

Another page had a photo of Private Sickle paper clipped to it. She was in a wet suit, holding a surfboard, her hair slicked back. She stood on the beach next to a seaweed-covered sign with a biohazard symbol on it warning people not to walk, swim, or surf in the area.

"Shame about that one. The authorities think she was eighteen, maybe twenty-one at the oldest. Still trying to track down her real name and parents. She used a couple aliases. Was in and out of juvenile jail a few times. We're not sure if she was radicalized or just a kid who fell in with the wrong people." The birdlike man frowned. "Unfortunately that's as much as we know about her for now."

Alexander's mouth was dry. "What a waste."

"Very much so. But also, I have to say your efforts were very much not a waste. When you put people in the field and let them make their own way, they will never disappoint, I always say. From what I understand, you met an interesting woman in Las Vegas."

"She had nothing to do with this," Alexander said. "She's just a friend."

"Oh, we know that," the birdlike man said. "There's a reason I asked you to stop in Las Vegas, and it wasn't because I thought you were a gambling man. Las Vegas is two cities. It's Sin City, sure. But it's also like Athens: a point of convergence for fringe groups, terrorists, and spies. It was a fishing expedition on my part. But thanks to that lady, you caught a fish named Paulo. He's been popping up quite a lot. You know anything about him before now?"

"Not at all."

He was, Alexander learned, the second most powerful man in the west of Mexico: charming but also calculating, using his influence to grow a multibillion-peso empire, the same way Silicon Valley had.

"We initially thought the Mexicans were interested in making a move on California. Never quite seemed to add up, though. They have no need to colonize. If anything, they're nationalists through and through. Keep Mexico solidly Mexico, if you understand my meaning, although I'm sure taking back California would be sweet revenge to some of the old diehards."

"But you don't think that's what they were after."

The birdlike man shook his head. "For all we know, the Mexicans could have designs on Deseret or even us, for that matter. Although I suspect they wouldn't try it, even with all their machismo. Southern California? No way."

"Paulo told me he was part of Los Tigres Trafficantes. Just seemed like a big-time dealer to me."

The birdlike man laughed. "That's one way of putting it. But when you're the leading producer and supplier of a drug that has turned your country into an economic powerhouse, the government takes a big interest in you. In this case they're enabling him. We're going to watch him from now on."

"In Los Angeles?"

The birdlike man nodded. "Los Angeles, Las Vegas, Jalisco, too." He smiled. "We know he acts like he's untouchable, but he's not. Mexico's not infallible. No country is, not even us. Come to think of it, that explains why your alien friends live like squatters in the autonomous part of Deseret. What do they call themselves?"

"Shoeless Joe and Catfish Hunter."

"Right, those are names they use for earthlings to understand. Their real names are unpronounceable. Anyway, they're the unofficial ambassadors of Deseret."

"Really?"

"Outside of Vegas, those areas of Deseret thrive on alien tourism. Keeps them distracted from our Star Wars drills. Every time they see a flashing light, they think it's because of aliens."

"But," Alexander said, "they *are* aliens."

"You know what I mean, though," the birdlike man said.

"They also said they have homes in Los Angeles and Mexico, but they live on another planet."

"That's right, working the mines on that outpost for a decade or more. Far as we know, there's a few hundred of them up there, living happier than pigs in shit, too. But those two fellas came down because they got bored. After a while they found they really liked it here. Can you imagine? Advanced enough to create spacecraft that can travel thousands of light-years and all they want to do is listen to baseball."

"When they're not busy brokering a peace deal."

The birdlike man frowned. "Yes, we still haven't worked that out yet.

How they finagled that we can only speculate. Like Paulo, wealth buys influence. We're still following the aliens' money trail—because God knows they have a shit ton of money. Good news is, they don't seem to have evil designs on the planet."

"They seemed likeable enough to me," Alexander said. "If anything, they just want to help maintain the status quo in California."

"Nevertheless, we're expanding our surveillance just in case, and we've got people working to find out who they're in cahoots with."

Alexander flipped through the rest of the folder. The report confirmed everything the birdlike man had said in more detail. On the last page was a photo of a group of men he'd never seen before, dressed in dark suits and standing inside a graffiti-covered tunnel. There were three letters above their heads in fresh spray paint that dripped down the wall.

The birdlike man cleared his throat. "There they are."

Alexander looked up, perplexed. "There who are?"

"Your next assignment. You've seen Southern California. Now it's time to head north, son."

Chapter 18

"What is reality? I'll ask that question again. What…is…reality? To say that each of us lives in our own reality is fundamentally incorrect. There are in fact two versions of reality. And the majority of us make the unconscious or subconscious decision to believe in one version over the other, and this becomes our great, unshakable belief system for better or worse.

"You and you and this lady in the front row—all of you belong to the great either-or. You swarm with one hive mind or the other. Or if you'll permit me to muddle the metaphor, you're two schools of fishes that are swimming through two schools of thought. Each believes the other is wrong and is prepared to square off at all times against the other. Any idea that challenges your accepted version of reality is met with resistance and anger. Why, you believe so much in your one version of reality, you'll do anything in your power to discount any idea that might challenge it. That's how set in stone we are.

"Hear that? Boy, I do. That's the sound of a studio audience and those at home wagging their fingers, saying, 'Morris Readwater, you don't know me!' Oh, yes, I do. I know you like the back of my hand. I know you because I used to be like you.

"Me? Talk to a Texan? I'd rather be shot with their guns. Me? Listen to a sermon? I'd rather burn in the hell I don't believe in. And I'll be damned if I engage with a libertarian on the subject of taxes or a vegan on animal welfare. I'll stick with my own brand of reality; thank you very much.

"I'm sorry to disturb your reality, friends. I really am. I know it can be a bit painful. But if you are watching this tonight, then it's because you are curious. How else are we ever going to know what's really going on if we don't take a peek? It sure as hell isn't going to be from watching the talk show of your choice or watching the movies or reading the magazines or anything designed to cater to your preconceived opinions.

"And it's not going to be from getting in the echo chamber known as social media night after night to high-five each other for confirming our biases and trading insults with people who shared an article you don't agree with—something you probably didn't even read.

"Look, if you are really willing to admit it and be honest with yourself, you have this nagging suspicion that this kind of behavior is running its course. You're tired of confirmation bias, tired of being a choir member who gets preached to on a nightly basis. You know deep in your heart that you're going through the motions, and you can't figure out why that is. Maybe it's because that narrator you've been listening to is unreliable? Hmm?

"When someone likes what you said online or gives you some kind of prop, are you getting the same dopamine hit as before? Do you really have the strength to argue anymore? And—here comes to kicker—are you really still sure of your convictions anymore?

"Those of you new to this seminar are gripping the chair right about now; am I right? I can picture it. You're mentally white-knuckle, resisting the urge to turn me off or feed me the same talking points you've been using for years to debunk me, about how in fact the other side is wrong and you are right. Face it. Your anger is a facade to hide your fear that *you're* the one who might be wrong.

"What if doors open showing you a corridor you've never seen before, one that's filled with more doors you never opened? What if everything you know is upended? It's going to get uncomfortable.

"Let me ask you this: when was the last time you felt uncomfortable? If the answer is you can't remember, then there's an issue. Here's why: if you're comfortable, you don't grow. But what happens if we get uncomfortable? We squirm. And we stretch. And we cross our arms. And shake our heads, right? Looks like resistance.

"Tonight, I'm talking to those of you here and those of you watching at home; I want to say, you have a great power to turn your resistance tendencies into exercise—to make your mind stronger, sharper, more objective, and ultimately, make you a more successful person.

"I didn't hear you. What is Morris Readwater going to help you do? That's right! Make you a more successful person. And we do that by allowing you to discover your own duality, tap into both sides, break down those two realities and fuse them into one.

"The only way we can even begin this process is to get you to see that the answer to the question 'What is reality' is not 'Whatever I believe it is' or 'Whatever I'm told it is' or 'Whatever my parents or teachers or the local news or my favorite comedian told me.' With those kinds of answers, you might as well just be a sheep with big ears. Right? It's not productive. It's not helpful. And it will not make you a more successful person.

"Look, this isn't going to be easy. But then, if you still wanted easy, you wouldn't be watching me; would you? Ha-ha. You wouldn't be here. I promise we'll take it slow at first. Think of the next, well, forty-three minutes as an introduction to Reality 101.

"Now, before we really get in to the nitty-gritty, I want to say two things to you. The first is, I'm not a change agent. My goal in teaching you tonight is not to convert you to another religion or make you move to a commune in Cascadia or switch your political sides, as we've had enough of an upheaval in that arena lately. I'm not presenting you with one side or belief system to follow. I'm only here to show you that these dual realities have been crafted around you and that if you let the other reality in and understand it, then this behavior really will make you a more successful person.

"Will it be difficult? Not as difficult as you think. Can we do it overnight? No. But stick with me here: by showing up or turning on this station, you've already taken the first step in the Be More Successful™ program. And later at the end of the show, I'll give you some tips and tools to make sure you continue on this path. And at the end of the program tonight, ten of you in the audience will win tickets to the Reality 101 seminar that I'll be hosting in Pasadena, Costa Mesa, Downtown Los Angeles, and Newport Beach. And for those of you watching at home, don't worry. We'll flash up an eight-hundred number, and the first ten callers will also get tickets to the seminars.

"Now, are you ready? Let's do this. On the count of three: Let's Be More Successful™."

Chapter 19

The flight to San Jose should have taken three and a half hours, but fog at SJC and a thunderstorm in Texas delayed Alexander's take off by four hours. He spent some of the time whiling away in a dismal airport restaurant and bar, picking at a wilted lettuce salad and drinking coffee that tasted like it had been brewed in an old sock. He pushed his plate away in disgust, signaled for the check, and then wandered through the terminal.

Few people were there. A group of sullen-looking kids in UT shirts sat hunched in the corner. Three businessmen perched with arms folded in front of the TV, watching the same news from the previous hour on repeat. He bought a bottle of water and then sat in front of the window, watching the planes sit there doing nothing.

Despite the birdlike man's praise, he was in a foul mood. The resentment built as he watched the torrential downpour soak the baggage handlers, while women who stood behind the ticket counters went from hopeful optimism to silence until finally beating a hasty retreat through an employees-only corridor, leaving the irate passengers to seethe on their own.

California's decision not to honor the mutual defense pact was the first domino to fall, causing an uneasy rift on the continent, a quagmire in the Middle East, and an ongoing civil rebellion between the North and South. Why had no leader explained this when he was in the service? Not that it would have mattered—he went where he was ordered to go, as soldiers do. And why hadn't the birdlike man come out and explained how the dots connected in the first place?

Alexander never claimed to understand the intricacies of geopolitical strategies or foreign policy. But there was something wrong in finding out the truth after the fact. He'd buried friends and foes alike in Iraq and watched people die in California. In both instances, the reasons for the missions were either outright lies or left unexplained. In both instances, the soldiers were tiny puzzle pieces in a larger portrait they couldn't picture.

The army only told you that you were fighting for liberty around the globe and for security. You come from the almighty Texas, where, blessed with our strength and faith in God, we are always on the right side of history. If this were really the case, why was there a need to keep so much from soldiers like him?

The birdlike man was no different. Alexander was convinced beyond a doubt that his show of transparency was nothing more than that—a performance designed to appeal to a soldier's ego. He wasn't fighting for anything noble, only for Texas to get the upper hand.

"Those men in that picture might be the deadliest in all of California. They're part of a group called the CVB. No one knows what the name stands for. But we sure as hell know what *they* stand for, and that is the destruction of the government. They want complete and total anarchy."

"Sounds like teenaged punks to me: manifestoes and safety pins."

The birdlike man's face was grave. "This isn't an adolescent fantasy we're talking about, son."

"Are they anything like Biker and the Southern rebellion?"

"Much more powerful and persuasive—they've turned members of the Californian navy and air force. We're sure they're working with outside interests, too, Silicon Valley most likely. You know how those companies are. They don't see people as people, just parts of a computer program they can rewrite at will. Wouldn't surprise me if they were socially engineering the Northern resistance movement.

"But a collapse of a government, even one as liberal and ass-backward as California is something we cannot have, especially not now that we're in control of the Southern ports. If California dissolves into anarchy, any number of things could happen." The birdlike man held up a finger.

"One: the CVB destroys the country within a few years the same way the Socialists in Venezuela did." He held up another finger. "Two: the CVB fails, and a junta takes over." He held up a third finger. "Or three, another country sees it as their chance to take control by force."

"What about Texas? The Southern Californians are already on our side."

The birdlike man shook his head. "Our military resources are stretched thin as it is in the Middle East. We can't afford to shift troops. Best they could do is put the Texan National Guard at our borders to keep it from spilling over."

"If what you say is true and the CVB are more militant, why send me?" Alexander raised his pant legs. "Maybe you've forgotten?"

"That only proves you've been a soldier and a fuckup. I'd rather have someone in my outfit who's been on both ends of the stick."

"It was one thing when you sent me to LA, but how do you expect me to prevent this from happening? If what you say is true, that they've turned service members, this is a much larger deal. I'm no supersoldier."

"And you're no James Bond, either."

"Who?"

The birdlike man shook his head. "Never mind. My point is you've got character. You are the man for the job. You blended into the South like a chameleon, and you'll do the same in the North."

He pointed to the framed portrait of the Texan flag on his wall. "I'm not going to give you some jingoistic pep talk about us being the world's policeman. Wouldn't work on you anyway. But if California falls, it will cause a nasty ripple effect, believe you me. And that's something I won't allow on my watch."

The birdlike man sat on the front of the desk. "Besides, for all its faults, I do believe that country is worth fighting for. Now, get over there, find out what all you can, and report back ASAFP."

Before he'd left, Alexander had stopped home to do laundry, sleep in his own bed, and return to some semblance of normalcy if even for a night. He unlocked the door and pushed hard, breaking up a large pyramid of mail that had accumulated since he'd left.

Nestled among the bills, junk mail, and magazines he didn't remember subscribing to was a small package about the size of a pack of playing cards. There was no return address. He shook it and listened, but no sound came from it.

He opened the box and was surprised to find a small hard-packed brick of flower and a note printed on an index card:

For your travels and your troubles. Stronger. Smarter. More refined. And totally undetectable by drug dogs or pig cops. Enjoy your time in the north.

Paulo.

PS *Marie-Eve says* bonne chance. *She is moving back to Quebec.*

Just as it seemed the passengers were ready to mutiny, the rain stopped, and the airline attendants ventured back out to call row numbers. Alexander was surprised to find he was seated in first class. There was no one seated next to him, either. He swore he'd go easy and only have one vodka tonic, but one became five, which did nothing to brighten his mood and increased his paranoia. His mind went through a slew of conspiracy theories.

The Rompecabezas was a tracking device, and they were keeping tabs on him. Paulo was working for TexIntelSecuriCorp and had a vast network of people in California who could easily tail him. The birdlike man was actually working for California. TexIntelSecuriCorp was in fact a Silicon Valley company. The flower Paulo mailed him was tainted.

One thing was for sure: it went through security with no problems, even as he was stopped because of his prosthetic legs. Maybe Paulo wasn't the problem, after all.

For all he knew, the birdlike man was sending him to die for witnessing the atrocity in Los Angeles, fearing Alexander would turn whistleblower. As if he would ever do such a thing. His allegiances were not to the company or the country, but that didn't make him a traitor either. Even when he'd been a soldier, Alexander had belonged to no tribe. He might have been a lot of things, but he was not a rat. Nor did he ever view himself as a noble hero, letting the world know about hidden evils. If the world was too stupid not to see the evils, then that was their problem. He was a lone soldier, always would be. The closest he'd come to any sort of loyalty was with Marie-Eve, and even that was a quick blur, over as soon as it begun.

The pilot's voice came over the PA, announcing their intended landing and apologizing for the umpteenth time about the delay. Alexander lifted the plastic shade to look outside. All he could see was a thick fog, purple with dusk.

Instead of a rental, he was staying in a hotel. The birdlike man described it as a significant upgrade to his last living quarters. They'd send him further instructions on where to find the CVB when he got there. Then he would need to act fast to set a plan in motion. Who were the CVB really? He had no information beyond what the birdlike man had told him and what he'd read in the reports. And that was the most troubling part.

The reports had revealed that TexIntelSecuriCorp knew much more about the uprising in Southern California than he was told. And now that he'd been lied to once, Alexander was now supposed to take the birdlike man's transparency at face value? That wasn't going to happen.

He would meet with the CVB, all right. And he'd find out all he could about them. But this time, if he felt their cause was just, it would be his turn to spread disinformation. He was going to change the battle plans. To hell with TexIntelSecuriCorp, he thought, and to hell with Texas, and to hell with California, too. Alexander was through being a pawn.

Chapter 20

He was met at the San Jose airport by a driver holding a sign with his name scrolled on it in black. The driver was in his mid-sixties, pot-bellied, and wore a rumpled navy suit. He looked like the type who took pride in spending only seconds grooming before leaving the house every morning.

"Took you long enough. Been here so long I almost ran out of cigarettes. If you need to do your business, do it now. It'll take an hour before we get to the hotel."

They exited the airport, driving past the strange mix of old mission-style homes and brand-new sprawling tech campuses. The driver slowed to navigate past a group of employees cycling home.

"They're like a two-wheeled cult. We spent all this money widening the streets to give them their own lane, but do they ever use it? I'm part of one of their ride-share businesses, and they have bikes that are worth as much as my car. Tell you what: if I were in charge, they'd be first against the wall."

Alexander looked outside the window.

"First time here?"

"Yes."

"Some people like this part of California. Me, I can take it or leave it. Place has changed since the tech heads moved in. Used to be no one bothered you. These guys are remaking everything in their geeky image and jacking up the prices, so regular folks like me can't afford anything. Seven fifty for a cup of coffee—they call it 'pour over.' What the hell is that? You want me to pay extra to watch you make a cup of coffee in front of me?"

"It's not as bad down South."

The driver looked at Alexander through the rearview mirror. "Not from what I hear. There's this guy on the radio who says we should have let them secede because the economy is so bad down there they'll take the rest of the country down with them. Not that I got anything against them. I've got relatives out in Joshua Tree. They're struggling, but at least they can afford to live. Some of these idiots up here are paying six thousand a month in rent. Meanwhile the only place I can afford is an hour and a half away. Jeez, this rain—will it ever let up?"

Alexander tuned him out the rest of the way. He had a feeling the man would have kept up a tirade whether he was in the car or not. Forty minutes later, they pulled up to a retro-looking hotel that overlooked Monterey Bay. Just a short walk away, the electric lights of a boardwalk amusement park flashed.

The driver opened the door. "Help with your luggage?"

"I can manage, thanks."

"Suit yourself. One more thing, though. They told me to tell you there's a rental car in your name—a Subaru. They were out of self-driving cars."

They'd given him a suite on the top floor with a private balcony overlooking the bay. He sat outside, letting the cold fog envelop him. He smoked the new strain of flower. It didn't seem any different.

In the distance, high-pitched screams came in waves from the amusement-park thrill rides. He pictured couples on dates, families with kids, lining up for hours for a roller coaster that lasted less than ninety seconds. Scores of them came and went unaware their lives might be upended at any time. Not knowing was better than knowing, he thought. Ever since he was a kid, he'd always lived that way.

Inside his room, the Rompecabezas vibrated. He flicked it open and waited for the code to decrypt.

MTV, Mary Tyler Moore, Peppermint Twist, Crossfire, I'd Walk A Mile For A Camel, Lady Day.

When it decoded, the message read, "Jury Room, this Sunday evening after nine."

The next morning, he ate breakfast in the downstairs restaurant, feeling angry he hadn't ordered room service instead. The contrast between both parts of the country was astonishing.

Southern California was filled with a mixture of working-class immigrants, eccentrics, people who were just trying to get by, and a small percentage that were wealthy beyond comprehension. From what he'd seen so far, Northern California was uniformly rich and almost completely white. From the families with young children sitting next to him to the older couple on a romantic weekend getaway to his server who went on and on about where they sourced their bacon, whatever that meant—all of them wore the same cloak of elitism, as if any moment they'd break out in lectures should he do or say or think the wrong thing.

He sipped coffee from an oversized mug and listened to snatches of conversation so foreign in meaning it might as well have been in another language, which he guessed it was, in a way.

"They raised twenty million in funding based on a half-assed presentation deck. Can you believe it?"

"I'm concerned that my alpaca sweater is cultural appropriation because it's from Latin America and I'm from Marin County."

"My cat identifies as a male, so I named her George. Does this place have bottomless mimosas?"

"I just don't understand why we have to go outside to vape."

"'The weekend' is not very inclusive to those who have to work on those days. It really needs to be renamed. In fact, the whole concept needs to be rethought."

"There's no worse form of violence than using the word 'violence' incorrectly."

"I'm going to be fair and assume by holding the door for me that it was an unconscious bias and not because you wanted to shove me into a traditional gender role. Otherwise, you're being a helpful misogynist, which is the worst kind."

"The problem with the working class is that they refuse to adapt. When the coal mines close after twenty-five years, then you go back to school. If there are no jobs in your hometown, you move. What is so hard to understand?"

"Our app is finally out of beta testing."

"Do you make your kombucha in-house?"

If this were what Silicon Valley had wrought, Alexander thought, he'd rather have SoCal's crumbling fantasy. Every word that reached his ears made him want to stab someone.

Though his breakfast of eggs Benedict and bacon was described in rich detail on the menu, it tasted unremarkable. He ate as fast as he could, charged it to his room, and went back upstairs to shower, watch TV, and pass the hours until evening.

That night, Alexander hopped in his Subaru Outback and drove the short distance from his hotel to the Jury Room. He crossed the San Lorenzo River, wondering what he would do or say when he got there. Engage the enemy, he thought. But "enemy" wasn't the right word, not yet.

To his surprise, the bar was smoky. He ordered a Jack and Coke. A lazy brown mutt walked up to investigate his crotch. Alexander patted its head. The dog sniffed once and then left to go back to its place in one of the worn red vinyl booths.

"He doesn't like you," the bartender said. "Greets all strangers the same. If he likes you, he sniffs twice."

Alexander scanned the room. Everyone had sleeve tattoos, including the bartender. The threadbare pool table was empty. The brick wall matched the color of the booths. Strange artwork hung on the walls and ceiling and sat on the tops of empty bottles on shelves: doll parts, spray-painted stuffed animals, risqué playing cards, military dolls covered with glitter.

"You can smoke 'em if you got 'em," the bartender said. "It's against the law, but no one rats us out. Even the cops come here to smoke."

"Thank you, sir, but I don't smoke."

"Ah, you're from Texas, right? Let me guess: Rapid City?"

"No, I'm from the first state."

"An original, huh? We don't get too many of you around here all that often. What brings you in?"

"I want to see the CVB."

When he heard this, the bartender picked up a rag and wiped the bar. "I don't believe I caught that."

"Yes, you did."

The bartender considered this. "Now, are you sure about this?" Alexander stood up to his full height. The bartender put up his hands in defense. "I'm only asking because it might end up being the last thing you do."

"Doubtful."

The bartender shrugged his shoulders. "They're in the back room. Just knock."

Alexander drained his drink, threw ten Californian dollars on the bar, and went to the back room. The door opened before he could knock. Inside, he recognized one of the men from the CVB sitting with a stranger whose face was obscured by backlighting. He had no problem making out the gun pointed at him.

"Who are you, and what do you want?"

Alexander held up his hands. "My name's Braxton Alexander, with TexIntelSecuriCorp. They know all about you. They sent me here to try and break up your plans. Instead, I'm disobeying orders, knowingly and wittingly. I want to join you, and I believe I can be of service."

The man from the CVB motioned for the other to put the gun down. Then he did something that surprised Alexander. He smiled.

"Well, come in and shut the door. I gotta hear this. I want to understand why you have the *cojones* to think we would believe anything you say."

The other man stayed in the shadows but relaxed his posture.

Alexander was cautious as he took a chair. "I don't rightly know, sir. But maybe if I fill in some blanks, it'll give you some indication."

He spoke for an hour, telling them everything without holding back. It turned into a cathartic therapy session. He recounted his early days in Texas, the war, the catastrophic events in LA, how he questioned and ultimately denounced TexIntelSecuriCorp.

When he had finally finished, he wasn't sure how much they believed or how much he believed.

The man from the CVB leaned back in his chair. "So you're biting the hand that feeds you."

"From what I understand, you're doing the same to California."

"More like cutting the head off and then letting the body bleed out while we set fire to its house and dance around in circles while it burns to the ground. Other than that, sure, it's exactly the same. Why join the CVB? You don't have a dog in this fight."

"I could give you lots of made-up reasons, sir. They'd all be convincing, too. Problem is, not one of them would be accurate."

The two men waited for Alexander to continue.

"I'm just looking for a cause I can believe in, even if it isn't mine."

The second man turned around to reposition the light, revealing his face for the first time. Alexander's smile of recognition turned to shock when he realized he was looking at an alien, but the alien sitting before him wasn't Catfish Hunter or Shoeless Joe Jackson but one he'd never seen before. This one was built the same and had the same smile. The biggest difference was his blue-colored skin.

"See? I told you he was legit."

Chapter 21

"Hi. In case you're just joining the live stream, this is Lauren Seibring. I'm here at Berkeley, where so-called students are holding a protest march called 'Peace, Equality, and Freedom.' I say 'so-called' because the majority I've run in to look like they haven't seen the inside of Sproul Hall in twenty years, let alone a shower. But they can sure throw bricks and set cars on fire. I see y'all have been commenting on that, and I just want you to know that when I'm out here in the field, it gets really difficult to read your comments on Periscope, so just remember for the duration of this protest: I am keeping my Twitter DMs open.

"If you can hear this noise behind me, they are shouting, 'Hey-hey, ho-ho, fascist tactics have got to go.' Let's see if I can get one of them to go on camera and explain what they mean. Not sure about you but I've seen no evidence of fascist tactics anywhere except for those who claim to be part of the peace movement.

"You, sir, I'm Lauren Seibring with Middle Media. What brought you down to the Peace, Equality, and Freedom March today?"

"Same as you, I'm live streaming. You must not recognize me in my antifascist all-black getup. I'm trying to blend in. Ever notice the people who claim to be antifascists love to dress like fascists? Let that sink in. I'm Phillip George Kendall with The Rightist Network."

"Have you found out much since you've been here?"

"Oh, plenty. First of all, if you're a Welshman like me with a contrarian opinion, the supposedly antifascist people will jump down your throat and beat you with a bike lock if given half the chance."

"Are you saying that's what happened? You've been assaulted?"

"Not yet but it's only a matter of time. And of course, this is something the mainstream media won't cover, just like the fact that the people here are paid to march and protest by one very rich tech trillionaire who is based in Latvia at the moment. That's right. Far away from all the violence and bloodthirsty rioters, a man in Riga who claims to be anticapitalist sits counting his trillions of dollars, hoping for the downfall of the hardworking capitalists of Silicon Valley in the great Northern California. And no doubt, he's live streaming the march on my very channel, on a phone that Silicon Valley built. Let…that…sink…in."

"Well, thanks for sharing."

"Absolutely, and I just want to say thanks to my audience and your audience too, because I have gotten more subscribers in the past forty-eight hours than I have in two months. That's the power of the people, right? Not this trillionaire-funded riot."

"Good to see you. OK, let's just keep moving here. As for that Latvian trillionaire, Middle Media is not prepared to call that a fact as it is still unconfirmed, but you know how those British guys are—anything for clicks.

"Let's see if we can get anyone to—Hello? Dude? You in the black jacket? Or you with the Rorschach blotch on your mask? Girl, can I? Hi, Lauren Seibring here with Middle Media. Can I—the fuck?"

"He just pushed me. He just physically assaulted a woman, and you're supposedly an antifascist? This is being live streamed to more than one hundred thousand people. Do you understand what my gang of Idiot Savant fans will do to you? You'll wish you were arrested. Do you hear me, fuck nut?"

"You OK?"

"Oh, here's someone. I want to get your thoughts. Lauren Sei—"

"Hey, Lauren. Huge fan. You actually are the reason I got into live blogging. My nom de plume is Jimbo Bobbins. It's like Bilbo Baggins but—"

"Did you see what that man did to me? He literally shoved me. I am literally shaking with rage and fear right now."

"Sorry, I didn't. I was busy trying to get a Wi-Fi signal. Do you know if there's Wi-Fi around here? I'm almost out of data."

"Um, I work for Middle Media. They cover our data plan. I am, as you know, the third most influential female citizen journalist on YouTube—even though they've managed to demonetize me."

"Yeah, I know. Listen. Are you going to be in Berkeley long? I managed to snag a time-share apartment that's a three bedroom for the week. Figure this might only be the beginning. The real shit might go down overnight and throughout the week. We might have a real riot on our hands."

"Or it might fizzle as is usually the case. Anyway, you've been live streaming this riot all day?"

"To my five thousand followers, live. Thanks for following me, guys. Hey, Lauren, maybe you could follow me, too."

"Right, so, anyway, have you seen much? Found anything out?"

"Not really, they just keep chanting the same thing over and over again. Hey-hey, ho-ho—"

"We can hear it."

"Right. Everyone I've tried to interview just keeps walking by like they're in a trance or something. Except at one point I got a few of them to stop, but they just made a circle around me and kept protesting until a policeman made them get back in line."

"Whoa. Are you telling us on Middle Media right now that you witnessed police brutality?"

"Um, no, the policeman just, like, told them to stop circling me. So they did. Lauren? Hello?"

"We're now leaving this area because it's too intense here in Sproul Plaza now, and I'm feeling unsafe. Also it's kind of hot out, so let me get over to People's Park and see if there's any—hold on. Holy shit. You see that? That woman is doubled over. She's pouring water in her eyes. Hey!"

"Shit! Shit!"

"What happened?"

"We were just waiting for that Armenian guy to start giving a speech about how the antifascist movement is funded by anticapitalists who are in fact fascists when—"

"Pepper spray?"

"Oh God, it burns."

"What is it?"

"Urine!"

"What in God's name has the country turned into? This is so-called higher learning. To think it costs two hundred thousand Californian dollars a year to go here. Are you OK?"

"I'll be OK. If I could just get you to—"

"Anything. You need more water?"

"No, I just need you to wipe my phone off. I think the lens got wet."

"Sorry, girl, but I'm not wiping piss from your phone."

"OK, I'll do it. Can you just hold my water bottles?"

"Yes, but can you tell us what happened?"

"Well, shit was really fucked up. There were about a hundred of us here, waiting for the Armenian guy, what's his name—"

"Minas Petrossian."

"Yeah, we were waiting for him to show up. And a bunch of us were talking about how right he always is, you know? Like what he says about the mainstream media. They will play into any fears and stoke any controversy even when the controversies cancel each other out—because they just care about headlines."

"This is absolutely true. And this is why Middle Media is becoming a powerhouse of alternative media—because we care about truth."

"Plus he has such a wicked sense of humor; he's so catty. Anyway, we were waiting for, like, hours, and you could feel the tension building because those of us who are part of the counterprotest movement were just waiting for something to happen because all the time the antifascists were yelling at us and calling us supremacists and fascists. A fight broke out, too."

"A fight? That's horrible; I can't believe I missed it. Can you describe it for us? How many were involved? What kind of weapons?"

"Oh, just like, two people—it got broken up right away."

"But it must have escalated later, right?"

"Well, after a while everyone was on the move."

"See? What did I tell you, Idiot Savants? They plan these things. There's always a moment where it gets coordinated. Usually it's a teacher of some sort, pretending to be student. And then the walkie-talkie comes out, and it becomes a coordinated effort. Is that what you saw?"

"Um, no, people were on the move because the more we thought about it and the more we discussed it, the more we all decided this Minas Petrossian guy wasn't coming. He always makes these videos that say the same thing and promises to be this force of nature at these protests and swears he's going to show up, but he always cancels at the last minute. So we just all figured he was full of shit again, and a bunch of us just left at once."

"And that's when you got hit in the face with urine? A final fuck you? Some last parting shot?"

"Let me back up first. We'd been discussing who was behind these protests because they always bus in people, you know? And some people think it's a tech trillionaire, and other people think it's some other group. Hell, one guy even thinks Minas is behind it."

"You never know with him, to be honest. I mean, he is a foreigner."

"Right? So as we were leaving, a few people started whispering about some group called the CVB who were behind it. I'd never heard of them before, but they sound sketch."

"Neither have I. And believe me, our sources would have known about them if that were the case. We have many sources."

"This guy kept saying the CVB was behind this whole protest and orchestrating it. Like, it was just a way to keep us busy while they plot a bigger downfall of society."

"What are your thoughts on it?"

"I'm pretty open-minded, but it sounded like tinfoil-hat stuff to me."

"But when did you get hit in the face with urine?"

"Actually…"

"Did you get a look at who did it? With the number of smartphones around, someone had to have caught it."

"Well, actually…I did it myself."

"Sorry, what?"

"Yeah, see, I've got this YouTube channel that I'm live streaming from, and when there's downtime, I'm always trying to be informative and teach people stuff they can use. So I know a couple people like JailBirdy_76 and KokoMoHomo already covered pepper spray, so I thought I'd show people what to do if they got hit with a bottle of urine."

"So you threw piss in your face."

"I mean, it was my own urine. I'm not crazy. But I didn't know how bad it was gonna burn. I think I went through three liters of water just to wash it out. Definitely not a fun experience, but my subscribers need to know what's up."

"And how many subscribers do you have, exactly?"

"A hundred. And I think I'm going to set up a crowd-funding page to help pay for a new phone. Maybe if I inflate it a bit, I can get a rig like the kind you have, so I'm not holding it all the time."

"So…We're just going to move away from People's Park, and as you can hear, the chanting has finally died down. First time it's been relatively quiet all night. I think I'll shower as I'm suddenly in need of one, as you can imagine. Then if anyone in town wants to join me for dinner, just DM me, and I'll let you know where I'll be; but I want you to know I do have my security with me at all times. My Idiot Savant fans are always welcome. But all foes need to stay away. This is Lauren Seibring with Middle Media singing off."

Chapter 22

They tied his hands behind his back, put a hood around his head, stuffed him sideways in the back of the Subaru so he wouldn't be seen by other drivers, and covered him with a blanket. He wasn't sure who did the driving but assumed it was the man from the CVB. Like the gray alien, the blue one was short in stature; it would have been hard for his feet to touch the pedals and see out the window at the same time.

They took a meandering route on purpose. The car went up and down hills, made turn after turn, stopping and going at endless lights. The overall effect in the dark, lying sideways, was disorienting to the point where he no longer knew how long they'd been driving or where. It could have been minutes or two hours. They might have left Santa Cruz long ago, or they might never have left the same ten-mile radius.

The man from the CVB spoke only once when they'd all been loaded in the car.

"We're taking you for quality assurance. You won't be harmed along the way. If you don't pass inspection, you're toast. Understood?"

Alexander nodded, unsure if they were even looking in his direction.

"My friend here still has his weapon. I wouldn't try anything."

"I won't."

After driving in silence for an undetermined amount of time, Alexander asked them if they'd mind rolling down the windows. "It's kind of stuffy what with this bag on my face. I'd rather not pass out before we get wherever it is we're going."

He heard the whiz of power windows lowering, but not much, a small crack on either side at most. But he could feel the cool air through the bag, and the sounds would at least give him a sense of where they were.

No traffic sounds, smell of forest pine, overwhelming damp—his ears popped, indicating a change in elevation. He had no doubt that they'd left Santa Cruz.

The Subaru rolled to a stop. The back door opened, and he was lifted out. They walked on a gravel path about ten yards when he felt a clammy alien hand on the small of his back.

"We'll wait here."

"Whatever you say."

In the distance a strange melody played, reminding him of an ice-cream truck. He heard children singing but could not make out the lyrics. He counted the seconds in his head: one minute...two minutes. The song ended and began again.

He heard footsteps jogging back toward them. The alien removed his hand and started undoing the handcuffs. When he was free, Alexander snatched the bag from his face, blinking to restore his sight and gasping for air.

They were outside on what seemed to be some sort of mountain farm surrounded by Douglas firs. The smell was so sharp he could almost taste the sap on his tongue.

He stood in front of a large store that was overdecorated with Christmas lights: unblinking ones, ones that flashed at hyperspeed, traditional bulb-shaped lights hung over modern LEDs wrapped around lawn ornaments in the shape of reindeer, Santa, and elves. A pious nativity scene with three glowing solar lights coming from the Three Wise Men jockeyed for attention next to a modern one made from holograms complete with a yawning baby Jesus. There were neon signs in purple and orange and even brown. And halogen floodlights with colored stencils on them displayed green Christmas trees on the gravel.

The entire effect was surreal and disturbing, as if a once neighborly competition for the largest Christmas display created by a suburban homeowner had gotten so out of hand that madness had set in, turning the domesticity into a manic compulsion.

On the rooftop, Santa and his reindeer looked ready to take off. And just beneath it, hanging from the gutters, spelled out in electric red, white, and green wreathes, candy canes, and snowflakes was a giant sign that read "The Christmas All The Time Store."

Alexander's head swiveled between the man and the alien.

"Let's go," the man from the CVB said.

"In there? Is this a joke?"

The man from the CVB jerked his thumb toward the door. "Now."

Alexander walked to the automatic door, hesitating as it slid open. The baffling displays on the outside could not prepare him for the deluge inside. What he noticed first was the smell. A strange potpourri of pine and peppermint and cloves and cinnamon seemed like it was being pumped from the air ducts. It was stifling and made worse in no small part by the amount of lights that blazed from every conceivable part of the enormous showroom. Every crevice was crammed full with decorations. Alexander realized his jaw was hanging open and snapped it shut.

There seemed to be no specific layout to the room. A Christmas tree stood next to a Christmas sled on which mechanical ornaments winked. Animatronic snowmen were face-to-face, waving their gloved hands at each other. Strings of plastic popcorn were laid out on the floor, while a tangled snake's nest of lights lay in a giant heap to one side. A dozen four-foot-tall nutcrackers, all with mouths agape, stood in rows, staring at him with their wild eyes. Paper snowmen's faces swayed from the wind of a ceiling fan that also blew red streamers.

A giant tree covered with bows stood in the middle of the store like a totem. He took a step toward it, recoiling when he heard a whistle blow. With a mixture of awe and horror, Alexander watched as an amusement-park train snaked its way through the room, driven by a blue alien, who wore a train conductor's hat and engineer's overalls.

The train was not painted in Christmas colors but in camouflage. The alien wound his way toward the center display, waving to Alexander as he did so. His entire face was blithe. A bizarre, toothy grin was plastered to his face, giving the impression that he was the winner of a lottery whose untold riches only he would appreciate.

As if breaking the spell, the man from the CVB motioned him toward the tree. Noticing a small red flag to one side of the train tracks where it met the tree, Alexander walked toward it and waited.

After what seemed an absurd amount of time, the train arrived to its destination. The train conductor alien held a finger in the air as if to say, "Wait a minute," and pointed in the opposite direction.

It was then that Alexander realized the music had stopped and the space was silent. The alien had pointed to a solitary gold display wrapped with festive green garland. On top of the display was a red stereo.

He watched the record lift from the turntable and hover a moment before settling back down again. For the first time, he could clearly hear the lyrics sung by the chorus of children. It oozed like treacle.

> *Welcome to the Christmas Village*
> *Where it's always Christmastime.*
> *Lights and tinsel make it twinkle,*
> *Gifts for yours and gifts for mine.*
>
> *Deck the halls, silver balls,*
> *Stockings, lights, and wreaths galore.*
> *Houses made of gingerbread*
> *Who could ask for more?*
>
> *Baby Jesus in the manger,*
> *Bringing peace to all.*
> *With mistletoe and cocoa,*
> *You're sure to have a ball.*
>
> *Menorahs for our Hebrew friends*
> *Gifts for Chinese New Year,*
> *In the Christmas All The Time Store,*
> *The greatest gift is cheer.*

The alien in the train motioned for his friend to turn the record player off, which was done in a great hurry and with a loud snap.

"That song never fails to get me," the train conductor alien said. "I would visit this store even if it weren't a front. The holidays are such a wonderful time of the year; don't you think? Christmas is never bad." The train conductor alien paused as if caught up in the emotion. He then shook it away as if rousing himself from sleep. "You're Braxton Alexander, with TexIntelSecuriCorp, yes?"

"I am."

"And you are interested in leaving, yes?"

"Correct."

"Good, you're just in time. There is much work to be done. We have a quality-control program for you to pass, of course, but with your references it shouldn't take long, not long at all."

"References?"

The train conductor alien winked at Alexander. "From Shoeless Joe and Catfish, of course. Oh, and one Senor Paulo Aveleyra, who sends his regards. Well, don't look so surprised, young man." The alien glanced at the empty seat behind him. "Take a load off those metal legs of yours. We've got people to see and time is a-wasting."

Alexander opened his mouth to say something, thought better of it, and did as he was told.

Chapter 23

An entry dated October 12, 2004, from RunningUpThatHill.co.cal

If you've been reading this blog with any regularity, then you know the best kind of trail for me is one that is not only challenging but one that is off the beaten path. Sure, there's always the Dipsea Trail or Miwok, but I have no interest in (pun alert!) running into other people when I'm training.

Pacers are great for a real race, but I don't want anyone near me as far as I can see when I'm training. I don't know why, but I can really get into the zone when there's no one around me for miles. For another thing, I am at one when I am in unspoiled nature, and there's no eyesore like the site of microtrash junking up the place because some a-hole who doesn't respect Mother Nature decided to leave his empty glucose pack on the ground like a pig.

And to be completely selfish but honest, I'd rather eliminate my natural waste behind a bush without worrying someone's going to catch me in the act, if you know what I mean. Hey, at least one's organic. Also, I carry composting toilet paper with me, and I'm smart enough to know to dig a hole in the ground when I'm gonna do a dump run and then cover it, so predators don't come sniffing around. (Please check my links page on the right to learn more about the best hygiene practices.)

Lately, one of the other things that has become a requirement for my training runs, beyond a challenge devoid of other runners and one that is off the beaten path, is something that comes with a sense of history.

I'm almost ashamed to admit that I didn't know about Wrights Tunnel or its accompanying ghost town until now. Sad since I've been running in the Santa Cruz Mountains ever since I started school three years ago, and maybe this isn't news to anyone, but it sure was to me.

Now, before I go any further, you may not believe this, what with it being only a few weeks away from Halloween, but I *swear* this is a 100 percent true story that happened to me, and it still gives me the willies.

Early one morning I went out for a trail run I'd been keen on trying for a few weeks but hadn't been able to because of the ankle sprain and midterms. But when both were over (finally), I headed up on a fairly warm but dry morning.

I hesitate to even call it a trail because it's not like it's well worn or anything, but there is definite evidence of runners beating down the grass before, if only sporadically.

So I'm about five miles into it and feeling loose and warm when something appears out of the corner of my eye, and I look up and see this large railroad tunnel. It was crazy. I stopped running because I just had to take it in.

At the mouth of the tunnel was a gigantic puddle, as if every time it rains the water collects there, and maybe it does. Vines were covering a lot of the bricks, but the actual opening was completely free of debris. I could see graffiti covering the inside up to the point where the natural light wouldn't reach. Knowing those guys, I'm sure they bring lights with them, but I didn't think to bring my flashlight, which was a mistake. Mental note—when trail running, always bring a small amount of emergency supplies.

All of a sudden, this dude walks out of the tunnel and scares the living daylights out of me. He's covered with mud and has scars on his face. He looks like a homeless guy or a drug addict or maybe one of those survivalist militia types—I don't know. But I'm standing there in my blue-and-white one-piece suit, still panting, and he's staring at me with the wildest eyes I've ever seen on a human.

"You scared me," I tell him. But he doesn't say anything at first. He just keeps staring at me.

Then he jerks his chin in the direction of the tunnel and says, "Know what that is?"

I tell him I have no idea. So he tells me about Wrights Tunnel, also known as Summit's Tunnel. Apparently a long time ago, back in the 1880s, this area was full of thriving mountain towns. Some even had resorts, if you can believe it. It's not that there was much industry up here, except logging maybe, but there was a stagecoach trail, which then became the place where they laid train tracks.

So this was the site of Wrights Station, at the top of Los Gatos Creek, not quite nine hundred feet above sea level. The man said no one knew anything about this guy Wright, but he must have been famous enough to have a town named after him.

The man said it took almost three years to complete the tunnel. The South Pacific Coast Rail Road Company financed the whole operation. They wanted the train to snake its way through the mountains all the way from Los Gatos down to Santa Cruz. Problem was it was pretty much doomed from the start.

Back then it was the Chinese who primarily worked the railroads, the man told me, because they were fast. They were treated horribly, would die on the job, get carted out, to be buried only at the day's end. The man said it didn't help there was gas trapped in the mountain and that the tunnel was running over a fault line.

One day an explosion killed more than thirty of the Chinese workers. Rather than call it quits, the man said they pushed on until the tunnel was finished in 1880. The 1906 earthquake in San Francisco destroyed the tunnel and cut off service in that area.

The man said that despite the constant upkeep to the tunnels, the mountain towns declined one by one. They dynamited one of the entrances in 1942, and the last cities called it quits. All that was left, he told me, were two ends of the tunnels.

When I asked how the hell he knew so much about the area, he said he had a lot of time to kill. He told me his name was Mountain Charlie, and he'd been living in that area since the early 1820s.

"I built the first toll roads round here. Got mangled in the face by a grizzly as payment. Been wandering the tunnel ever since, looking for my eyes."

That's when it dawned on me why I had such trouble looking at his face. His wild stare was the result of coins he'd put where his eyeballs should have been.

At this point I tell him thanks for the history lesson, but it was probably high time I ended my break and got back to running. He agreed and told me it would be best if I avoided stopping by the tunnel if I came up that way again.

There's only one time I've ever run faster downhill, and that was the time I came in second at Tahoe. My quads were burning like hellfire by the time I got to my car, but even then I didn't stop. I drove until I made it back to campus and then took a long hot shower and rubbed soap in my eyes to get the sight of his eyes out of my brain.

After that, I went to the library and did some research and found out that there was a Wrights Tunnel and there was Wrights Station that turned ghost town in the early 1940s. His story was true.

But here's the strangest part: there is even a myth about Mountain Charlie, who may have been a real person who lived up there and got mauled by a bear. But I know for a fact the person I met was not the same person at all. Beyond the obvious reasons, some trail runners who posted in my forums (thank you!) told me this area is a hub of activity for drug dealers who grow their own marijuana and other drugs. The guy was probably just trying to keep me away so I didn't dip into their crops.

Not that I ever would. If you've read this blog before, then you know I am seriously against drugs of all kind, illegal or otherwise, but especially performance-enhancing drugs. My body is a temple, and there is simply no reason to defile it with something that promises short-term gain but usually ends up giving you long-term side effects.

That's why I'm happy to report that Running Up That Hill finally has a sponsor that I can trust, and that is Speedy G's Glucose energy gels and drinks. Made with organic chia seeds and plant-derived glucose, Speedy G's natural glucose candies, drinks, and powders will give you the energy you need for the long haul without preservatives or synthetic ingredients. Plus, it won't leave you crashing by the time you hit mile fifteen like some of those other brands. They have it in raspberry, blueberry, and lemon-lime. I've tried them all, and they all taste great. (Pro tip: do what I do and mix raspberry and blueberry for an extra kick.)

You'll see the link at the bottom of this post, but you can also click on the banners. And I hope you will if you decide to try it, because I'm an affiliate member, so you'll help support me by buying through this site.

Let me know in the comments what you think of Speedy G's!

Chapter 24

The train meandered through the store until it reached the back entrance, where it picked up speed, chugging along at twenty miles per hour. They traveled through the Douglas fir farm that seemed to stretch for miles in all directions.

"Now, you just make yourself comfortable, young man," the train-conducting alien said. "Be there in no time. My name's High Pockets Kelly, by the by."

The other blue alien sat behind Alexander, put a warm hand on his shoulder, and said, "And I'm Pepper Martin. Friends call me Pepper. I think we'll be friends; don't you?"

The man from the CVB sat in the fourth seat. "We took the liberty of checking you out of your hotel."

"And why's that?" Alexander asked.

"Because if you pass quality control, then we don't want you anywhere your organization can find you. And if you don't pass quality control, then you won't return either way."

"Now, now," the train-conducting alien said with distaste, "don't let's put the fear of God in him just yet. He did come highly recommended. And let's face it: TexIntelSecuriCorp is itself quite the exclusive outfit. I'm sure he'll do quite well."

Their path took them up the mountain along a winding route through trees, past a rushing creek, illuminated by the train's pencil-thin headlights. The wheels seemed to float along, making very little in the way of noise. Even in the dim light, the tracks shined bright.

As if sensing his thoughts, High Pockets said, "We only put them in last month. Still under construction. They're electric, you see. Makes for silent transport and saves us a lot of time."

"Nearly there," Pepper said.

The train reached a plateau and headed left toward a very large tunnel. Floodlights hung from the brick archway. Graffiti covered the half-mile length in thick layers, as if each year different people made a pilgrimage to find one open section they could defile and, finding none, started over by spraying silver. The squiggles and letters writhed in the train's headlights. They exited the tunnel and slowed to a stop at the end of the train tracks.

"Here we are," High Pockets said. "Toot, toot. Hope you enjoyed the ride."

They were in a large natural clearing. To the right was a large encampment where dozens of black-clad men and women milled about. The man from the CVB told him to wait with the aliens and jogged toward the encampment.

Pepper glanced at his watch. "Five minutes to go before quality control begins."

High Pockets smiled. "If there's time afterward, we might even let you join us."

"Join you in what?" Alexander said.

"Why, game seven, of course," High Pockets said. "Nineteen forty-six. Ted 'the Thumper' Williams meets his match."

"We haven't heard it yet," Pepper said. "Have you? If so, please don't spoil the ending for us. Surely you're a fan of baseball?"

Alexander shook his head.

Pepper frowned. "Pity. What about cryonics?"

The man from the CVB jogged back, interrupting the alien. "You are to report to the field marshal and Major Dog Patch immediately."

"Let's do this." Alexander said. "I'm ready."

He started walking toward the encampment, but the man from the CVB turned him around. "Not that way. Go to the center of the clearing."

Alexander took a few steps and marveled in spite of himself at the sight of the sky awash in so many stars. He saw only one figure in silhouette that came into view with each new step. The man from the CVB held up a hand for him to stop before the silhouette gave the nod.

"Major Dog Patch San Onofre," he said. "And you are Sergeant Braxton Alexander, Texan army, retired, now employed by TexIntelSecuriCorp."

"Correct."

"Let me be clear: we could have killed you at any time since you arrived. Only reason we haven't is because of the Mexicans."

"Hey, what about us?" High Pockets whined. He and Pepper frowned in unison.

Major Dog Patch ignored the question. "We want to know how serious you are. See, we're not as naïve as the Southern Californians." He pressed something on his sweatshirt and looked up toward the sky. "Nine Mile! Where the hell are you? Put down those meat robots, and get your ass in gear."

Alexander listened for a response of some kind, a voice or the sound of running footsteps, but none came. There followed an awkward silence for a few minutes. The aliens shifted on their little feet. The man from the CVB pulled out his phone. Realizing there was no reception, he shoved it back in his pocket. Major Dog Patch stood blank and immobile, like a toy someone had turned off.

Just as Alexander was about to walk away in frustration, a strange faint whirring noise came from out of nowhere. To Alexander's astonishment, he watched as a floating hologram flickered on. The hologram was that of a man, who walked over to Dog Patch. The hologram man wore a brown pith helmet, safari shirt, and green military pants. He looked like he was on his way to a costume party. The hologram man saluted Dog Patch.

"Meat robots? They're called sex dolls, Dog Patch. You're quite the one to judge, considering there's not one skirt in a fifty-mile radius you haven't chased."

"We've got a guest here."

"Surfers, hippie chicks, librarians—you really have no sense of shame, do you?"

"Just drop it, will you?"

"I had to clear out the sales girls in the Christmas All The Time Store because of you. Have you seen the clutter ever since? Looks like a hoarder with a hard-on for red and green moved in."

"Can we drop it already?"

The hologram folded his arms and shot him a look. "At least my sex robots are productive." Before Major Dog Patch could respond, the hologram man spoke to Alexander.

"Do you know who I am?"

Alexander shook his head. "No, sir, I can't say that I do."

The hologram man nodded. "Field Marshal Nine Mile Beach, leader of the CVB. Major Dog Patch is my second in command, in charge of the day-to-day duties. We're the only ones with titles. All other CVB members you will address either as sir or ma'am. You will not know their names. Is this understood?"

"Sir, yes, sir," Alexander answered as though by reflex.

The field marshal nodded. "Good. Are we done here? Because I'm supposed to be in a parallel universe fighting an alternate war right now, and I'm already late."

Major Dog Patch said, "That can wait. He needs to go through quality control. He needs to be indoctrinated."

The field marshal rolled his eyes. "Braxton Alexander, raise your right hand and repeat after me: 'I am now indoctrinated—'"

"Don't half ass it," Major Dog Patch snapped.

"But this war is boring," Field Marshal Nine Mile said. "We haven't even begun to get it off the ground. Oh, very well. Braxton Alexander, before we begin, you may ask me anything. And I will answer any questions, as I am able. Go on," he said, motioning with his hologram hands. "Ask away. Go on. What are you waiting for?"

"What's the CVB's mission?"

"To bring down the government of Northern California in order to create an anarchocollectivist utopia. Our stated goals are to abolish both private ownership and central governments. We are not taking a slow approach to this. We'll rip the bandage off with as much brutality as possible. Quicker the better."

"Why destroy the Northern California government? I keep hearing it's the most progressive one on the continent."

"Yes, they tell everyone that, and they are full of it. Besides, it's still a government—just like the most altruistic corporation is still part of a capitalist system. We won't abide by either anymore."

"Who's funding you?"

"Our resources come from multiple channels. Many interested parties wish for our success."

Major Dog Patch held up a hand. "There are an equal number who would like to see us all dead, too. This is the reason Field Marshal Nine Mile Beach only appears in hologram."

"Affirmative. Even as I talk to you, I am firmly ensconced in a secure location known only to my two assistants and me. When the war is over and won, I'll abdicate my leadership and finish creating the utopia we've already begun. And then turn my attention to the parallel universe war, which is exponentially more interesting. I would love to tell you all about it, but it would take too long, and also I'm not allowed to." Though he did not turn his gaze from Alexander, the last sentence was spoken loudly to Dog Patch.

"What makes you think you'll be any more successful at it than the Southern Californians were?"

The field marshal's smile was grim. "Besides being better fighters and better planners and better at life in general? That's easy. We learned from their mistakes."

Chapter 25

They put him to work at once, helping to lay more railroad tracks alongside a group of fourteen CVB members he was not introduced to. A member showed him how to spread ballast and level it while, just behind, concrete sleepers were laid out using another machine. The sun came up just as they were off-loading the rails.

Major Dog Patch explained they needed to connect the rail to an older but still functional railroad, which would then create an alternate route to San Jose. When Alexander pressed him on the purpose, Major Dog Patch told him he'd find out when he was through what he kept calling the indoctrination.

That first night, his back ached and his phantom limbs throbbed. But like any good effort that produced results, however incremental, he was pleased. Anything he could do to show eagerness would help gain their trust.

After a campfire breakfast of coffee and beans, in which he witnessed Major Dog Patch attempt to grope at least two of the female combatants, they drove him to a safe house in the Russian Hill area of San Francisco.

Major Dog Patch handed him his suitcase. "Good first day. Get some rest. We'll come by at six this evening to pick you up."

The studio apartment was small but inviting with large bay windows that faced north toward Alcatraz. Alexander showered off the dirt and sweat, slept for five hours, and then got lunch from a nearby restaurant. When he returned, Alexander opened his suitcase and found his stash of flower was gone. The Rompecabezas was undisturbed. He opened it and sent a message back to HQ: "CVB have moved me to safe house in San Francisco. They are anarchocollectivists. Planning total destruction of Northern California government and economy. They want to indoctrinate me. There are blue aliens here. They might be colluding. Awaiting your orders."

An hour later, there was still no response. He went downstairs to wait on the street for Major Dog Patch, watching the sunset from the slanted street, glancing at his watch every thirty seconds.

"Seems like you're waiting for something," a raspy voice said.

Alexander turned to see a woman in a trench coat, sizing him up. "I'm waiting on a friend to pick me up."

"Maybe you're waiting for something else, too?"

"Such as?"

"Whatever you're into, babycakes, I'm sure I've got it: reds, whites, blues, LSD, smack." The woman patted her trench coat. "I'm a genuine pharmacist."

Alexander looked at the hands, noted their size, and wondered whether the woman was perhaps not a woman after all. "What about flower?"

"I said I was a pharmacist, not a florist."

"Maybe you call it chocolate?"

"Only candy I sell is nose candy."

Alexander shrugged. "That's what they called it down south. Guy I met there gave me a sample."

"Maybe that's how they roll down in SoCal, but I don't give out free shit. No free ass either. Fuck the sharing economy. Those nerds ever set their sights on my business, I'll be assed out quicker than you can say Silicon Valley."

Just then, Major Dog Patch showed up. "Making new friends, I see. Hi, girl; what's your name?"

The woman tightened the belt on her trench coat and stalked off.

"You took my flower," Alexander said.

"We've got a strict no-drugs policy."

"Flower's different—the Mexicans developed it."

"You're not helping your case."

"It makes you smarter."

Major Dog Patch took his eyes off the road to pierce Alexander with a glare. "Listen, idiot. I don't know why, but the field marshal spontaneously decided you're part of the CVB until we say you aren't anymore. But if you want to be with us, then you don't do drugs. It took everyone else months and months to get in, and all you do is show up with alien references and some Mexican drug dealer, and you're part of the crew. Regardless, the no-drugs policy holds. Besides, there's still a shit ton of work to be done."

"Like what?"

"More of the same—that railroad needs to be complete before we can do anything else. You think we're going to roll up on a highway with all the weapons we have after what happened down in LA?"

And so it went for a month straight. Every night, they'd take him back to the mountain to lay more ballast. And every morning at sunrise, they took him back to his apartment and his view of Alcatraz peeking through the fog.

The doldrums of manual labor on top of the more abstract mission from TexIntelSecuriCorp took its toll with surprising speed. Alexander felt the soreness of backbreaking work and was crushed by permanent exhaustion. Added to the physical symptoms was the existential anxiety of trying to determine whom he could trust, which side he should fight, and how best to fight if at all. Drifting into uneasy sleep in the mornings, he'd gaze out across the bay to that prison landmark, feeling empathy for those desperate men who'd tried to escape the inescapable.

The other CVB members only spoke to him about the tasks at hand, under strict orders not to disclose personal information. Attempts to get on Major Dog Patch's good side were rebuffed. Most of the time he was seen coming and going from the women's barracks. Field Marshal Nine Mile Beach was nowhere to be seen.

He heard nothing from TexIntelSecuriCorp for twenty-eight days. On the morning of the twenty-ninth day, the Rompecabezas vibrated. He'd just stepped out of the shower and was still dripping wet when he opened it. The message was longer than usual. He toweled off, waiting for it to load in its entirety before decoding:

We can corroborate your intel about the CVB. They have a manifesto already written and have been broadcasting it on pirate radio the past few months. However, the messages we've read are sometimes incoherent. They may be spreading disinformation to distract from their real intentions. Seems the college students in the area are malleable and extremely gullible due to their horrible education. Even now our operatives are investigating and will pass on information as soon as we can. As for you, let them think the indoctrination is working. You're a true believer now.

We have no reliable information as to the whereabouts of Field Marshal Nine Mile Beach, if he is indeed real, and we aren't sure that he is.

Your disclosure about the blue aliens is extremely distressing. It may be that they are at war with the grays and using the North and South Californians as pawns to fight their war. Isolate them and find out.

Forty-eight hours later, Alexander hammered in the last spike of the railroad to the sound of applause. He was surprised at how strong his upper body had gotten in four weeks' time.

The hologram of Field Marshal Nine Mile Beach appeared by the long line of Douglas firs.

"Like a modern-day John Henry, Braxton Alexander has completed the line of track and will pave the way for victory. We now have routes from here to San Jose and an underground railroad from San Jose to San Francisco. The armaments will flow from our stockpile under the Christmas All The Time store. And then we'll use the same route to populate our mountain utopia once the war is over and the infrastructure of San Francisco, Sacramento, and Berkeley has been leveled."

The hologram flickered, and the field marshal's smile disappeared. "However much we appreciate your actions, Alexander, let none of us forget that this effort could only have been done through our collective strength. Here's to the CVB."

"Here's to the CVB," they shouted in unison.

The aliens rushed over, pushing and shoving to be the first to shake his hand.

"Good on ya," Pepper said.

"I just knew you'd be a fine addition to the CVB team. I just knew it," High Pockets said.

"A celebration is in order," Pepper declared. "We'd love to take you to breakfast. There's a great place we know in San Francisco: never closes, serves dinner twenty-four hours a day. What do you say?"

Alexander watched them blink in unison. "I'd love to."

Chapter 26

"You're listening to the *Minas Petrossian Show* coming to you live from Berkeley as part of the Podcast One Company, where we've decided that, though my speech was shut down at the last minute, I will stay here anyway and broadcast to as many voices as possible, as I refuse to be silenced by anyone, especially ugly people who wear all black.

"As many of you have heard, the Peace, Equality, and Freedom March was a total fiasco, and I for one am glad. We know that the people who claim to espouse the values of free speech and equality have shown themselves to be the most totalitarian and vicious. It's as if we're sort of living in an *Alice in Wonderland* world, but what else is new? If only their costumes were as fabulous.

"Does it not get so boring wearing black all the time? I understand these neo-fascists are cowardly and have to blend in a sea of anonymity, rather unlike yours truly, who stands out wherever he goes like a flamboyant praying mantis. It's why my fans love me and why I keep getting more and more of them every month while these regressive cretins are lockstep in a death march in the army of same, spouting the same bumper-sticker drivel as the worst pundits on television. Hacks.

"Peace, equality, and freedom—let's break those down, shall we? Start with peace. The only ones who aren't being peaceful are the protesters. All you need to do to make them angry is challenge their opinions on everything from gender roles to revisionist history to the failed coup in Southern California, as if questioning their identity politics is an actual threat to their own identity. And they take the bait each and every time. I can literally do it in my sleep at this point. Ugh, can you imagine waking up every morning and having to declare yourself a nonbinary albino feminist who believes that speech you don't agree with is the same as a physical violation? How can one be so mollycoddled? By the way, do albinos refer to themselves as people of color or people of noncolor? It's so hard to keep up.

"Equality: who is not equal? I know the answer, of course, but it's not who the protesters think. As an Armenian outsider, I can tell you, Northern California is the most equal place on earth for women, men, black, white, you name it. There is no inequality except as it pertains to government overreach, which seeks to oppress the entrepreneurs of Silicon Valley who are trying so hard to turn this area into a capitalist utopia, except for the ones who are intent on demonetizing speech they don't agree with. Thankfully, as you all know, I am so terribly rich that when they demonetized me, it didn't matter.

"But subtracting that one issue for the moment, there really is no reason to be upset here. This is why they need to invent reasons to protest. Are my ideas really such a threat that people will take to the streets to avoid hearing them? And instead of meeting me head on with rebuttals, instead of listening to my speeches respectfully and having a lively, spirited discussion of their ideas, they just goose-step their way around the campus, their really expensive campus that Mummy and Daddy pay for because—news flash—making think pieces won't cover the two-hundred-thousand-Californian-dollar-a-year tuition.

"And then lastly, there's freedom. Now one would assume that word pertains to all, since it's part of the same slogan as the word *equality*, but no, that's not the way they think. Understand that these words don't have the same definition to these people as they do to you or me. These words only pertain to their groups. How else would you describe the abhorrent events that happened the other day as a peaceful rally?

"Why, do you know one poor girl had urine thrown on her by these so-called intellectuals? Can you imagine? They stand up for equal rights when it suits them but have no issues violating a woman whose viewpoints they disagree with. Revolting is it not? We are trying to get her on the show. Even now I have three of my interns devoted to finding her. And let me say this: I am personally putting up five thousand Californian dollars of my own personal savings for any information leading to the apprehension of this piss-throwing thug.

"Now, many of you are saying, 'Oh, Minas, why couldn't you just be the stronger person and give your speech anyway when so many of your fans have braved the line of fire to come out to show your support.' Believe me, I truly want to. But as you know, they are making it quite hard for me to speak at Berkeley and indeed many other colleges and universities in the northern part of the country. As you well know, they don't want my ideas of individualism and freedom to spread. I know exactly why, too. They believe I'm a threat. I am the real anarchist.

"I suppose in a way, I am, albeit a fabulously handsome one. After all, anarchy is just another word for freedom—real, true freedom to be who you are and say what you want without consequence. Unfortunately the reality is that for all the success Northern California is having in the technology sector, they are regressing in terms of the educational system. And in Berkeley's case, what they've done to me and keep doing to me is suppress my right as a resident of California to speak. And the way they do this is in addition to demonetizing my YouTube channel and by trying to get me to pay a king's ransom for security.

"It is true I am fabulously wealthy, as you all know, and this really isn't about money. I mean, I am currently wearing designer high-top sneakers that cost as much as one month's rent for someone in Pacific Heights, but that is neither here nor there. I care about the security of the people who believe in the free exchange of ideas. Twenty thousand dollars to protect my interns and me is not a lot of money. But I could not guarantee the safety of my listeners, and that is very distressing to me.

"What's that? Oh, good, it seems that we have tracked down the poor woman who had urine thrown in her eyes by these despicable people. We'll see if she can get here in time, and we'll try to do a live segment in the next block.

"That will just add one more thing on my plate to get to today, so, Minas, stay focused for once. Where was I? Oh yes, so the Peace, Equality, and Freedom March was a joke. The student protesters wouldn't even be out there unless they were being paid, and now we know that they're being paid to protest by Berkeley professors. This is absolutely true, and later in the show I will be naming names, make no mistake. It is truly disgusting.

"What's even worse to me is the fact that that group you've been hearing about so much, the CVB, is also behind this. Now, as far as I know, no one knows who this group is or what their goals are beyond using the useful idiot students and their professors to sow disruption. I have my theories as to who they really are, but ultimately I suspect they are loud nothings. I really do. They are a tempest in a teapot. And the reason I think so is simple: the less substance something has, the more people are attracted to it. How else would you explain the nightly news programs?

"Also, think about this: the CVB doesn't even have a logo. I haven't seen any. Have you? And no, I don't count those chalk scrawls those kids make on the campus sidewalks. Poor darlings. If that isn't a display of arrested development, I don't know what is. No logo means there's no substance.

"Now contrast that with my fabulous logo for those of you who are part of the Minas Mod Squad. It's a perfect illustration of yours truly, complete with my lovely coiffed hair when I wore it platinum. Now, of course, it's more of a blood-red lacquer because I need to stand out even more than ever.

"Did you know being a Minas Mod Squad member means you get access to me all the time? There's the Minas cam, the podcast downloads, behind-the-scenes photos of our production, one-on-one interviews with the interns. And this month we're doing something new: the Daily Sound Off, a forum where Minas Mod Squad members can have their say. And each day yours truly will curate the best of the best and highlight them for all to see.

"If you want to be a part of the Minas Mod Squad, we're running a special this month. Use the code MINAS and the fifteen-ninety-nine-a-month access is now just eleven ninety-nine a month for the first six months. Oh, and I almost forgot: one other cool thing I'm doing for the Minas Mod Squad is what I call the Easy Access pass. Whenever I give talks from now on, you'll be able to purchase tickets before anyone else. Because who doesn't like easy access, right? I know I do.

"If I'm not mistaken, I believe my next talk is scheduled at...Where is it? Oh yes, UC Santa Barbara. I'm supposed to go head to head with a nasty woman who believes all men should be castrated in the name of equality. It must be something in the water down there; I don't know. But I do know it will be an amazingly fabulous experience you won't want to miss."

Chapter 27

Little Joe's was San Francisco's oldest restaurant. Once a railroad dining car, it had gone through extensive changes over the centuries, evolving into a building that took up a city block. The original structure was still in use and so exclusive that reservations were made months in advance.

The maître d' rushed over to the aliens, leaning down to wrap them in hugs and shower them with air kisses. "High Pockets and Pepper, I haven't seen you in a month. Our profits have gone down fifteen percent. Usual table?"

Little Joe's was warm and inviting. The maître d' led the way through the packed front room to a chestnut-colored booth that was intimate and secluded.

"I won't even bother with today's specials because I know you both too well. Will your friend be having the same?"

"Why not?" Alexander said.

They ordered steaks with creamed spinach and beer.

"Oh, it may be a tad old-fashioned, but we just adore this place," High Pockets said.

Pepper nodded. "We ordered baseball steaks. Their beef is dry-aged for thirty days. You can cut it with a fork; it's so tender."

"I wish I'd have known what kind of place this was," Alexander said. He was still in his sweat-stained denim jeans and flannel work shirt. On the other hand, the aliens wore blue blazers with blue shirts and bow ties. The overall effect was blue on blue on blue.

"Don't give it another thought," Pepper said. "This place is very unfussy."

Their food arrived. It was indeed very good, Alexander thought, better beef than Texas, who prided itself on its cattle production.

"Now that you are—quote, unquote—indoctrinated, we simply must get to know you better," High Pockets said.

"Now that we're allowed," Pepper chimed in.

"And vice versa," Alexander said. "There's something I've been meaning to ask for a while now."

"Please do," Pepper said, spreading his arms wide. "We are open books."

"Are you and the grays at war with each other and using California to do the fighting?"

They looked at each other in stunned silence. They then turned to face Alexander. After an awkward silence lasting ten seconds, they burst out in laughter.

"Oh my dear," Pepper said, wiping tears of laughter from his eyes. "I'm choking. I can't even…"

"Us," High Pockets gasped. "At war…with the grays…using California."

Alexander's cheeks flushed. "It's not really all that far-fetched."

When their laughter died down, Pepper was first to speak. "My dear boy, I want to thank you for the good laugh, as I have not laughed that much in ages. I do apologize."

"As do I," High Pockets said. "It's just, you see, we and the grays, as you call them, have absolutely no reason to go to war with each other, let alone use humans to do so."

"Perish the thought," Pepper added. "Earth has its problems, of course. But how bad could a place be if they gave us Whitey Ford?"

High Pockets finished his beer. He exhaled once to finish catching his breath. "You met Catfish Hunter and Shoeless Joe Jackson, from what I understand. Surely, they didn't come across as warmongers?"

"No."

"You see? Why, we're not even in the same industry. First of all, if—and that is a very big if, mind you. But if we were to go to war with each other, it would make more sense to do it from our respective planet, where we are populated, as opposed to down here, where there are so few of us."

"Perish the thought," Pepper said. "Our last war was more than ten millennia ago. And as my dear friend here reminds you, we wouldn't even be corporate enemies. The grays work on that lonely little asteroid mining their rocks, whereas our line of work is in gemstone synthesis. We take rocks from a certain not-too-distant planet and turn them into precious and semiprecious stones."

High Pockets held out his blue hands, showing off rings with stones set in them, one on each finger. They were unlike anything Alexander had seen before. The one on his left ring finger caught Alexander's eye.

"May I?"

"Certainly," he said, removing the ring.

Alexander held it in his hands. It had the same wavy patterns as a tiger's eye stone, but the colors were alternating blue, not gold. The colors bobbed back and forth. The more he looked, the more he felt as if the gemstone were looking back. He managed to break his gaze and return it to the alien.

"I know what you're thinking," Pepper said. "It's not sentient."

"We're just that good at production"—High Pockets nodded—"at the risk of sounding arrogant, that is."

Alexander picked up his glass, but it was empty. "If you aren't fighting against the grays and you don't want to harm us, then what are you doing with the CVB?"

High Pockets smiled. "I can tell you're an Occam's-razor kind of fellow, so I'll answer it succinctly: Field Marshal Nine Mile Beach needs our gems."

"Well, one gem in particular," Pepper said. He held out his right pinkie finger. He wore a translucent gray ring. With gentle pressure, Pepper squeezed the ring. Alexander watched in disbelief as a hologram image of Pepper appeared floating over the remains of the creamed spinach.

"We keep him in hologram gems," High Pockets said.

"And what does he do in exchange?"

"He pays handsomely for it." High Pockets looked at Alexander in surprise. "Surely my dear boy, you must know how expensive it is to live in San Francisco?"

They ended up dropping him off at a cramped Italian coffeehouse in North Beach. He was going to ask why, but they bid him farewell, telling him to try the cappuccino, as it was the best in the city.

Alexander couldn't think of any reason not to, so he pushed open the door and did as he was told. His back was in knots from the month's work. He was in desperate need of a shower and a long day's rest. And he smelled like grime and soil.

He ordered his drink and sat at the window, looking outside at the passersby on Vallejo Street. The weather was unseasonably hot for that time of year. Older men in newsboy caps sat outside, drinking espresso from tiny cups. Women in short sleeves walked past. A homeless man made the rounds of trash cans, realizing too late they'd been collected earlier that morning.

A crashing sound came from behind. He turned to see that a man wearing a strange headset over his eyes had crashed into a display of cups.

"My bad," he said. "Still getting used to these."

"Gotta take it slow, bro," said another man, who wore an identical headset. "You'll get the hang of it."

There were half a dozen men in all, fumbling like zombies with outstretched arms. Alexander walked up to the woman behind the counter to return his cup and saucer.

"Look at them," she said. "They come here and strap on their virtual-reality headsets and pretend to live in alternate worlds. Why do they insist on taking up seats here? I wish they'd all just go the hell home."

"Sorry," he said.

"Work in retail long enough, it's impossible not to have total disdain for humanity." She smiled in spite of her anger. "Sorry. I didn't mean you."

"This is probably a long shot, ma'am, but you wouldn't happen to know of anywhere to get flower around here?"

The woman shook her head. "Last I heard the supply's dried up. I'm not even sure you can get it down south at this point."

"Well, thank you anyway," he said.

"Wish I had better news. Hey, if you happen to find some, you know where I am."

Alexander left the café. Wired from coffee, he walked around Washington Square until the buzz wore off. When at last he sat on a bench in front of a Catholic church, his forehead was beaded with sweat. Three old parishioners hobbled up the steps and into the cathedral. Within a span of twenty minutes, three different drug dealers approached him. None had what he wanted.

Assuming the woman in the café was right, why would the Mexicans cut off the supply? They might be waiting until the new refined version was ready to ship. Then again, the woman might have had no idea what she was talking about. It could have been a rumor she'd heard from someone who heard it from someone else. Like playing a game of telephone, the more removed you were from the source, the more muddled the real message was. And right now, Alexander thought, there were plenty of things not adding up.

Chapter 28

"If you are just joining us, welcome to Precious Gem Week on the *Shopping at Home Show*. I'm Marsha Bascomb. It's actually our one-year anniversary show, and today you're going to get a peek at some of my favorites, like this amazing bracelet. Now, you know how much of a fan I am of charm bracelets. But how about taking a charm bracelet and replacing those charms with freshwater pearls and real gemstones? Well, our price on this is just one eighty-five, and you can get that with four easy payments if you choose. These are all moonstones, very limited, very elegant.

"Now, the next thing I want to tell you about is this necklace. I absolutely love green, and the chrome diopside is really stunning with an easy-to-use clasp. Oh, and did I mention it's two carats of diopside and genuine diamonds? Appraised at five hundred fifty dollars, because it's Gem Week, that price is only two hundred fifty dollars. What a treat.

"But what I want to do now is go ahead and jump in and introduce to you, Mrs. Julie Battista. Now, Julie, as you know, is our lady who procures all those lovely diamonds and precious gems from the most famous houses in New York and Amsterdam, so she can dress the ambassadors and the supermodels and even celebrities on their red-carpet rides and movie premiers. And she sends out some pretty high-tech robot security guards to ensure all of those lovely pieces go straight back to the diamond houses when they are done, with them. But, as a *Shopping at Home Show* exclusive, Mrs. Battista has a one-of-a-kind collection of gems that are as good as the real thing because they are the real thing, but at a price you can afford. We call them body doubles, you know, just like those celebrities who use body doubles when they are doing stunts or some racy sexy scenes—isn't that right, Julie?"

"That's right, Marsha. Sexy is the word. But it is important to reiterate to everyone watching that even if we do call these body doubles, everything you see in the Battista Collection is one hundred percent real. Don't let the prices fool you. This is the real deal, and no matter your price point, we have something that you can feel special about owning and consider a worthy investment."

"So true, Julie."

"Now, this is going to be really quick because I just know the minute you see them, you'll be picking up that phone without even listening to what I have to say, so let me take a deep breath before I begin. Here goes: these are already going. For instance, the Alexandrite is—is it gone? No, apparently we still have a few left in size six, but only a few. In our red tiger's eye here, size ten is already sold out, so let me take that off so you don't feel tempted. OK, so here we are; we have a few Alexandrite left, and let me put it on—isn't it amazing? So bold and exciting. The bounding is amazing, with fifteen-carat gold; it really is just a masterpiece, and at only two hundred fifty, it is a real value."

"Marsha, I have a confession to make."

"Uh-oh, what could that be, Julie?"

"I've been holding out on you and your audience—until now. I really have been saving the best for last in this collection."

"Oh my, I don't know if I should be upset or excited or both."

"Let's go with both, Marsha."

"Fair enough, this better be good."

"Oh, it will. Now, I want you to do me a favor and feast your eyes—I mean, literally feast your eyes—on this amazing set of minirings as I call them. Look at this mesmerizing Lapis Mazuli."

"I think you mean lapis lazuli."

"No, Marsha, I said it right the first time—Mazuli with an *m*."

"I have never seen anything like that."

"Right? Because nothing like it has ever existed. I'll let you in on a secret. These three body-double gemstones are all lab developed, and it took five years to perfect them. That's right, Marsha: five years."

"That is just…Wow. I am speechless. Mazuli, huh? It looks like it's moving."

"Doesn't it? Well, you'd better take some deep breaths because we have two other ones to offer for you today. The Lapis Mazuli is just one, and before we move on, I should say we are out of size six already, but all the other sizes are in, and because it is part of the exclusive Battista Collection, made only for the *Shopping at Home Show*, you can only get it here, and that means you can only get it at this unbelievable price today of just two hundred fifty dollars. And these are appraised at four hundred dollars normally."

"Amazing."

"But, Marsha, let me just tell you we offer the same twelve-carat gold ring with two other gemstones as well: the first, Topaze."

"Topaze?"

"Yes, with an *e*, like topiary, with an 'aze' sound, as it is."

"Ha-ha."

"I don't know how else to describe it, but this Topaze, Marsha…I mean, just look at it—the warm honey color is so warm and lovely. It's no wonder ancient Egyptians associated it with a sun god. But now you can get this amazing body-double version for, again, just two hundred fifty dollars."

"I'm holding it up right now, Julie, and I love how much it matches my skin."

"Doesn't it? But my final treat for you, and it is also going fast—it seems we're out of sizes nine through eleven already—is this final new color. This brand-new color the Battista labs have invented is called Griseonine."

"Griseonine?"

"Exactly, from the Latin *griseo* meaning 'gray.'"

"Ah, Julie, that explains it. This little gray stone is positively exquisite. It's so translucent—almost colorless."

"It's like looking at one thin onion layer."

"And, Julie, you say these are all developed in Battista labs?"

"That's right, Marsha. But don't let that fool you. We didn't create these out of nothing. We used some of the same properties of gemstones worth three, five, even ten times the amount to create these versions."

"Careful or you'll be putting us out of business."

"Well, thankfully for you these are only available for a limited time. We've pitted these against some of the finest gem houses in Europe, and they could not believe their eyes. These are truly flawless in every sense of the word. But—"

"Sorry to interrupt; it seems we're out of size five now."

"Thank you, Marsha. And yes, as I was saying, these are flawless but at a fraction of the price. Now, as a special deal for you, in honor of Gem Week and the *Shopping at Home Show*'s one-year anniversary, I am pleased to offer these body-double Battista gems for only one hundred ninety-nine dollars. Now, that's a discount of more than sixty percent. So if you are looking for something precious but affordable, that will fool even the most prestigious gem and diamond houses in the world, you simply must act now."

"If you at home won't, I know I will—that's for certain. Ha-ha!"

.

Chapter 29

What must have once been a regal banquet hall in downtown San Francisco was now dark and musty, a faded distant memory. Cobweb-covered lights hung from the vaulted ceilings. The tables were laid out with cheap place settings. Napkins were stained; tablecloths, dotted with cigarette burns. The space smelled like decades' worth of wedding-reception beef, chicken, and stale tobacco. Plastic flowers in elaborate displays sat on each table. If there had been a raffle of some kind, it would not have surprised Alexander. The strangest part of the banquet hall was a giant disco ball hanging above them in the center of the room, a strange spinning anachronism casting square lights all around them.

Major Dog Patch strolled from one table to the next, chatting up one woman after another. His shiny dress shoes were a sharp contrast to the threadbare carpet that looked like it had been installed dirty and had never seen a vacuum.

They were enjoying what Dog Patch called with pompous irony "a last bacchanalian feast before the war to end all wars began." The spread was modest: bulk wine, nondescript meat, and too-salty potatoes with wilted vegetables and desserts made to send the diner into sugar shock.

Despite his full initiation into the CVB, Alexander still felt like an outsider even though the continued silence from TexIntelSecuriCorp made him more determined than ever to abandon his old life. He sat alone, eating and drinking in silence, listening to the constant chatter that surrounded him.

Two weeks ago, he'd stood before Major Dog Patch and the hologram of Field Marshal Nine Mile Beach in the Christmas All The Time Store. The lights where turned off, except for one overhead star-shaped paper lantern, casting five shafts of light across two dozen black-masked CVB members who stood in a wide semicircle to witness his final rite of passage.

They'd spent the day clearing away the decorations, making room for a large shipping container that contained automatic weapons, grenade launchers, and three small but very powerful unmanned aerial vehicles for remote assaults.

"We don't usually go in for such theatrics," Dog Patch said. "But to truly be one of us, you must sacrifice as we sacrificed."

He brought out a dagger from underneath the cashier's table. The sheath was adorned with an intricate pattern of gold and green. A ruby was affixed to the hilt. Dog Patch unsheathed it, revealing the same markings on the dagger.

"Take your shirt off."

Alexander did as he was told, his hands fumbling on the buttons.

Field Marshal Nine Mile Beach spoke in a solemn voice. "We all bleed together. And in shedding blood, we become one."

He was still dropping the shirt when Major Dog Patch sliced his bicep. The point of the blade just penetrated the surface of the skin, no more than two inches in length. But the sight of blood and the pain caused a sharp intake of breath.

Before he could react, a CVB member cleaned the wound, covered it with gauze, and wrapped it with a bandage. The baptism under Christmas lights was over before it had begun. As soon as the ceremony was over, the semicircle separated, and the members sealed up the shipping container.

Now seated in the banquet hall, he had a dull lingering pain as the only reminder of his initiation. Other than this, nothing had changed. Alexander still felt like he was kept at a distance, like a freelancer rather than a comrade-in-arms. He looked around the room, hoping he'd find High Pockets and Pepper. They weren't there. Come to think of it, he hadn't seen them since they'd taken him to eat, and that seemed like ages ago.

Alexander was seized with a distraught suspicion. What if, despite their assurances, the aliens were actually fighting each other, orchestrating their war with the Northern and Southern Californians as instruments? It wasn't really that far-fetched, especially if the Southern California rebellion was the grays' move. As a response, perhaps the CVB was the blue aliens' turn. And what a surprise it would be if they'd managed to entice Alexander to defect from one side to the next like a roving game piece. He shook the thought away, choosing to believe them. They just seemed too damn sincere to doubt.

Besides, any other number of explanations was possible. Both blue and gray aliens were conspiring with Texas to cripple California as a whole and using him as an unwitting go-between. The Mexicans were working to take back California, either with the help of Texas or on their own.

The possibilities were endless. But it didn't matter because there was no proof beyond what he could see with his own eyes. The simplest explanation was always best. Wasn't it?

"May I have everyone's attention?" Major Dog Patch tapped a glass with a spoon. The room fell silent. "The field marshal wants to speak."

The hologram of Field Marshal Nine Mile Beach appeared in the center of the room, dressed in formal military attire.

"Men, women, soldiers, comrades," he began, "long ago, the West was settled by pioneers who forged the mighty rivers and cut a path through the uninhabitable. They scaled mountains, tamed the wilderness, and let nothing stand in their way. The shifting geography and impossibly long coast became one land with one people. We were the shining example for all. Even our dirt was festooned with gold."

The CVB members applauded. Field Marshal Nine Mile Beach held up a hologram hand to regain their silence.

"But where did that progress get us? The gold rush ended on a heap of empty promises and greed. And out of the scrap heap, Hollywood was born in the South and Silicon Valley in the North. And with it came arrogance, elitism, decadence, and cultural decay. The economic gap widened with sickening speed. We no longer live in California," his voice boomed. "We live in Sodom and Gomorrah. This is ancient Rome before the fall."

Alexander watched in horror as the hologram started to flicker and fade. And yet the voice continued.

"Civilization is in decline, and only we are smart enough to recognize it and hasten its demise."

The field marshal appeared in the flesh in the center of the room. At the same time, a small hologram of the field marshal appeared on Alexander's table, hovering just over the roast beef. He looked around the room but could not see the hologram on any other table. Alexander felt the eyes penetrating his, pouring into his skull.

"Like Noah from days of old, I chose you. Together, we will cause the flood of anarchy to destroy civilization. Then we shall begin anew. I chose all of you because you are able to fight and build and rebuild. You've been instructed and will act accordingly. When the time comes, and it will come soon, you will know what to do. Won't you?"

"Yes," came the response.

"Will you know what to do?"

"Yes," came the response.

Alexander tore his eyes away from the hologram to look at the real person standing in the center of the banquet hall. The person he saw was not Field Marshal Nine Mile Beach, but Shoeless Joe. He blinked his eyes, and the figure altered its appearance, becoming the Bedouin who'd supplied him with the dreamfish. Then the face turned into the birdlike man and then Sgt. Biker.

Alexander turned to face the tiny hologram once more, but it was gone. He stood up, knocking over his chair. Perspiration oozed from every pore. He walked through the banquet hall, passing the chanting CVB members, who were blind to his sudden departure.

The air was stifling; the walls were closing in. He half ran down the narrow corridor, heading toward the faint exit sign, which shone dimly like a distant beacon.

With the sound of Field Marshal Nine Mile Beach's thundering voice still echoing in the room, Alexander burst through the doors onto the empty sidewalk. He wanted to run but forced himself to walk to the corner, gasping for breath in the damp night.

Putting his hands on his knees, he doubled over, waiting for the wretched feelings to subside. Somewhere in the layers of noise coming from the city and his breath and beating heart, he heard one faint scratching sound as if someone had struck a match by a microphone.

As if propelled by second sight, Alexander gathered himself and took off running, his metal legs clomping across the street. He'd just cleared the intersection when the explosion rocked the banquet hall. He dove to the ground, turning in time to see it exploding in slow motion, not outward, but imploding like a purposefully controlled demolition.

Chapter 30

From the back two pages of Chat Magazine*'s last issue, vol. 450.*

Thirty-eight years is a long time to run a magazine, and we've covered everything that was worth covering and interviewed everyone who was anyone. Now that we're hanging up our spurs, so to speak, we decided to go out with one last hurrah and interview the person who graced our cover more than anyone else—the delightful enfant terrible Al Bronson. If it reads as a rambling monologue rather than an interview, it was at Bronson's insistence.

"Yeah, you covered a lot of ground, so what? I covered three times as much as you did, for damn sure. I'm going to be ninety-eight next week, no joke. Still spry. Maybe it's all the sex; I don't know. Does it matter? It's none of your business.

"You know, I've done so much that when people talk about me, they forget about all my accomplishments. The worst thing about getting old is trying not to become an et cetera. I always tell people, 'List it all, even if we're here the whole night. Where am I going anyway?'

"What I remember most, in no particular order: Saltwater taffy—the good shit, not the synthetic shit. Artistic movements. Not just my own art, mind you. I might have been harsh on the postmodernists and the environmental artists and body modificationists. OK, that last one still sucks, but whatever. Point is there was a time when everything was better.

"Some things are good now: the ocean, the fog. City Lights is still here, incredibly, even though people don't read. Marin County—I guess most of the Bay Area. I don't travel like I used to. Seen enough as it is. My neighborhood's enough.

"Is this really how you want to end your magazine? I know I have a reputation that you never know what you're going to get with me, but I hope I don't let you down. Sometimes I don't have the energy to be witty. I don't like having to make an effort these days, not for people I don't give a shit about.

"The one thing that you can't replace is the music of the seventies, right around the time you started interviewing me. Now *that* was the heyday. I still had my natural hair color then, and this was before all the diseases when you could just do whatever. But anyway: the music. Some of that stuff I still listen to all the time. The clubs were the best. I will go on record as saying after the seventies ended, there was no reason to ever step foot in a club again. It just wasn't worth the time or the cover charge.

"If I wasn't at the Ramshackle, I was at the Rathskeller. To this day I don't know how I managed to stay up for so many days at a time. I guess I make up for it now as I seem to sleep nine hours a night every night now. But those two clubs were like my place.

"Thing I loved most was to walk in and find a crazy machine. You know what a crazy machine is? It's that girl or guy who is so wasted and out of control but somehow wanting to converse as if it were a normal day at lunch or something. Always around two or three, I'd just get this second sight, and I'd know a crazy machine was in the room. I'd be in my booth as usual, and I'd just slowly look around until I saw them, and then our eyes would lock, and—boom—they'd come over, and I'd have myself a crazy machine. I attracted them back in the day.

"I wouldn't be dancing with them then. No, they'd have thrown up over their fabulous outfits if that were the case. No, we'd just sit and talk. And then after an hour or so, I'd get bored and leave. Crazy machines are only fun as long as you can disassociate yourself from the fact they are inherently sad people. And just so you know, I'm talking about famous people, not everyday people. Artists, rock stars, actors, politicians—they were all sad, lonely people. I liked to think I was doing them a service— like I was a priest.

"Oh, that's the other place I forgot: the discotheque. Remember it?

I can't remember the name, but it's on the tip of my tongue, though. I know it didn't start with an *r*, like the other places, though. But if the Rathskeller and Ramshackle seemed exclusive, the discotheque I'm speaking of was on a whole other level. Do you know they had a fake restaurant on top of it? It's true. Well, it was more like a banquet hall than a restaurant. But it was made up to look like one of those old, dark Victorian things, like something you'd imagine in a castle. But I swear it was never open. Not once in the years I went there did I see it open. But the entrance to the discotheque was right there. You opened the great double doors, and then there was another set, which led to the banquet hall, but it was roped off, and the lights were always off, too. Very strange.

"The bouncer would point to what looked like a side door to the left, and you'd go in there and then down a full three flights of stairs. Talk about underground. Once the bouncer pointed, you were on your own, and gosh, it was so dark sometimes; all it would take was one drunken misstep, and you'd have a waterfall of people tumbling down, down, down.

"That is, if you were even allowed to get that far. And you wouldn't have been able to. One of your journalists tried to interview me there, but they wouldn't let him inside. If the place were still around you still wouldn't be able to get in. They had a no-press rule. They *hated* everything about the press, called them all two-faced hacks, ambulance chasers, liars—that kind of shit.

"Anyway, the weird part was there wasn't much to the place. I mean, it was huge, and the people were outrageous, and there were these nightly bubble parties, but otherwise—

"That's right, bubble parties. Oh, my dear, you are so cute. Well, I'm talking about the kind where they just hose everyone down with soap and water, and you dance in this sudsy liquid. You have to remember there was tons of cocaine then, so people were really into stupid shit.

"So besides the bubble parties, there was a huge bar, but it mostly looked like an empty space, like it could have been a Masonic lodge or something. Maybe at one time it was—who knows? Those places came and went so quickly. I think I lived at all three of those clubs for as many years before they all closed. The places would get raided, or the owners, arrested. It was a very intense time.

"The only other thing I remember about the discotheque was that it had this huge disco ball—just one, the size of a moon. It was obnoxious. But all of the glitterati hung out there, and you'd see these endless lines of nobodies trying to get in, and they never got in, and that was even more absurd because the place was so big, but there'd only be a few hundred people inside. I don't know how they stayed in business.

"Well, I *know* how they stayed in business, which is why the owner went to jail, but that's another story for another time. Aren't you glad you interviewed me? You didn't really think I was going to tell you anything juicy or important, did you? This magazine's always been about superficial things. Why would I spill the beans on anything important now? At least I'm being honest.

"Thirty-eight years you managed to hang on. How many celebrities are even left besides me? And you know, for the record, I was never comfortable being called that. I am and will always be a true artist, no matter what *Chat* or its readers might think.

"Oh, I suddenly remembered why I stopped going to that discotheque. It wasn't the people or anything like that. The bubble parties got on my nerves—and worse. Whatever soap they used, I was allergic to, and I'd have to leave after an hour and take a shower because my skin would itch something terrible.

"Does anyone know if that place is still around? I wouldn't be surprised. Nothing shocks me anymore, not at this age. So if you told me it was still around, I wouldn't be surprised. We live in interesting times, don't we?

"You know that phrase, right? I think the Chinese came up with it. 'May you live in interesting times.' I love that phrase—because it sounds like a good thing on the surface, but in reality it's actually a curse. It's really quite brilliant."

Chapter 31

"You're watching *Eyewitness News Special Edition* with Jessica Abercrombie. Tonight, an unspeakable tragedy occurred in downtown San Francisco when the Oleg Ukrainian building was rocked with explosions in what is being described as a horrific tragedy.

"Incredibly, no one outside the building was harmed, and firefighters and rescue crews on the scene are describing it as an incident that was specifically manufactured to destroy only that building. For more on this story, we are going live to Mason Richards, who is at the scene. Mason?"

"Yes, Jessica, I am standing here just a few blocks from the building, where, as you can see, police and the Californian National Guard have cordoned off the area. No one is allowed any closer as they work to clear the area."

"And how are they going about this process?"

"First, they are doing a drone sweep of every building within a five-block perimeter. If any suspicious package is detected, they send in the dogs and bomb squads. This is painstaking work, Jessica, as they have to sweep one building at a time, one floor at a time."

"Now, you said you've spoken with security team members there who are planning a press announcement."

"That's correct. This announcement should occur shortly, they've told us, but whether 'shortly' means five minutes or three hours, it's hard to say. They're not taking any questions and have instructed us to wait until presumably all the information is gathered."

"I assume they are in touch with the president."

"The president has been notified as well as his chief of staff, but that's all we know at this time."

"What about fatalities, Mason? We are hearing the banquet hall was booked tonight."

"That's what my sources are saying, Jessica, but we are still trying to confirm this. We know the space can hold several hundred people, so if there was indeed a gathering here tonight, it would be catastrophic and frankly doubtful that anyone inside would have survived."

"Has anyone been taken to a hospital?"

"None confirmed at this time."

"Troubling. Mason, is it too soon to call this a terrorist incident? Or too soon to assume Southern California is behind it?"

"We can't assume anything at this point, Jessica, nor rule anything out. Without any confirmation from the authorities, it would be reckless to declare this a terrorist incident. The fact is at this moment we simply do not know."

"OK, let's switch to social media. I'm going to put up some tweets that have come through the last hour. This one from @Kim_Chi, who says, 'Was on the street when the building just dropped like a house of cards. Terrorism?' Another from @CrumpetMaster33 reads, 'I swore I saw a plane hit it. #coverup.' And lastly, this one from the president of Cascadia releasing a statement: 'Our thoughts and prayers go out to the people of California. Cascadia stands with its ally and will pledge whatever financial or military support is needed.'"

"Jessica, sorry to interrupt, but I am standing with someone who says she witnessed the incident."

"Take it away, Mason."

"You are asking to have your face obscured, so we're blurring it, and we are also going to mask your voice. Presumably you won't give us your real name, either."

"I'd rather not. You can call me Melinda."

"OK, Melinda, tell us what you saw."

"Well, I was walking my dog sometime around nine thirty or so, when the building shook from side to side, and it just collapsed in on itself."

"Can you tell us anything else?"

"Well, like what?"

"Did you see how it happened?"

"Oh, well, I think I might have seen a plane, kind of like what happened in the United States years ago."

"A plane?"

"Yeah, I mean, a small plane, not a big one—like it hit in the middle. Or maybe it wasn't a plane but like one of those drones."

"Drones?"

"That's right. I think I saw a drone hit the building."

"Did you see any people trying to escape?"

"No, not a soul—that's why it's so weird. I'm a local activist here in this neighborhood, which is why I don't want people to see my real face. But as an activist, I'm usually first to know about the goings-on. This is just a mystery."

"There you have it, Jessica. That was Melinda, not her real name, believing this was a drone attack."

"I know San Francisco used to have its problems with drones, but the regulations took care of those issues years ago. If what she's saying is accurate, this would have to be one powerful drone, and I'm just not sure—oh, we're going live to the press conference, which is beginning now."

"Chief Inspector Robins, spelled like the bird with an *s* on it. Thanks for your patience. Now I'm going to read a statement detailing what we know at the moment, and I'll reserve time for a few questions. But please understand the information is trickling in, and we won't be divulging anything that hasn't been given clearance. Is everyone ready?

"All right. Tonight at approximately nine thirty p.m., the Oleg Ukrainian Banquet Hall building imploded. There is thought to have been somewhere between three and five hundred people inside. We are continuing to sift through the wreckage, searching for survivors, but at this point in time, it is doubtful anyone lived. Again we still can't say for certain, but this is what early indications would suggest.

"It is fair to call this an act of terrorism, but an unusual one in that we suspect the people who were killed in the building were themselves terrorists. More information is coming in even as we speak, but from what we understand, the group was an anarchocollectivist organization called the CVB. I'll repeat it so you have it correctly—the organization is called the CVB. We don't know what it stands for at this time.

"About twenty minutes ago, the president of California received a communiqué from an organization taking responsibility for the attack. We are not prepared to read their statement at this time, but what I will say is that the president and his cabinet members have all read it and have been or are in the process of being debriefed. Now I'll take questions."

"Chief Robins, I'm with the *Daily Herald*. Can you tell us more about the terrorist organization who took responsibility for the attack?"

"Not at this time. You, in the red dress."

"Do you know what caused the building to collapse?"

"We're still working on it, but we believe an explosive device or multiple devices were set off in the basement, but again we still aren't sure and won't be until the bomb squad is able to enter the building. You, in the blue suit."

"Was the Californian government aware of the CVB?"

"I can't confirm or deny that. I should add that in light of what happened tonight as well as in Southern California recently, the president is appointing a special task force to focus on rooting out homegrown terrorism. Further details will be announced in the following weeks ahead.

"At the moment, that's all I have to say. Please just let us do our jobs, and when we have tangible information, we will share it with you. Thanks for your cooperation."

Chapter 32

The assistant project manager had the type of mustache that hadn't grown in all the way (and looked like it never would). A small patch below his left nostril stayed bare, as if rebelling against the rest of his face. If he'd been in working in the field, the birdlike man would have demanded he shave it off. But since this was not the case, there was nothing he could do except to silently question its existence.

The conference room was full of executives, all in dark suits. Someone pressed a button to lower the automatic blinds, shutting the sun out of the room. For a moment, they sat in darkness, with only a red light from a conference phone and the faint glow of screens illuminating them.

The assistant project manager inserted a disk into a DVD player. The flat-screen televisions in the conference room were soon broadcasting a homemade video of two men and one woman sitting in front of a backdrop depicting a yellow flag.

The assistant project manager pointed to the backdrop. "It's a corruption of the Deseret flag. They came up with it themselves. I believe the woman stitched it. Not a bad job."

The three people on camera took turns making strange expressions. They genuflected. They raised their fists to the sky with eyes possessed. Their mouths moved, proclaiming in no uncertain terms their beliefs, but no sound was heard. It was if they were playing terrorist charades.

The birdlike man glared. "The hell, son? Fix the volume."

The assistant project manager snatched the remote control. They watched him raise it up to seventy, but still there was no sound.

"Get IT up here," someone said.

There followed an awkward moment where the three terrorists were frozen on pause until the IT guy showed up, brushing crumbs from his face. After some fiddling with the machine, the IT guy shook his head.

"Damn fools didn't record the volume."

"Really," the birdlike man said.

The assistant project manager sighed. "We could bring in some lip readers and subtitle it."

The room groaned in unison.

"Son, this isn't a foreign film."

"You're right. Sorry. It was a weird idea. Besides, it would take too long."

Someone asked, "Is California aware of the filmed message?"

"They have been made aware of its existence," the birdlike man said. "We furnished the info through the usual channels. They'll be expecting it."

"Well, we can't share this with them," the assistant project manager said.

"Maybe it's a blessing in disguise," the IT guy said and then shut his mouth, realizing he was speaking out of turn. But the birdlike man nodded in encouragement. "Well, it's just, you know, if the government doesn't get the video, that means it won't get leaked to the media either. More is left open to interpretation and speculation."

"I reckon so," the birdlike man said. "Let the rumor mill crank on its own. Leave more to the imagination. The California media will demand answers the government can't supply. The government will demand answers from Deseret and won't get much. Wouldn't be surprised if some heads rolled during the midterm elections, too. Might even help SoCal after all." His smile vanished. "How'd we end up with three of them?"

The assistant project manager smiled, which due to his unfortunate facial hair made him look menacing. "The young man we approached went ahead and recruited his brother and sister, too—all on his own. He didn't want to be known as a lone wolf."

The IT guy tried to press play on the video but hit fast forward instead. The people in the conference room sat watching the three terrorists as they continued their silent decrees in a high-speed farce before he managed to get the DVD working at normal speed once again.

The IT guy wiped his forehead. "They sure recorded a lot of footage: thirty minutes."

The assistant project manager laughed. "Thirty-four minutes and twenty-three seconds to be exact. Even if they'd been smart enough to record sound, we would have had to edit it. What is it with terrorists and overly long manifestoes? Doesn't anyone ever read their writing out loud first? Doesn't anyone practice? So much repetitiveness all the time, it's frankly unprofessional. It's bad enough when it's in a foreign language, but in English? Get in and get out is what I say."

The birdlike man ignored his ranting. Another executive spoke up.

"Deseret might have a problem on its hands now."

"Only a pretend one. But if we've made them believe it's real, so much the better," the birdlike man said. "The Mormons are supposed to be pacifists. Now they have a crisis of conscience. They'll need to have a come to Jesus or whoever, and ask themselves how this could happen. How could they have spawned terrorists? It'll keep them unnerved. But of course, we'll be on hand to publicly offer any and all assistance, just like we will with California."

They sat watching the silent film for a few more minutes. When the three terrorists picked up their bombs and strapped them to their chests, the room had enough.

The assistant project manager stopped the DVD. "Are we absolutely positive they neutralized all the members of the CVB?"

"Quite," the birdlike man said. "It's going to come as a shock to the folks in the navy and army and in Sacramento when a few people don't show up for work tomorrow. But that's the price they wanted to pay. And pay they did. Can't imagine how they'll explain that away. My guess is they won't even try. The truth's expensive, though."

The assistant project manager held the DVD in his hands like he'd just picked up after his dog. "I'll put this in the records room, just in case." He left the conference room, muttering about manifestoes.

The birdlike man touched a button, raising the blinds once again. The Texan sun was obscene. As they filed out of the conference room, one of the executives turned to him and asked if anyone had heard from Alexander.

He shook his head. As he left the room, he thought there was a good chance Alexander was alive. He had survival instincts. He knew which risks to take and which to avoid. And, despite his claims to the contrary, he couldn't help but stick to a moral code. He knew Alexander all too well. Underneath that harsh exterior was a patriot through and through, one who was smart enough to know how to pick the right battles and how to stay on the winning side.

The birdlike man thought the soldier would make a great politician. In a decade's time and with a bit more refinement, he could run for office and win handily. The birdlike man allowed himself a smile of satisfaction. He knew how to pick recruits.

Chapter 33

"Welcome to *Hot Takes*, with Cynthia Wellesley, Charles Naughton, Matty Matthewson, and me, Harry Goldberg. First, my opening monologue: 'Government Corrosion in the Face of Implosion.'

"In the wake of what happened in San Francisco, the mainstream media refuses to ask the questions all of us want answers to. Who was behind the incident? How many people died? Why were they singled out? It's literally Journalism 101, and instead of rolling up their sleeves, these multi-million-dollar pundits are carrying the football for Sacramento. And I for one have had it. Charles, is this a fair assessment of the media?"

"Are you kidding me, Harry? No, not at all. I know you love to take the antimedia, antigovernment stance, but the news outlets have been asking plenty of questions and getting answers."

"Oh please."

"Harry, what have we learned in the past forty-eight hours? Three terrorists blew up a building in which another much larger group of terrorists was plotting something heinous—the destruction of the Californian government. How can you say we aren't being told anything? Matty, what do you think?"

"Well, Charles, it's just like you to take the side of Sacramento, but really, why should we believe them? You saw how they painted Southern California with the same brush, just because they want equal rights. I mean, what do we really know about this group? About either of these groups? Cynthia?"

"Matty, the truth is we don't know anything about these groups. One was supposedly called the CVB?"

"Yeah, the CVB—what does that even stand for, Charles? The Chocolate Verbena Bonbons? Cozy Venetian Blinds? We don't even know they had that name. It could all be misinformation."

"Oh, Harry, here you go again with your antigovernment crackpot theories."

"Excuse me, Charles, if that is your real name, ha-ha. What information do you have to substantiate any of this? We've so far had one—no, two press conferences. In the first, we weren't told anything because it was too soon. Now it's two or three days after the fact, and I'm sorry, but they just seem like they are throwing out random theories to see what sticks. Matty?"

"I have to agree with Harry, which, as you know, is something I almost never do. You heard that police chief tell a couple of different stories in that second conference. First he said they were antigovernment, and then he said they were in cahoots with Southern California. And that other organization, the people who blew up the building, is supposedly from Deseret? Come on. They have given us zero in the way of details about this Mormon group. The whole thing stinks to high heaven. And it does feel like the journalists aren't even trying."

"Well, I'm trying—very hard to get a word in edgewise. You boys really need to let a lady speak sometimes."

"Believe me, Cynthia, if we had a lady at the table, we would."

"Very funny, Harry. Just keep in mind, and that goes for everyone here (Charles especially), that the government's fundamental function is to keep us safe from harm. And when they can't do that, they need to explain why they can't. And if they can't, then as far as I'm concerned, any level of skepticism is healthy."

"Well, I would agree with you there, Cynthia."

"Thank you, Charles."

"But I will say this, at the risk of being contrarian—"

"You, Matty? Contrarian? Color me shocked."

"OK, Charles, enough. Even you might find this point relevant since I happen to agree with you. I mean, at the end of the day, we're journalists sitting around this table. Sure, we can thumb our noses at the other shows on our competitor channels, but they're journalists too, after all. They don't get anything from carrying the ball for Sacramento, not at this point—and certainly not on this particular tragedy."

"Great point. I mean, would you decide to risk your career without knowing what reward you were going to get?"

"Well, Harry, if your track record is anything to go by, you probably would."

"Good one, I'll have to remember to get you back in the B-block. Don't go anywhere because *Hot Takes* will be back after these messages."

Chapter 34 (The Ending)

After the blast, he'd gone to the safe house, packed, wiped everything down, and headed out. He caught the second new update from the San Francisco Federal Police. They still weren't saying how many people had been killed in the blast or, indeed, who had rented out the banquet hall that evening, which meant either they had no idea who had, or they knew exactly who had and weren't saying.

He thought of using the Rompecabezas to send a distress signal but didn't. Instead, he put it in his suitcase, took a taxi to the airport, and booked a plane for Dallas without telling anyone he was returning.

The person at the ticket counter told him the next flight out wouldn't leave until five the next morning. Alexander bought two large coffees and spent the next three and a half hours watching the news.

At four thirty, the newspaper deliverymen replaced the vending boxes with the latest editions. He bought the *Northern California Gazette*, *Southern California Times*, and *Cascadia Post*, reading them all on the flight.

He arrived in Dallas, took a taxi home, and spent the rest of the day switching between left- and right-wing news stations. When they began to repeat, he switched to radio.

The Rompecabezas started buzzing. He opened it, read the encrypted message, and tried and failed to decrypt it. Every few hours, he'd get another warning. Each time he tried to decrypt the message, nothing happened.

Before going to sleep that evening, Alexander took stock of the news he'd absorbed the past twelve hours. No one, it seemed, knew anything of value. The newscasters and their guests all had a particular point of view, but it was all based on fiction.

How in the days of CCTV, mobile phones, and digital journalism could there be such a void of information? The only way, he thought, was if someone had clamped down on the narrative. Alexander went to bed, now fully convinced of who was controlling the flow of information.

The next morning, he showed up at TexIntelSecuriCorp, unannounced.

"It is so good to see you, son. Have to say, the others weren't sure you'd survived, but I just had a feeling about you. Let me be the first to shake your hand. Mighty glad to have you back."

The birdlike man's grip was firm and his smile genuine. He pointed to a chair in front of his desk and went to pour them both a drink. He handed Alexander a tumbler, clinked the glass, and downed it. Alexander didn't raise his glass. Nor did he drink. "What's the matter? Don't like whiskey?"

"What I don't like are things being kept from me," he said.

"Now, hold on, now—"

"You hold on," he yelled. "I was in that building. It was only dumb luck that made me leave."

The birdlike man shook his head slowly. "We had no idea that was going to—"

"Spare me the bullshit," he said. "You knew all about the guys down in LA, down to the day of attack. You had files on Biker. Why should I believe you about San Francisco?"

"I told you going in that certain things would be divulged to you (or not) on a need-to-know basis. But I've been on the level with you this entire time. That's the God's honest truth."

Alexander reached into his pocket and pulled out the Rompecabezas. "Yeah, like this all-important message was a 'need-to-know' one, right?" He placed the device on the desk. It continued to vibrate. "Go on; look at it."

The birdlike man opened the machine. He read the message out loud: "That gum you like is back in style." He hit the decryption button.

"Been flashing that message for two weeks now. Still don't know what it says. Kind of don't care much anymore, to be honest."

"This is Mexico's fault—"

The gun appeared in Alexander's hand, cutting his speech. "You've got ten seconds to tell me what the fuck happened."

The birdlike man raised his hands. "I'm talking. OK? I'm talking. Just keep your trigger finger still."

Alexander lowered the gun, keeping his eyes fixed on the birdlike man.

"I'll tell you exactly what happened. We had a bead on the CVB from the beginning, just like I said before I sent you there. What I didn't tell you is that Northern California asked us to help."

"And you just thought that little tidbit was a need-to-know piece of info, huh?"

"Understand, son, this assignment was not officially sanctioned by Texas. If they would have known, they wouldn't have let us do it."

"Then why help them?"

"We already achieved our goal of gaining control of the Southern ports. There was no need to cause instability up North and create a power vacuum, not when they were transparent with us about the CVB."

"Who planted the explosives?"

The birdlike man swallowed. Alexander raised the gun.

"Sacramento—they had no idea you were in that building. That's why we sent you that message the day before. 'That gum you like is back in style.'"

"What's it mean?"

The birdlike man kept his eyes fixed on Alexander. "It means: 'Don't go to the dinner. Great job, come on home. You're getting a promotion.' Now that's the truth—I swear."

Alexander lowered the gun and sat down at the same time. The birdlike man lowered his hands and did the same.

"Why the hell did you need me there? And don't give me that boots-on-the-ground horseshit. I'm tired of empty phrases."

"Northern California requested you. They were convinced you were the reason Southern California failed in their rebellion."

"But I told you when I returned: I had nothing to do with it."

The birdlike man filled his tumbler with another measure of whiskey. "Hell, son, they didn't need to know that. They came to that conclusion on their own. When they requested you, we just figured, well, hell, it won't hurt to keep them in the dark. No point in disappointing them." When his smile was met with Alexander's glare, he continued. "I'm sorry the message wasn't translated. If it makes you feel any better, I knew you'd be just fine all along. You've always had a survivor's instinct."

Alexander put the gun on the table and picked up his drink. "You used me just to spread even more disinformation than you already do. If I had been sacrificed, you wouldn't have given two shits."

They stared at each other in uncomfortable silence. Alexander finally broke his gaze.

"Hell, you don't really believe that, son."

Alexander pretended to think about it. "No, I don't guess I do."

"Course not. It just wouldn't add up. Why would I have scouted you out just to let you die? And why on God's green earth would we want to let you die if we wanted to promote you?"

The birdlike man got up from his desk, walked over to a bookcase, and pulled out a binder. He flipped it open and started reading to himself in silence. He came back and put the binder in front of Alexander, open on the very last page. "That's your entire file. You can read it all. But start on the last page."

Alexander picked up the binder and read. "In his short time with TexIntelSecuriCorp, Braxton, Alexander A., has exceeded all levels of expectations as a new employee. It is unanimously agreed that he be removed from the field and given an expedited promotion to Scout, with yearly salary of five hundred thousand Texan dollars, plus bonuses."

Alexander looked at the birdlike man in surprise.

"You've made a big impression on everyone here, and at the risk of giving you a big ego, even the president was impressed. They were fixing to give you a medal of honor. Took all I had to convince them not to. We need to keep you a secret."

"Because you want to promote me to do what you do."

"That's right, son. I'll show you the ropes at first—just you and me. We'll work together to choose the right vets who are ready, willing, and able to continue fighting the good fight. From now on I'll teach you how to find 'em, how to persuade 'em, and how to put them in the field. And I'll also teach you what to keep from them and when to share those hidden secrets to keep them motivated. As of right now, you are working from home from now on. That means we need to replace you ASAFP."

Alexander nodded. "So that'll be my first assignment: find someone to replace me."

The birdlike man smiled. "Uh-huh. It'll be the first in a long line of hand-selected soldiers you'll be leading in the effort to ensure the great Texas flag continues to wave high and proud around the world."

"If you told me years ago that someday I'd be a leader, I wouldn't have believed it," Alexander said.

"Well, just think, son. Soon it'll be you who's in charge of picking the best of the best and telling them how to serve. You're no longer a foot soldier. You're the director now. How does that sound?"

He could pick misfits just like him. But instead of all that doublespeak, he'd be transparent, explaining the entire system to them, teaching them how to bring down the system from within by using their very own trusted tactics: misinformation, doublespeak, sleight of hand, intrigue, and shady political alliances.

He'd teach every candidate to play the part of the model soldier: loyal, zealous, unwavering in his or her belief that TexIntelSecuriCorp was always right. Behind the window dressing, their real role would be that of a monkey wrench in the machine, a giant thorn in the side of power, a weapon driven by betrayal that could come from anywhere.

Alexander thought about the amount of damage he could do with those who hated the system as much as he did—far more damage than any bomb or gun could cause. Because his kind of damage would be undetectable until it was too late: the proverbial frog slowly being boiled alive in a pot of water.

The birdlike man coughed. "I said, how does that sound to you, son?"

Alexander picked up his tumbler, leaned back in his chair, and raised his glass to the birdlike man. He put the tumbler to his lips to drink, said something he didn't catch. It might have been, "I think it sounds just great," but on the other hand, it also sounded like, "I think you should go fuck yourself."

"What was that, son? You're fading in and out."

His body flickered for a moment. It started turning into random dots and pixilated static. The birdlike man squinted and could, it seemed, still make out Alexander smiling from ear to ear. From the other side of the country, Alexander laughed. From his chair in the office in Texas, the sound was garbled and metallic. He started to speak, but what came out of his mouth was a surge of white noise that overtook the room. Inside the cacophony were random words the birdlike man couldn't understand. The sound was deafening.

He was halfway through yelling "Just what in the hell do you think you're doing?" when Alexander's hologram vanished.

Chapter 35 (Alternate Ending)

The Subaru eased its way down the mountain pass. Sitka spruces loomed on either side. The sun had set behind them, covering the highway in one long shadow. He drove in the slow lane with his foot on the brake, letting the big rigs pass with angry horn blasts. With a quarter tank of gas left, he hoped the sign depicting the miles to the nearest town was accurate. Otherwise, he'd be stranded. And there was nothing worse than being stranded on the side of the road at the base of a dark mountain.

After the blast, he'd gone to the safe house, packed his clothes, wiped everything down, and headed out. He'd thought of using the Rompecabezas to send a distress signal but didn't. Instead, he put it in his suitcase and threw the suitcase in the trunk.

He'd been driving due north for close to sixteen hours straight. He had no reason to go north any more than he did east, south, or west. It wasn't a fight-or-flight reaction; nor was it from instinct. Alexander drove because he couldn't think of anything else to do.

One minute they were there; the next minute, buried under rubble. He watched the building come down and saw the ease with which the steel and brick and mortar could just cave in. He heard no screams. No one escaped. The war to end all wars was over before it began—so much for utopia.

He listened to the radio for the better part of the drive, hoping the news-program talking points would change into something more meaningful. After six hours of the same repetitive nonsense, he snapped the radio off.

The most shocking thing to Alexander was just how little was known about the incident. Press conference after press conference yielded no usable information. A statement from the mayor's office said they had no idea how many had died, no credible leads on suspects or motives for the explosion. Southern California was quick to deny involvement. They did offer support, as did Texas and Cascadia, the country he'd never seen until that day. He passed through customs with ease. The border agent remarked with a sense of wistful pride that he'd been born in Texas and that any fellow Texan was OK in his book. Alexander managed a wan smile but entered the country feeling nothing but a profound sense of alienation and loss.

He made it down the mountain and rolled into a truck stop called Lovey's just outside of Ferndale city limits, if it was possible to call a population of ten thousand a city. An attendant ran out to help, wearing a heavy flannel jacket with a Lovey's patch on it.

"Almost nobody pulls up to full-service anymore," the man said.

"I didn't have a choice," Alexander said and pointed to the dashboard. "I was running on fumes. Didn't want to risk it."

"You're a lucky man. Fill her up?"

"Please. Don't suppose you service vehicles, too?"

"We don't, but the place next door does. Won't close till eight, so there's time."

Alexander got out to stretch his legs. Then he used the bathroom to pee for what seemed like ten minutes. When he returned, the attendant was wiping imaginary bug juice off his windshield.

"That'll be fifty Cascadian, if you've got it. Otherwise, we take cards."

Alexander handed him a card, signed, and drove to the other station, where a man who looked almost exactly like the first attendant came to help.

"You got a brother over there?"

"Sure do," he said and smiled. "Twins. I'm older and smarter and better looking, though. What can I help you with?"

"I drove it for sixteen hours straight. Started to have radiator trouble. Smelled like burned plastic."

The man whistled. "Let's take a look."

Alexander waited a half hour. The man came back with bad news. "Radiator's shot I'm afraid."

"Shit."

"Best I can do this time of night is order a new one. Might have to hang around a day or two until it comes."

"Two days?"

"I feel your pain, sir; I really do. Tell you what, I won't charge you for the estimate."

"I appreciate that but…two days. Shit," Alexander said.

"Well, be glad you're in Ferndale," the man said. "Don't look like much, but it's the last stop before the Deseret border. That means we've got tons of motels, hotels, restaurants, and bars. Hell, more people stay and drink here than live here."

Alexander popped the trunk and removed his suitcase. "Guess I'm one of those people now, at least for a few days."

The mechanic pointed to the suitcase. "Better answer your phone and let everyone know you're in Ferndale."

Alexander walked across the parking lot and headed into a diner. He was starving and in desperate need of coffee. He ordered chicken pot pie and a bottomless mug and fished out the Rompecabezas while he waited for his food to arrive.

He opened the machine. The vibration was steady, as if it were a heartbeat. The encrypted message repeated itself three times: *That gum you like is back in style.*

Over and over it repeated and buzzed. He hit the decrypt button, but nothing happened. He tried again with the same result. When his food arrived, he turned the machine off.

After dinner, he walked down the street to an access road with a row of hotels and motels. The first one he tried was booked solid.

The manager of the second hotel was an older woman with tired eyes who explained the same thing: "There's a military reunion in town."

"Oh? I didn't know Cascadia fought in any wars."

The woman shook her head. "Canadians—they take Ferndale over this time every year. They fought a war when this part of Cascadia was still Canada. Most of 'em are eighty years old by now," she said.

He tried two more motels with the same result. Alexander's energy was draining. The weather was turning colder. He spotted a large hotel on a hill above the others and walked up the winding drive to the top, sighing in relief when he learned they had room. He paid in advance for three nights, letting them know he might need to stay longer.

The rooms were all business-class suites, complete with a kitchenette, minibar, and den. He tossed his bag on the bed, undressed, and stood under a hot shower. He fixed himself a scotch and tried the Rompecabezas again. The decryption button still didn't work.

He went to sleep for twelve hours straight, only waking when his phone rang. The mechanic said the part would be in the next morning and assured him he'd be on the road by noon.

All he could do was wait. Alexander stared out the window. From the hotel's vantage point on the hill, he saw a stunning snow-capped mountain to the west and Deseret to the east. Nearby were lakes and rivers that were known for their fishing.

He thought of renting a car, maybe driving to Deseret. But he couldn't be bothered. Instead, he walked down the hill and ate lunch at the same diner, strolled into Lovey's to get a paperback book, and then walked back to his hotel.

When it came time for dinner, he decided to try a Mexican restaurant that wasn't too far away. It was surprisingly good. They even stocked an impressive list of tequilas.

"Let you in on a secret," his waiter said. "The Mormons who are less than pious come here from over the border most every Friday and Saturday to drink. You'd be surprised how much they like their booze."

He walked off the enchiladas and tequila on his hike back up to the hotel. Once again he stood under a hot shower. Then he checked the Rompecabezas again: same message, same lack of decryption. He snapped the machine off and went to sleep.

The second morning, he woke up early enough to watch the sunrise over the mountain. For a brief moment, Alexander thought, what would happen if I just moved here? Sure the town wasn't much, but I would make it work, settle down, maybe meet a nice girl who worked in town, go fishing on the weekends.

The phone pulled him out of his reverie.

"You won't believe it, but the delivery was early for once. My men are putting in your radiator even as we speak. We should have you all ready by ten, ten thirty at the latest."

Alexander thanked him and hung up. He had a continental breakfast in the hotel lobby, scanning the complimentary paper as he did so. There was no new information about San Francisco. In fact, the papers had moved on to a different big story. A radio host he hadn't heard of who was known for pushing conspiracy theories was involved in some sort of sex scandal. The radio host claimed it was all a conspiracy to keep him from telling the truth. He didn't bother with the details.

Alexander shut the paper, checked out of the hotel, and walked down to the mechanic's place.

"Funny, I was starting to like it here," he said.

"Ferndale will do that to a feller. But you wouldn't say that in the middle of winter when it's minus forty out and it takes a half hour to get the ice off your car."

"That's true," he said.

Alexander paid the mechanic. "So where are you headed?"

He answered, "North, I guess. I suddenly have some downtime and thought, why not go somewhere I've never been before?"

"Well," the man said, "safe travels, wherever you end up."

Alexander got in the Subaru, putting his bag in the front seat next to him. He left the town and got on Interstate 5 again. He wasn't far from Vancouver, which had been in Canada when he was a kid.

Canada made him think of Quebec and Marie-Eve. It was clear across the other side of the continent. And anyway, she might not still be there. It was the Mexican who'd said she'd gone back, but who knew if that was really true? He'd thought of calling to confirm but realized somewhere along the way he'd lost Paulo's business card.

He drove to Vancouver but didn't stop there. Instead, he headed east in a roundabout way, first going northeast and then southeast, winding his way past towns with strange names: Merritt, Nakusp, Kamloops.

At a rest stop, he opened his suitcase and checked the Rompecabezas.

The device still vibrated. And the same message, stuck on repeat, now took up the whole screen, in an endless scroll.

That gum you like is going to come back in style.

Although he could not decrypt the message, Alexander settled on a translation that seemed to fit: your debts are paid.

He'd fought too many battles, lost too many people. But in the end, he didn't turn his back on Northern California. Even if their cause was as hopeless as the rebels in the South, and the cards of fate were stacked against them, at least they'd had a cause.

He'd risked a lot for both sides in California, put his life on the line even more than in the Middle East. Over there, he hadn't believed in the cause. The price he'd paid was high. But even if his legs were gone, his soul somehow remained intact.

He got out of the car, taking the Rompecabezas with him. The device still beat out a rhythm he could no longer follow. There was a good chance that TexIntelSecuriCorp might think he was dead, after all that had transpired. Why not keep it that way.

The rest stop was set just off the highway, close to a scenic wooded picnic area. Alexander walked to one of the tables, sat down, and pressed the decryption button one more time.

When nothing happened, he powered down the machine. Then he stood up and threw it deep into the woods, as far he could make it go. It disappeared somewhere in the trees. With any luck, he thought, the snow would soon fall and bury it for the next six months. It wouldn't even matter if someone came along and found it. The Rompecabezas was untraceable. Soon, Alexander would be too. He got back in his pickup truck, feeling directionless and sure of himself.

Chapter 36

A short message from the narrator.

Up until now, the narrator has done his or her best to be reliable and present this story in a way that is nothing if not completely factual. One could argue that with each new piece of information, the story has shifted slightly. Some readers may view these shifts as being to the detriment of what might have been an otherwise generally accepted linear narrative as defined by conventional standards.

But that line of thinking might depend on your favored media of choice, how you skew politically, which baseball team you root for, what your unconscious and conscious biases are, or whether or not you're from Texas or California or from another country entirely.

Mind you, the above statement is not to be read as an accusation or judgmental assertion on the narrator's part. After all, the narrator does not know any of the readers, and the readers don't know the narrator. So let's not get the wrong understanding about each other, not at this late date, as that would not be fair to either side, so to speak. If anything, this story was written to bring us together.

Again, it must be stressed that to the best of the narrator's ability, the facts presented in this story are 100 percent accurate, as the narrator perceives the story to be, which is in itself admittedly a bit of a problem, as everyone, including the narrator, has different perceptions that are based entirely on myriad factors, including zip code, socioeconomic background, age, race, gender, politics, and cultural ancestry, as well as historical, sexual, and culinary allegiances, the last of which is of course the most important in shaping a point of view.

Before we try to proceed, there must be some kind of common ground upon which the narrator and the reader agrees. After carefully considering and rejecting such matters, the narrator has chosen what is most likely the one and only thing we can agree upon, or agree to disagree upon as the case may be, and that is regarding culinary matters that divide us.

You see, there are two kinds of people in this world: those who like ketchup on their French fries and those who like mayonnaise on their French fries.

While it has been thought that the love of mayo on French fries is purely a European predilection, this has been found not to be the case. The narrator has personally witnessed people in Deseret, California, Cascadia, and even Texas enjoying the emulsified egg-yolk based goo with their spuds. And that's only sticking with one land mass. The same is also said to be true in parts of Asia and Latin America, although the narrator has not spent much time there and does not want to deal in duplicity or hearsay and will not attest to such theories without evidence.

Sticking only with this detail and discounting the negligible population in this world who are equal fans of putting tomato- and egg-based sauces on the tuber in question, the fact that there is an either-or proclivity in something this wholly inessential is a great way to highlight the overall hopelessness of society as a whole.

The sharp divide between the ketchup and aiolist factions should be seen as a very large and disheartening indication of just how bad our belief systems have diverged. It is a wonder the entirety of civilization has not collapsed at this point in time. But this also brings up an important point, as perhaps our point in time is important enough to highlight as the #TeamKetchup #TeamMayo divide, if not perhaps even greater.

At this point in time, the narrator is collecting his thoughts to finish what will surely be a short message to the reader assuring in all earnestness the intention of telling a factual and true story with absolutely no trickery involved.

But it hardly needs to be said that by the time the reader's eyes reach this part of the story, it will be a different time altogether. It makes no difference either, the duration between when the narrator finishes telling the story and when the reader finishes reading the story. Be it an hour, a year, or ten years, there will most certainly be a passage of time. And it must be said that this time lapse represents a chasm where any and all manner of things might occur that will alter the story or, more precisely, the reader's response to the story. For all the narrator can say, there is a very real chance the narrator's response to the story changes subsequently.

Another thing in the "all manner of things" that might occur: new facts could always come to light to the narrator. Events recounted in the story might upon further reflection turn out to have never happened or didn't happen exactly as conveyed. New events could theoretically come to light entirely.

The narrator would be remiss if he or she forgot to mention the importance of events that occur within the readers' lives too, which may have varying degrees of importance because it will have an effect on how this story is perceived. If, say, someone shared with you an editorial on Facebook that angered you or your daily status meeting got pushed back three times or someone cut you off in traffic, then you might be in an angry frame of mind when reading this book. And while the narrator is by no means suggesting the reader book a few hours a day in an isolation chamber until this book is finished, the overall point is that there is a lot to take into account.

At the same time, however, and at the risk of raising some ire in a few of the readers who are sensitive, the narrator must also stress these factors, these "all manner of things," could also just as easily be discounted or ignored entirely.

Perhaps it's optimism setting in upon the near completion of this pithy addendum, but there is a part of the narrator that sincerely believes that we do have the power to remain objective about our world (albeit not without a great deal of effort) and come to our points of view in an agnostic way, with little to no influence, a way that will ultimately lead to a better and more respectful discourse, that if no one comes to an agreement, at least both sides aren't at each other's throats. In some ways it's akin to walking while chewing gum or patting one's head while rubbing one's stomach: a bit tricky, but nothing the police would ever put on a field sobriety test.

At the same time, there's no reason to suspect the other part of the narrator buys any of that malarkey, because it most certainly does not. That part of the narrator is a hard-boiled cynic who views the world through eyes wide open instead of being wide-eyed. The narrator was not born yesterday. The narrator is not jejune. And civil discourse is the stuff of fantasy, because at this point in time (that phrase again) we are so divided from one another that it really is as if we are living in two different realities where never the twain shall meet except on bumper stickers that read "Coexist." For all any of us knows, this is a treatise on fatalism masquerading as a novel.

The third theory, and one that probably holds the most water, is that it is a little bit of both or sometimes none of the above. Just like the proverbial river, one cannot step into this same story twice, let alone the same chapter.

For instance, there is very little reason at this point in the chapter to assume that the narrator who introduced himself or herself just a few very short pages ago as reliable is in any way reliable despite his or her initial declaration. How could he or she be? Ponder this for a moment: out of all the times to insert oneself into the story, this one chose now, not, say, between parts one and two, which might have acted as a lemon sorbet palette cleanser. Nor did he or she have the decency to lay the groundwork by appearing periodically throughout the story by way of clever asides, random quips, footnotes, breaking of fourth walls, and the like.

Unless of course there is a chance the narrator was doing so all along, without saying so, and is only saying so now. Throwing this out as a hypothetical example: What if the narrator was listening to *The Outer Reaches* radio show or watching *Hot Takes* on television or live streaming Lauren Seibring and just filtered those bits of news into the story? Isn't that the way all of us go about our days? Filtering and absorbing news, entertainment, and infotainment? Blithely spreading digestible clickbait headlines and rumors as fact and deriding actual facts as fiction?

Who honestly knows anymore? Certainly not the narrator—that is, unless you, the reader, are now quite convinced the narrator has not lost the plot at all but is once again talking out of two mouths like a living, breathing Janus.

At the risk of accusing the narrator of becoming compromised, let he or she humbly submit to you the reason for appearing now is of vital importance, and that is to get you to reconsider your point of view about this novel in general and Braxton Alexander in particular.

Now that you've reached the end of the story, the narrator wished to present you with two endings to ponder, two scenarios holding a certain degree of plausibility to both.

Let us assume for a moment that scenario 2 (chapter 35) is the correct[1] ending. Braxton Alexander rejects TexIntelSecuriCorp and becomes a leader by not allowing himself to be led.

Now let's examine the possibility that scenario 1 (chapter 34) is the correct ending. Braxton Alexander, knowing full well that TexIntelSecuriCorp has been the sole manipulator throughout part 2 (and even, it can be inferred, part 1), goes to confront the birdlike man but then decides instead to put on a show of accepting a promotion,[2] embracing the company, and becomes a leader with the intention of destroying the company from within.

Of course, there is no way of knowing in either case how successful his attempts will be, for various reasons, including how much he does or doesn't know when it comes to the whole story.[3]

---

1   Correct in the sense of being satisfactory for the reader and not correct in the unconditional Greek absolute sense.

2   It could also be inferred that with the narrator's deliberate word choice of "promotion," there is a parallel between the corporate structure and the military-industrial complex structure, but this might also just be a happy accident.

3   The narrator is specifically referring to Braxton Alexander's own story and events that have occurred either directly or indirectly, which include but aren't limited to the thoughts of his superiors in parts 1 and 2, the sincere and ulterior motives of the Californian and Texan governments, and how this was reported by

As an aside, and with the full intention of keeping this adjunct a concise one, the narrator wonders how many of the readers know who Paul Harvey was. Without Googling this, and thereby being led astray into endless and most likely irrelevant days of research, the narrator will now explain to the reader the gist of who Paul Harvey was.

Paul Harvey was a sort of folksy American news broadcaster who used a quite unique style of storytelling in his broadcasts, especially during a particular commentary segment called "The Rest of the Story," in which he would take a very interesting story and then wait until the end to reveal something very important about the story. For instance, upon concluding a story about Davy Crockett, whom we had always heard had been born on a mountain in Tennessee, Harvey would reveal that, in fact, he hadn't been. The stories Paul Harvey regaled the older generations with were always true and always ended with his signature line about the listener now knowing the rest of the story, with a delightful emphasis on the word "rest." (Several of these broadcasts exists on various websites should the reader's interest be piqued.)

One of the narrator's favorite examples of such a story that was on the Paul Harvey program was about the man who wrote "Yes, Virginia, There Is a Santa Claus." This is yet another example of the duality of media—in this case, an editorial written by a journalist named Francis Pharcellus Church.

Church's commentary was written as a response to an eight-year-old Virginia O'Hanlon, who innocently wrote to a newspaper to enquire whether or not Santa Claus was real. The answer to the editorial called "Is There a Santa Claus?" was an unequivocal yes. So masterfully simple in its response, the editorial has been passed down every year since it was written and has become as important a part of the holidays as Irving Berlin's "White Christmas," David Bowie's "White Christmas" duet with Bing Crosby, and snow.

The rest of the story in this case is that despite how well written the response to cute young Virginia was, the journalist in question, Francis Pharcellus Church, was a hardened, cynical war correspondent and atheist, who not only had no time for superstitions, but did not even want

"the media."

to write a nice response to the eight-year-old in the first place and did not want his name attached to the piece when it was published. The narrator suspects he would have had little patience for the Christmas All The Time Store, although, to be fair to the ironically named Church, this is only a guess. Perhaps he, too, would have changed his mind upon seeing such amazing decorations, especially the hologram Nativity set with yawning baby Jesus. (The narrator will now make a note to go online later and see if such a thing exists.)

Stories like "Yes, Virginia, There Is a Santa Claus" represent the folklore and myths and legends of an America that, while it may not obviously be represented in this book directly, is most certainly represented in this book thematically. Anything built on a myth is open to question; is it not?

War correspondents who are curmudgeonly dicks aside, this modest supplement to the story is merely the narrator's way of letting the reader know that everything in this book is true as it happened in the fictional story, or at least has a reason for being, even if the sole reason for being is a red herring or something that only exists to negate itself or is perhaps even, if the narrator is being honest, some eccentric detail written on a whim.[4]

Before the narrator forgets, there is a moment in part 1 where the board game Risk makes an appearance. And while this seems like it was thrown in as somewhat of a lark, the idea of being able to teach military strategy through a board game is not without precedence; chess itself was one such tool, and armed services around the world make use of simulators and video games to prepare one for battle, without engaging in real battle. Still, there is something about the game of Risk, which is one more fitting analogy to this story.

Risk is a game that was created by a French director in the late 1950s

---

4   And if you really think about that one for a minute, it's even more absurd considering the source material of this novel is a very loose plot as concocted by the members of Camper Van Beethoven for their album *New Roman Times*, which was released in 2004 on Pitch-A-Tent/Vanguard Records. A special thanks must be given to David Lowery, Jonathan Segel, Victor Krummenacher, Greg Lisher, Chris Pedersen, and David Immerglück for the inspiration and creative freedom to allow me to take this story where it felt like going. In the narrator's defense, a few of the songs are instrumentals, so you know…creative license and all that.

when we were, at least theoretically, in peacetime.[5] Despite more than a half century since its inception, the game has held a certain appeal, at least enough to spread throughout the world in various languages and themes.[6] So there's no reason to think Biker's tactic of trying to teach one of his younger soldiers military strategy through a licensed board game is an infantile one. Or put another way, it's no more infantile than a video game. Biker could have just as easily plunked Sickle down in front of a PlayStation to play the latest version of *Call of Duty* or some such and taught her that.

Except he really couldn't have unless it was player versus player (PVP) as opposed to player versus environment (PVE) because video game AI generally becomes predictable after a while, which wouldn't have done anybody any good. And playing PVP would have opened up a whole other can of worms because one would need to ask who the other players are and where are they, and does Sickle have a head seat and would she as a woman want to broadcast her voice, and so on. In light of this, it is easily seen why the narrator went for what seems like a more nostalgic but no-less-germane choice.

Board-game digressions aside, it is now high time to explain the reason for this brief epilogue. In short, the narrator feels it necessary to broach the topic of this book having two different endings, which could potentially be a land mine for even the most patient and open-minded of readers.

For instance, why are there two different endings? What is the reader supposed to infer from that? And how did Alexander turn into a hologram ring if that is really what happened? And what's even up with the aliens, let alone their love of baseball?

Unfortunately, the narrator must respectfully refrain from explaining these details. But the narrator does have a sincere intention in attempting to add some closure to this all-too-fleeting postscript. Again, it must be stressed without belaboring the point that this is written not to offer up an explanation for the ending(s) to this story (surely, the reader doesn't

5   More or less, discounting the Cold War for the sake of expediency. And "we" being the West, or at least the United States, to some degree. The narrator realizes we don't want to be here all day.

6   There are *Lord of the Rings*, *Star Wars*, *Dr. Who*, *Game of Thrones*, and *Metal Gear Solid* versions, to name just a few.

want that) but to at least offer a way in which the reader might approach the alternate endings to the story, if said reader feels it necessary to choose one as being the—quote, unquote—correct one.

If in the decision-making process some help might be needed, here are two options one might try. Read the penultimate chapter, and ending one, and then wait a half hour or so. Then read the penultimate chapter and the alternate ending, one after the other. See if there's an ending that jumps out over the other, and then the reader might just have an acceptable ending for herself or himself.

Providing some friendly word of warning, it is worth mentioning that the narrator has not actually tried this technique. He or she cannot be held responsible for the effectiveness or the logic of such a suggestion. It may in the end be nothing more than a shot in the dark.

And anyway, if the narrator is being frank, whatever ending the reader prefers (including both endings simultaneously) will most likely be dependent upon a cornucopia of elements including the reader's zip code, socioeconomic backgrounds, age, race, gender, political affiliation, and cultural ancestry, as well as historical and sexual factors and, above all, in terms of culinary proclivities—that is, which side one falls on when it comes to ketchup-versus-mayonnaise-on-French-fries.

www.ingramcontent.com/pod-product-compliance
Lightning Source LLC
Chambersburg PA
CBHW070741180626
46818CB00007B/2939